GARRETT

a
BACHELORS OF THE RIDGE
novel

KARLA SORENSEN

GARRETT

Cover Designer: Najla Qamber, Najla Qamber Designs
Cover Photography: Perrywinkle Photography
Interior Designer: The Write Assistants

To the readers of romance.
It's a label that I proudly claim for myself, because readers of romance are part of a community that is intelligent, fierce, loyal and above all; believers in happily ever after.

CHAPTER ONE

GARRETT

Most people who knew me would tell you that my life was pretty good. Not like, *I lived in a mansion and had a playboy bunny for a wife and she loved to cook* good. More like, *I hated my job and worked for my father and he didn't* know *I hated my job and I felt like nobody took me seriously* kind of good.

Yeah. That kind.

Despite my shameless whining, I really did enjoy my life. I had kick-ass friends and a house that I owned. My sister and I were close, and I received a steady, ridiculously inflated paycheck from a job that held a title that was just as ridiculously inflated.

Chief Operating Officer of Calder Financial Services, Inc. sounded big and important, because it was. We were a financial firm in Denver that employed over fifty people, and my dad had poured his entire life into those brick walls for the last twenty-five years. But every single time I sat down in a mindless meeting that could have been wrapped up in an email, I wanted to gouge my eyes out with a popsicle stick, just to see how long it might take.

The people across the table from me would give me side-eyed looks when I suggested such a thing. *Gasp!* No meetings? How would they all function? Imagine the productivity levels if we actually had to sit at our desks and get shit done.

The horror.

Given that I had zero popsicle sticks, I jammed my fingers in my eye sockets while my dad preached at me from the opposite end of his office after the last perfect example of the kind of meeting I hated. Roughly twenty-five percent of the square footage of the top floor of the building was dedicated to his office, and I always marveled at how he thought it was necessary. Not that it wasn't nice. He had two leather couches, a full size conference table for twelve, mini fridge behind his L-shaped desk, and two solid walls of glass that showed nothing but the downtown Denver skyline. Specifically, the shining golden dome of the Capital building and the long stretch of the Rockies beyond it in the distance.

"Garrett," he barked and I dropped my hands.

"Yeah." I blinked a few times. "I'm listening."

"You can't do that in the middle of a meeting, son. You can't make statements like that, the kind that basically tell your senior management team that they're wasting their time with pointless bureaucracy."

"They are wasting their time," I mumbled, stretching my legs out in front of me and picking at a piece of lint on my charcoal colored pants. Fine. There wasn't actually a piece of lint, it just gave me something to look at besides my father's face.

Partially because it weirded me out sometimes, how similar we looked. Same height (roughly six-three), same hair (dark blond/light brown depending on the time of year), same strong nose (from his mother's side), same dark brown eyes. The other part was because I was so familiar with his tone of voice that I had no desire to see the matching look of disappointment on his mirror-image face.

Believe me, I saw it often. You wouldn't want to look either.

"Garrett," he said wearily, and the creak of his leather desk chair made me lift my eyes briefly. "This is how it's done. You can't ask people that have been doing things a certain way for their entire career to cut out a massive chunk of the decision making process at this firm simply because you don't think it's necessary."

"Dad, come on. We sat in that room for two hours this morning and the only clear thing that came out of it is that the danishes from the bakery downstairs suck and that we need to run an extra report at the end of each quarter." I lifted my eyebrows. "You seriously think that's a good use of company time?"

He held up his hands and leaned back in his chair. "I'm not saying it is. But you still can't do that in the middle of a joint staff meeting. That's not how a COO should— "

"Not how a COO should conduct himself," I finished, since I heard it on a weekly basis. Bi-weekly, actually. Speaking of should, that *should* beg the question of why he wanted me as COO in the first place.

Of course, I knew. It wouldn't help me to verbalize it. My younger sister Anna had a successful career as an interior designer, and no interest in working at Calder Financial Services. Which meant in order to keep it as a family owned and operated business, I was the heir apparent on the operational side.

Anna and I both owned shares of it, along with my parents, so it would take a lot for it to be owned by anyone else. But for my father to be satisfied with someone else running it? That was a horse of a different color, as they say. I didn't say that. That would be weird, as I was thirty-four and not eighty-four.

"I get as sick of saying it as you do hearing it."

I held up a finger. "I wouldn't necessarily agree with that statement. I actually think you love saying it to me. In fact, I'd go so far as to say that saying that to me makes you feel all warm and fuzzy inside, like someone just puked up gold at your feet."

My dad sniffed, shaking his head when I said it. "Do you take any of this seriously?"

"Nothing gives me greater joy than for you to remind me that I embarrass you."

"And to think," he continued as if I hadn't said anything, "I was just going to hand you a project that might make you happy."

"Spit shining your shoes?"

He pursed his lips just as there was a knock on the door, followed by a female voice. "Rich, you wanted to see me?"

It was, in fact, a miracle that I held in the groan that I so desperately wanted to let out.

The reason I say that is because while my father constantly reminded me that I should be doing better, almost every single person in the company loved me. They smiled when I walked past, showed me pictures of their grandkids or new litter of puppies because I actually took the time to ask.

There was one person, however, besides my father that constantly made me feel like I was a little kid pretending to be an adult.

Aurora Anderson. It was so unfair that the Wicked Witch of Finance inhabited the body of a gorgeous woman my age.

"Rory!" my dad said with a big-ass smile on his face.

Rory, I mouthed at her, with my eyebrows lifted and she pierced me with a narrow-eyed glare that actually made my balls shrink up. No one called her that around the office, so it delighted me to no end that I had something I could use against her.

"Sorry I couldn't be at the meeting this morning." She crossed the office and clasped my dad's outstretched hand. "I had an emergency at my condo a couple days ago and had to wait for the insurance adjuster."

"Clogged toilet?" I deadpanned and she took a deep breath, never once looking my way. To be honest, that was fine. As much as I hated Aurora, which I did, she sure as hell was something to look at.

She was slim and tall, at least five-nine or five-ten without heels, which she wore without fail. Her blonde hair was always loosely curled and pulled back into a low ponytail. Her skin was tan in the way that made me think she spent a lot of time outside. Shocking, because I typically thought vampires would burn the hell up out in the natural light.

Honestly, I wasn't even positive what her eye color was because she either glared at me or ignored me. That wasn't true. We interned together at CFS while we were both finishing our MBA, even though my internships had merely been a formality. The first day we met, almost eight years ago at that point, I had to struggle not to gape when I introduced myself to her. She had the deepest blue eyes I'd ever seen in my life. Almost a purplish blue.

Like flowers or sunset or some shit.

But then she'd opened her mouth, and blew it all to hell.

"I'm not here to make friends, Prince Calder. If you stay out of my way, then we'll both be happier for the foreseeable future."

"*Prince* Calder? You don't even know me," I'd said on a shocked laugh.

Instead of answering, she'd flicked those remarkable eyes over my shoulder at the empty office that already had my nameplate on the door. "Sure I do."

Then she'd walked away, taking her long legs and perfect hair and shockingly blue eyes away from me. I don't think we talked for six solid months after that.

If you could believe it, our work relationship had gotten even worse since we first met. But I couldn't fire her, even if it had been my call to make. For one, I had to grudgingly admit that she was incredible at her job. And also because my dad and Aurora's boss, the VP of Finance, were completely enamored with her.

In a professional way. Not in like, the creepy old man way.

So if I'd tried to oust her, they'd probably throw my ass on the curb before I could blink.

"Earth to Garrett," Aurora said, snapping me from my internal diatribe. The one I had often, where I fantasized about telling her to pack her shit and leave.

Since my dad couldn't see her when she was facing me, she rolled her eyes when I apologized.

"Okay," my dad interrupted before I could do something super professional like flip my middle finger up at her. "As I was saying to Rory, the two of you both think there are things we could streamline and subjects that could be handled more efficiently to cut down on meeting times."

I glanced over at her, but she'd shifted in her chair and was facing my dad again. She and I agreed on something? With a quick look out the window to make sure the sun wasn't dripping with blood or some other sign of the apocalypse, I nodded in answer.

"So, I'd like to assign you two the task of coming up with a new monthly and quarterly meeting schedule for the senior management team."

He stared at us, waiting for a reaction. Aurora was completely still, and I was trying to choke down my laughter.

I cleared my throat. "Dad, are you *sure* you want the two of us to do this?"

"Rich," she said immediately after I was done, not sparing me a single look. "I really think this is something that could be handled by just one person, with input from the senior management team via email."

But my dad silenced her by lifting one hand. "I get it. You guys don't like each other." Aurora and I immediately started talking, but he gave us a look that shut us up pretty quickly. "It's fine. And you know what? There's no rule that you have to love everyone that you work with. However, you *do* have to be able to set aside the things that you don't like, and be able to get your job done. And in this case, your job is to work together on this because I've asked you to." He paused, leveling a serious look at both of us. "Despite the fact that you don't get along, I think you'll balance each other well if you set your issues aside. Garrett, your desire to streamline our processes, the ideas that you have are great. And Rory, you have a practical outlook and a logical head to work with him on that."

Silence cloaked his office. Most likely because Aurora and I were both attempting to come to grips with the fact that this was the first time in eight years that we'd be working on something together. Not just together, but only the two of us together.

When I lifted my head, she was staring at me. Then she mouthed a curse word that I'm quite sure started with an 'F' and turned back to my dad.

The sides of my lips started to curve into a smile, so I coughed into the back of my hand to hide it.

"Okay, Dad."

Rory nodded and gave him a small smile. "Sounds good to me."

When I looked at my dad, he looked pleased in a way that made me ill. Like he'd just succeeded in some Machiavellian scheme to overtake a small country.

Then he rubbed at his chest and took a deep breath.

"You okay, Dad?"

He waved me off. "Heartburn. Shouldn't have had that Chinese for lunch."

Aurora stood from the chair she'd been sitting in and spared me a derisive glance. "When would you like this done, Rich?"

"Present me with your recommendations in two weeks and it'll go to senior management when I've signed off on it."

When she nodded and started her quick-paced walk to the door, I gave my dad an absent wave and jogged after her. I wished, I really, really wished that her ass did not look so spectacular in the simple black pants that she favored.

"Aurora," I called out when she picked up the pace. "Come on, you can't ignore me already. This'll be a shitty two weeks if you do."

"Watch me," she said over her shoulder.

I caught up with her and hooked a gentle hand into the crook of her elbow and steered us into the darkened conference room.

CHAPTER TWO

AURORA

"Get your hands off me," I hissed and ripped my arm away from him. Garrett held up his hands in surrender when I whipped to face him. Ugh. This man made me go from zero to fire-breathing dragon in about one point two seconds.

He flipped the light switch on so that we weren't standing in a dark conference room and took a deep breath. "Come on, Rory, don't be like this."

"You do *not* get to call me that."

Damn him, ooooooh, damn him and that highly amused grin that he gave me in answer. That's what made it so much worse. Garrett Calder was handsome. He was tall and muscled with broad shoulders that looked (I could only admit this in my head, because I'd likely choke on the words if they came out of my mouth) incredible in a suit. Oh, I'd have liked it so much better if he was a hunchback with two teeth and pockmarks covering the left side of his body.

You know, have the outside match the inside.

"But my old man does?"

With brisk movements, I straightened my blue cotton blouse and sniffed. "Yes."

Garrett leaned up against the door behind him, clearly not planning on going anywhere. Ass.

"How come?"

"You realize that I don't *have* to answer you, right? It's my prerogative who gets to call me a nickname and who doesn't."

When he snorted, I risked a look at him under my lashes. Still smiling that stupid smile. It was one of the non-professional things that I envied about him. The ease with which he smiled and joked, making the people around him happy in turn. The people who I reported to and the people who worked under me all respected me and liked me. But we weren't exactly friends. We didn't swap jokes or secrets.

But I'd take respect any day of the week, and twice on Sunday. So I straightened and faced him, giving him the full weight of my annoyed expression. "What?"

"Nothing." He shook his head, completely amused by my snippy response.

"You are so aggravating."

"And you are *so* defensive, Rory."

I narrowed my eyes and he smothered a laugh. "I'm not defensive. I'm simply explaining to you that it's my right to recognize that certain people are deserving of informalities over others."

He clutched a hand to his heart. "So many big words. Stop."

When I lifted an eyebrow, he gave me a mildly apologetic look. "Okay, fine. I'll stick to Aurora."

"Thank you," I conceded. "Can I leave now? This kind of proximity to you gives me hives."

"Better figure something out then, because not only will we have to work in the same room, but there will be no one to act as your buffer." He tipped his chin at me. "And I know you need those when I'm around."

This. This precise thing was my problem with Garrett. He never seemed to take things seriously. He held a position of power within a company that I very much believed in, and he was always on the verge of a joke. The fact that he'd done approximately nothing to deserve the job he was in rankled against every core value I held packed around my heart.

I worked fifty-five hours a week to make sure that I earned my spot as Senior Manager of Finance. My boss, Cal, never failed to acknowledge when I stepped up to the plate, and Rich had been the most fantastic mentor I could have asked for in my years since graduating college. CFS helped me get my master's with the financing program they extended to every intern who took a job with them, but I would have stayed without it.

Time and time again, I told myself that I'd give Garrett the benefit of the doubt. I'd be civil, maybe even attempt to get to know him better.

Then he'd open his mouth and I'd want to stab him. Repeatedly. With a rusty butter knife.

"I'll be perfectly fine. Your father has never had any cause to doubt my professionalism."

Garrett snapped his fingers. "That's it! I'll wear a wire when we're together." Then he clicked his tongue and gave me a sad smile. "When he hears the uninhibited vitriol that you spew my way? Better get your resume ready, Aurora."

I crossed my arms over my chest and smiled sweetly. "While I feel like I should acknowledge the multi-syllable words that you just used correctly in a sentence, I don't want to waste my time. Anyone can use a thesaurus." His lips flattened and he straightened from the door. I stepped closer to him. "Your father won't fire me, Garrett. Because not only have I been a perfect employee for this company since day one, he voluntarily took on the role of being my mentor." Then I pointed a finger at him. "That's why he's allowed to call me something that only very important people in my life can. Because he knows me. And he's had a major impact on my life."

I didn't know what I expected. I really didn't.

"Huh. Can't imagine what that must be like."

"What do you mean?" I rolled my shoulders and just, ugh, wanted to be anywhere else.

"My father as a mentor. I pretty much just get barked at."

Maybe he was kidding. But when I searched his face, he actually looked genuine. It made me want to laugh. It also made me want to fidget. Something sharp and pokey settled in my stomach when I thought about getting a piece of Rich that his own son didn't even have. So like I usually did when that particular reaction was triggered, I went back to my default. At least, my default with Garrett.

Sarcasm.

"If your interpretation of getting *barked at*," I lifted my fingers to make air quotes, "is being handed the COO position in barely six years while the rest of us actually have to work at getting promoted? Sweetheart, I'll start investing every cent into Kibbles N' Bits."

The look on his face gave me a moment of pause. Garrett looked … not offended, exactly. Uncomfortable. He looked uncomfortable. Like I'd unveiled something that very much bothered him.

Too bad, so sad.

If Prince Calder didn't like the idea that he'd been handed a promotion on a silver platter, it was *not* my job to assuage his conscience.

Regardless, I shifted on my feet and wrapped my arms tightly around my chest again. It was starting to feel warm in the room, which was ridiculous since the air vent was blasting frigid cold air down at us.

"Because you know everything about my life, don't you?"

"I know enough." It felt easy to say it, not quite as easy to believe it.

He spread his arms open, revealing the crisp white shirt and scarlet colored tie. "And she's a psychic, ladies and gentlemen. Let's all give her a hand."

"Don't you dare patronize me," I snapped.

"Then don't you dare judge me," he snapped right back, more fire in his eyes than I was used to seeing.

"Calling a spade a spade is not the same thing as making a snap judgement, Garrett. Don't forget I've had a front row seat to your rise to the top floor. You can't tell me it's not exactly the way I'm describing it."

Garrett rubbed his lips together while the words were still hanging in the air between us. I was breathing harder than I should, given the small amount of space we were sharing. Didn't matter that the conference room was cavernous. The pocket of space that we were sharing felt like a thumb tack. He finally blinked.

"Fair enough," Garrett finally said, his voice rougher than normal. "Should we just connect tomorrow morning?"

I nodded, staring out of the large wall of windows that opened into the hallway, actively avoiding his stupid brown eyes. "That's fine. The first half of my day is pretty open."

With that, he walked out and left me in the quiet. I gripped the back of one of the chairs behind me and fought for balance. I did not need to feel bad for Garrett, in any way.

So I closed my eyes and pulled in a deep breath, trying to exorcise myself of anything resembling pity for making Garrett feel bad.

Be a diamond, Aurora, my father's iron-edged voice echoed through my head. *Not because it's pretty. Pretty doesn't mean shit. Because they'll never be able to break you.*

"Get out of my head, General," I whispered into the empty room. But maybe it wasn't terrible, that anytime I had a moment of weakness I could clearly hear the lessons he shoved at me my entire childhood.

If I was honest with myself, he was the thing driving me anyway. He'd probably never know it. But that didn't matter.

I knew it. And I'd know when I made it past anything he ever thought I could achieve.

So I lifted my chin, straightened my spine, and walked back to my office to get the hell back to work.

By the time I made it home that night, my garden-level condo was blessedly quiet. With only the sound of my clicking heels on the hardwood floors, I walked through the open kitchen and dining area.

My eyes were closed before my back hit the cushions of the couch.

My phone dinged and I heaved myself up to a sitting position so I could root through my purse to find it. I smiled. My cousin Mia.

Mia- Please tell me you're home, in comfies and watching The Bachelorette by now.

Me- Close. Minus the second two.

Mia- BORINGGGGGGGG. You have to have something else in your life besides work.

I rolled my eyes, because this was a conversation we had often. It was hard to describe to someone who was your complete opposite that you were truly satisfied with a life that would drive them crazy. Mia was the ultimate extrovert, always had to be surrounded by people and going, going, going all the time. The fact that I willingly worked fifty hours a week and had no qualms about going out for a meal or to a movie by myself was akin to life of torture to her.

Me- Work makes me happy though. And no part of my life is a compromise. Isn't that what everyone wants?

Mia- I guess if by 'everyone' you mean only loners who hate people. Then yes, your life is what everyone wants.

Mia- You can't tell me that you don't ever get lonely. I call bullshit.

I ran my thumb over the letters of her text and thought about it, instead of shooting off my knee-jerk response of firm denial. Loneliness was a state of mind, for the most part. If I chose to focus on the fact that I had no one sharing my space, sharing my bed or sharing meals, then maybe I'd have felt lonely. But I didn't. There was no one to tell me that watching horrible reality dating shows, admittedly my biggest guilty pleasure, was silly. There was no one to play music too loud when

I wanted to nap on a Saturday afternoon or read quietly in the chair under the window looking out the front of my condo. No one to argue with my choice of restaurant when I wanted Chinese four nights a week.

Nope. There was no loneliness coating any part of my life. Sometimes, I thought that people wanted me to admit that I was lonely because my life didn't make sense to them. Like somehow admitting that I felt that there was a piece missing would make it more palatable for them. *Oh, you're sad? Fantastic. I feel much better about the way you live now.* Even though Mia knew me better than just about anyone in the world, I knew she didn't get it either.

She didn't *get* that at thirty-three, almost thirty-four, I wasn't falling over myself to find a man, even for the night, as was her style. When I didn't answer right away, I heard the chime of more texts come through. Instead of looking, I stood from the couch with a groan and went to change my clothes. The twelve-hundred square feet of my condo in Capitol Hill was a bit bigger than what I needed for just myself, but Mia occasionally visited from Washington, and I liked having an office at home in the second bedroom.

Leaving the lights off in the master, I yawned as I stripped off my black pants and silk blouse, tossing them on to the floor of the walk-in closet. Normally I wasn't so tired after work, but it's possible that my run-in with Garrett had more of an effect on me than I was expecting.

I'd run into Rich about two hours later and as was his way, he made sure that I was okay with working with Garrett on the project he'd assigned us.

"Of course," I'd answered dutifully.

"Good," he'd boomed, clapping me on the shoulder when he passed by me. "I know you'll do a good job of keeping him in line."

I smiled, thinking about that. If Garrett knew his dad had said that, he'd probably cause problems just to make me look bad.

Suddenly, the fact that I was tired pissed me off. One tiny incident shouldn't have that much sway over me. A quiet night moping on the couch would probably only make it worse, so I yanked open the drawer that held all my workout gear.

If I was going to feel tired, it would be because I'd worked out any frustration on the treadmill or the punching bag at my gym.

No way would I let Garrett be responsible for something like this.

CHAPTER THREE

GARRETT

More than just about anything, I hated being bored. Like it somehow was a representation of my social life. But when I felt the upheaval that was currently going on at work, it was even worse.

There weren't many TV shows that I watched, beyond Sports Center and whatever game might be playing, so flipping mindlessly through channels wouldn't do much good. And all that seemed to do was remind me of how I felt like I was spinning my wheels at work anyway. You'd have thought that a Chief Operating Officer wouldn't feel that way, but I did. I kept people happy in their jobs and made sure everything was running smoothly on a daily basis. Well, given that we weren't a huge firm, that wasn't as hard as it might seem.

For a while, I sat on the floor with my back against my brown leather couch, chucking a tennis ball at the wall and catching it when it bounced back.

Thrilling stuff, I know.

When I almost missed and took my nose off, I stood with a groan and grabbed my cell off the kitchen counter. Within three minutes, I knew my friends would be no help.

Cole, who lived on the street behind mine, wasn't answering.

Michael, who lived across the street with his brother Tristan, wasn't answering either.

Dylan, who lived two streets over with his girlfriend Kat, was at work.

Tristan wasn't on my call list, because he kinda scared the ever-loving shit out of me when he was by himself. Sometimes I thought he gained his power from broody looks and long silences that were only occasionally punctuated by monosyllabic grunts or random deep thoughts that no one understood.

Knowing Dylan wouldn't care, I pulled up Kat's contact info and waited for her to pick up.

"Did you know that an octopus has three hearts?"

I pulled my phone back and looked at the screen with bent brows, then brought it back up to my ear. "Are you drunk, Miss Perry? It's not even six."

"No," she answered patiently. "I'm watching a documentary on octopi and it is fascinating."

"Uh-huh. Thank you for answering my question of whether I should walk over to your house so I'm not so bored."

"Dylan's at work."

"I know. But you're not. And Leonidas isn't either."

"Leonidas is a dog."

I gasped. "*No*."

"You cannot be that bored, Gare Bear."

"Hey, we've discussed this already. You are not allowed to call me that. Every time I hear it, it makes my balls shrink up in protest."

"Umm, gross." Kat made a gagging sound. "Seriously though, you can't have even been home from work for an hour. Aren't you capable of being by yourself anymore?"

Instead of letting out the whiny nooooooo that I wanted to, I coughed into my hand. "It's your man's fault. I was perfectly fine until he lived with me for a while."

Kat laughed, but I was serious. Standing in my immaculate kitchen and looking into the family room that my sister had decorated, it just felt too big and too quiet.

"Maybe you need a dog."

"I can borrow yours."

"Maybe you need a girlfriend."

"That's exactly the last thing I need."

There was banging in the background and Kat made an exasperated huff. "Well, Garrett, I don't know what to tell you. But I need to go. I'm attempting to make dinner before Dylan gets home and it's hard enough for me to cook actual things without being distracted. Go for a run or something. Get rid of some energy."

When she hung up on me, I was still holding the phone to my ear like a freaking chump. When you can't pester your best friend's girlfriend into hanging out with you out of pity, it's a sad state of affairs.

Maybe Kat was right though. I'd canceled my gym membership about a year earlier in favor of working out in the yard or hiking with the guys for exercise. But it was hot as shit outside, and I wasn't in favor of dying of heat stroke.

So I changed my clothes and made the five-minute drive to my old gym.

Which was closed.

"Shit," I said under my breath while I stared at the new sign. Unless I suddenly grew breasts, they wouldn't be letting me inside to work out. While I flipped through my other options on Google Maps and turned my car to head to the next closest option, I realized what an appropriate turn of events this was for my entire day.

Chewed out by my father.

Forced to work with the one person in our whole company who truly hated me.

Nobody to hang out with me.

Gym closed.

I actually opened up my car door to make sure I didn't have a flat tire.

Which is why I should not have been surprised in the slightest when the first thing I saw after filling out my registration forms from a bored looking meat-head was a woman jogging on a treadmill who actually made me pause to look again.

That probably made me cliché—man checking out woman at the gym—but there was positively no way I would not look.

She was tall and slim, but toned in a way that told me she was here often. She had a thick headband wrapped around her head covering most of the hair against her scalp, but the messy bun was blonde.

The skin-tight pink pants that she wore stopped at her knees, and the only other thing she was wearing was a black sports bra.

God Bless America and the massive workout facility that I'd just waltzed into. Because she was the kind of woman, physically, that made me—the commitment-phobe who usually broke out in hives when women talked about getting married— want to get a whole lot closer and figure out a whole helluva lot about her.

Along her rib cage was a thin line of script that I couldn't make out. I blinked a few times, realizing what a creeper I probably looked like. Not four feet into the building and I was a full-fledged gawker.

I was about to walk to the weight machines when she turned her head to grab the water bottle and I caught a glimpse of her profile.

"No way," I muttered under my breath.

I looked up at the ceiling, hoping that among the exposed ductwork and steel beams, I'd find a divine answer to why I was getting completely shit on.

Dear God, I thought, *do you hate me? Couldn't you have just given me shingles or something? Maybe some kidney stones?*

For a brief moment I considered walking past her and going to the opposite corner so she wouldn't see me. But then I thought, nope. If I have to suffer from knowing she's here, then she needed to suffer too.

Aurora started slowing her pace by punching at the screen on the treadmill when I walked on the one next to her. There were thin black wires snaking up her neck that connected to earbuds.

Instead of starting my machine, I braced my forearms on the dashboard and stared over at her. For a long minute, I thought she might never look over. But when she did, I grinned and was rewarded by a jolt of her entire body. She slapped a hand over her chest while she turned the treadmill off.

"Holy *shit*, Garrett." Tilting her head back in the same way I had done moments earlier, she attempted to slow her heavy breathing as she pulled the earbuds out. While she did that, I was absolutely not looking at the soft sheen of sweat on her chest or the softly defined lines of her abs.

Some women looked unattractive to me if they were too muscular. Aurora didn't have that problem.

She looked strong. Strong and beautiful. Unfortunately, it would now make me worry that she'd be able to kick my ass if she wanted to.

When she glared over at me, it registered that it was the first time I'd ever seen her without makeup. Without the polish that she normally had at the office, she looked younger and softer.

"Stalking is a federal offense, Calder." With slow movements, she wiped at her neck and chest with a blue towel that made her eyes like, glow or some shit. They were *so* blue against the unlined skin of her face.

"Nice ink."

Her eyes snapped to mine before she made a sharp turn off the treadmill.

"Not gonna tell me what it says?" I jogged after her, angling my head to try and see it while she stopped at the free weights.

"Go screw yourself."

"Well now, that's an odd choice."

She sighed and crossed her arms over her chest when she faced me. "Shouldn't you go do some crunches?" Looking down at my midsection, she lifted an eyebrow. "You're looking a little chubby there, Calder. Maybe lay off the danishes at the next meeting."

I started laughing, because it was so ridiculous. I may not have an eight-pack or something crazy like that, but I definitely had muscles there that she'd be able to see from twenty paces.

"That's cute, Rory." I smiled even wider at the pinched, pissed off look on her face when I said that. So I leaned in and made a slow sweep of her body. "I'm surprised you can even sweat. Doesn't water make you melt?"

"Sticks and stones, sweet cheeks." She sounded bored, but there were twin pops of color high on her cheekbones. "I'd rather be a witch than a clown. How about the next time you see me here, you walk the other direction."

My face froze, but she didn't stick around long enough to see my expression. This time I didn't follow, because she'd just given me the verbal equivalent of a punch to the junk.

I'd rather be a witch than a clown.

The hot sweep of embarrassment that flooded my chest made me feel raw. Aurora Anderson had just put my biggest fear at work into eight measly little words. She'd pegged me with the same sentiment before, but for some reason it hit me harder when she said it here, in her stripped-down state.

Without her armor on, as I was used to seeing it at work, I stupidly didn't have any on either. So instead of standing by the weights, I marched back to the treadmill and only briefly warmed up before setting a punishing pace for myself.

With no music in my ears, all I could hear was her deceptively innocent, feminine voice saying those words over and over and over.

In my head, I knew I didn't love my job. It felt like more of a prison sentence than anything. Being cooped up in an office for at least forty hours a week, with discussions of Roth IRAs and mutual funds and life insurance and pension funds dominating my time was just about the worst thing I could imagine. They all took their jobs seriously at CFS. All except me. Hearing *her* say it, of all people, made my brain hurt.

She hit me in a place that she couldn't possibly know would affect me so much.

I wasn't positive when Aurora left the gym. After her parting shot, I didn't give her another look. Not a single one. All I knew was that by the time I pulled into my garage an hour and a half later, there were aches in muscles that I didn't remember existed. Truly, people who found joy in exercise should be tested for some sort of mental disorder. It would explain a lot about why Aurora looked like she spent a *lot* of her time there.

Spending time outdoors, going on hikes, that was what I preferred to do to stay in shape.

Why join a gym then? Maybe I was losing my mind too.

My head dropped onto the headrest behind me as I groaned. Thirty-four was too young to be that sore, that fast. From the console next to me, my phone chimed. But it was so far away. It would require lifting my arms, grabbing the phone, holding it up so I could read it.

And I was secure enough in my manhood to not give a shit that I whimpered when I did those three things.

The weights had been overkill, apparently. Maybe I should have eased into things a bit.

Dylan: Kat said you were pouting earlier. We're home now if you want to hang out. I can call the other guys too.

Go inside and fall face first into my bed? That would cement my old-man status, given that it wasn't even 9pm.

Garrett: I'll be there in ten.

The only thing I managed in those ten minutes was to stumble out of my car, grab a six-pack of beer out of my fridge and chug a bottle of water before getting back into the driver's seat.

Yes, I was going to drive one street over to Dylan and Kat's place, because my knees had suddenly decided to pitch a mutiny.

But a quiet, empty house would be too much for my brain after my run-in with Aurora. That woman managed to poke at me with maximum efficiency. Like she could see my weak spots with special goggles that lit up my body with a road map.

Insecurity: hit here.

Unhappiness: hit here.

Uncertainty about future: Oh, do I have the perfect spot. Right here, missy.

I was still fuming about it when I pulled my car into Dylan's driveway, so I took a second to take a deep breath and stare at the lit front porch of the place he'd lived for almost a year. We were all a bit of an anomaly, single guys who weren't downtown apartment dwellers. But a tiny shared space suspended above the same skyline that my office looked over had never appealed to me. I did enough of that type of living in college and the couple years after.

The thought of having my own yard to maintain and walls that weren't shared with anyone else was too appealing for me to walk away from. And given that I had zilch for college debt and a job that paid more than most master's graduates had, getting a house hadn't been a stretch for me.

All my friends were the same.

Other than Dylan, who I'd been friends with since late middle school/early high school before my dad moved us from Michigan back to Colorado, I'd met all my closest friends because of where I lived.

The Ridge of Alta Vista, a mix of condos and houses in a subdivision that was less than ten years old, was where we all called home. Cole Mallinson had been my real estate agent, someone that I'd connected with instantly. At the time, he was married, and lived down the street with a wife— now ex-wife— that I'd never even met.

Michael and Tristan Whitfield— brothers who were less than a year apart in age and about as polar opposites as brothers could be— lived across the street from me and had moved in about four months before I did.

Dylan was grandfathered into the group years later after he hauled his Michigander ass over to the Rocky Mountain state simply because he was one of my oldest friends. Kat, his girlfriend, was our pint-sized mascot and only female in the group.

I was still slumped in my car when the front door opened and Kat waved me in. In the space between her legs and the opened door, their mutt, Leonidas shot out and sprinted to my car. When Dylan had found him behind a dumpster at work as a puppy, missing one of his front legs, Kat had helped him get Leonidas fitted with a prosthetic leg. So basically, this dog was the *shit*.

"Hey, crazy man," I said after I shut the driver's side door behind me and scratched behind his flappy gold ears. "If I can't walk all the way to the door, can I grab onto your collar so you can drag my poor, old body?"

He swished his tail, turning a quick circle that made me laugh.

"You *drove* here?" Dylan asked from behind the kitchen island when I limped through their front door.

I flicked him off and yanked open their fridge to slide my beer onto the top shelf. Kat snickered under breath at Dylan's incredulous expression, which I only acknowledged with an eye roll before snagging a piece of pizza from the opened box on the counter.

"Can I have this?" I said around a full bite of spicy meat sauce and mozzarella cheese.

Kat smiled the little fairy sprite smile that always let her get her way around us, then pinched the sensitive skin on the underside of my arm while she passed me. "What would you do if I said I wanted it back?"

"Ummm, ouch," I said, using the back of the hand that was holding my food to rub at the place she assaulted me. "Dylan, rein your woman in. She's violent."

Dylan laughed, swooping down to give Kat a kiss against her smiling mouth. They did that constantly, with the kissing and the PDA. I was immune, thankfully. More so since I spent what should be an embarrassing amount of time as the third wheel to them. Dylan and Kat were the people I hung out with most, after their dog, and I was completely unashamed by it.

So he could slip her some tongue all he wanted.

Except, then Kat made a sound in the back of her throat, her hands started moving, and I had to turn my back to them. "I'm still here. And

I saw you grab his junk, Kat."

Probably just to be assholes, they didn't stop, instead making obnoxious pleasure-filled noises and smacking noises with their tongues.

If they wanted to play that game, I could to. I pulled out one of the stools at the island and propped my chin in my hands so I could watch them with avid interest.

Kat pulled away first, looking far too pleased at the fact that I'd just seen her squeeze my best friend's ass. Dylan shook his head at his girlfriend, but the completely ridiculous amount of love he had for her shone through.

"If you stick around long enough," he said, glancing over at me before smiling at Kat again, "maybe you'll figure out how to pick up a woman of your own."

I made a buzzing noise, standing to grab one of the bottles of the Breckenridge Brewing Nitro Vanilla Porter that I'd brought with me. "Not gonna happen. I've got one woman too many driving me up the friggin wall as it is. If I tried to fit one more into my life— even of the sane variety— I'd end up in a padded cell."

Kat clapped her hands and took the stool next to me, her eyes bright and curious while she punched me in the shoulder. "Who's driving you crazy?"

I was about to answer when Tristan and Michael walked in. Jerking my chin up in greeting, I kept my eyes on Kat. "You're nosy. Who said I was talking about anyone in particular?"

"Because your answer was way too specific." She smiled at the brothers Whitfield. "Hi guys, help yourself to some pizza if you're hungry."

She only grinned when I lifted an accusing eyebrow at her offer. "Just work stuff. Nothing new."

"You say that like you talk about work stuff all the time," Michael said as he snagged two massive pieces of pizza from the pie. "Every time someone asks you how your day was, you change the subject."

"Avoidance is usually more telling than a lengthy answer," Tristan said from the corner.

"Hey," I pointed at him, "that sentence was your entire days' worth of allotted words. Don't use them ganging up on me."

Tristan's full range of facial expressions ranged from a scowl to boredom to slightly less grumpy version of a grimace which he considered a smile. After six years of knowing him, I still had trouble reading him sometimes. So when he lifted one eyebrow a fraction of an inch, I knew he was distinctly unimpressed. "Am I wrong?"

"Oh, go loosen your man bun. It's cutting off the blood flow to your brain." Even though I said it to Tristan under my breath, everyone was staring at me like they expected me to actually explain myself. Then Kat gave me this excited smile, and the thing was she actually looked excited at the idea that I might share something about work with her.

Was I really that stingy with the details?

I didn't need to think too hard about that, in reality. The need to talk about work with my friends never struck me as important, because I didn't love what I did during the hours that I was in that office. Burdening them with my poor little rich boy issues was the furthest thing from my mind. Especially when I still felt unsure about what I'd do with my life if I didn't have to show up at CFS every Monday morning. But it was Kat's smile and the genuinely interested looks on my friend's faces that made me open my mouth.

"There's this woman at work," I started, twisting the bottle of beer in my hands. "Aurora."

Kat gasped. "Like *Sleeping Beauty*! Oh, I love that movie."

"Easy, Perry. This is not a fairy tale. Because that princess? Hates my guts. And she has no qualms about making that fact perfectly clear."

"She hot?" Michael asked with an unrepentant grin.

I wish I could have lied. I wish I could have looked him in the eyes and said that she was the ugliest woman I'd ever seen, was twenty years older than me and preferred the company of women so that they wouldn't entertain any ideas about how I viewed Aurora Anderson.

Instead, I had to tell the truth. "Dude, probably the hottest woman I've ever seen in my life." Kat punched her fist in the air and Michael gave me a nod like, *yeah, buddy, that's what I'm talkin' about.* I sighed. "Can someone grab me another beer?"

CHAPTER FOUR

AURORA

Most mornings, I kept the lighting almost completely off in my condo before I left for work. I don't know if it was residual from my upbringing of not wasting electricity unless we planned on helping contribute to the bill, or if the darkness around me made it so that I didn't dawdle after waking. The lights on either side of my bathroom mirror were usually the only ones I kept on for longer than a few seconds while I did my makeup and slicked my hair back into my standard low ponytail.

But that morning, I stood in front of the mirror for longer than normal after pulling on my bra and underwear. I turned to the side and dragged my thumb under the tattoo along my ribs.

The great rebellion from my eighteenth birthday.

Since my parents had never seen it, you'd think it wasn't much of a rebellious act. But for me it had been. It was the day before I moved out of their house for college, and the burn of the red, tight skin as I packed my belongings was the best kind of reminder as to why I was leaving. Not just leaving, but leaving and never planning on returning.

By the strength within I shall succeed

And I had. But tracing the thin, graceful letters that curved along the line of bone under skin, I couldn't help but wonder if what they'd drilled into me growing up had been the reason for my success all along.

No. Only so much of what I was had come from my upbringing. I hadn't passed through their house in fifteen years, and Lord knows I'd changed since then.

Pulling the silk blouse that I'd picked from my closet up over my shoulders, I watched the words disappear slowly. With steady fingers, I buttoned each button, leaving the top one open before tucking the ends of the shirt into my black pencil skirt.

Garrett asking about my ink zipped through my mind and I tried to blink it away. The memory of him smiling at me from that treadmill had legitimately made my heart lurch.

And the muscles of his arms. What was *up* with that?

He sat at a desk. Just like all the other men in the office. And none of the others looked like Garrett.

"Stop it, stop it, stop it," I chanted, staring down my reflection in the mirror. So I did.

Mind over matter and all that jazz.

Normally, I took my time eating breakfast in the dark dining area of my condo. But I found myself rushing through bites. Since I was on the garden level, with a small, private patio closed off with a half wall and wrought iron, the passing cars of early birds like me gave off plenty of light to be able to see the oatmeal in front of me. Even though it was my routine every morning, that day it felt more quiet, much more isolated. The complete lack of busy-ness in my life once I left the office normally didn't bother me. But I wanted to hurry through my morning, rush through the silence that filled all the space around me.

Work, as it had from the time I earned my first paycheck, was where I felt the most comfortable. So I finished my breakfast with hurried bites, knowing that I'd probably be the one to turn the lights on when I walked off the elevator.

By the time I eased my car into my normal parking spot at the corporate office park, I only recognized one other car.

"You have got to be kidding me," I whispered while I slammed my door shut behind me. The click-clack of my heels on the pavement echoed around me, a fitting tempo for my rapidly rising blood pressure.

Not once had he ever gotten to work before me. Not *once* in eight years, which was a fact that made me very proud.

So naturally, I was fuming by the time the elevator lurched to a stop. There was a wide swath of light spilling into the hallway from his opened door. Slowing my steps so I didn't sound like a hippo bearing down on him, I took a quick peek through the thin rectangular window to the right of his door.

And he was looking straight at me.

Shit, I mouthed and stepped into his doorway.

"Aurora, nice of you to finally show up." He was leaning back in his chair and tossing a baseball between his hands, catching it easily while his chocolate eyes stayed trained on me.

It was just after seven. The asshole.

"Garrett," I said sweetly, "I half expected there to be fire and brimstone falling from the ceiling. Only apocalyptic level emergencies would get you in the office before nine."

"Ooh," he groaned, clutching at his chest. "That's the best you've got? Not a morning person, eh?"

"Haven't had any caffeine yet." While I said it, I glanced around his office. Casually, of course. Just a quick sweep of my eyes in a way that didn't look like I was poring over every detail. There wasn't much of Garrett in the office. Generic paintings that had probably been hanging there since day one covered the walls in their heavy wood frames. He had a bookshelf on the wall opposite of his desk, but it wasn't full with books. There was a fifty-fifty mix of sports memorabilia and books on finance.

I snorted when I saw a textbook that I recognized from college.

"What?"

I shrugged my shoulders and looked back at him. "You just threw all your textbooks on the shelf to make it look like you actually read, didn't you?"

"You got me," he responded dryly.

Point to Rory. I smirked. "When do you have an opening today? I've got a start on compiling all the regular meetings and their purposes so we can work on streamlining."

Garrett swiveled his chair to the other end of his desk and snatched up a manila folder. "You mean this? Yeah, I know, I've been looking at it this morning."

"Where did you get that?" I snapped, pushing off his door frame.

"One of the perks of my job is that I have a master key." Then he winked. "Your office is so *tidy*, Rory. Almost makes me wonder if you actually get any work done in there. I hope you don't mind that I moved your pens around a little bit."

The growl out of the back of my throat was involuntary and his smile widened, carving a small dimple on the right side of his lips. If I'd had that freaking baseball in my hands I would have chucked it at his face.

"You had no right, Garrett."

Any hint of playfulness fell off his face and he leaned forward so that his arms rested on his desk. "Actually I do. That's why they *gave* it to me."

When I marched in and pointed a shaking finger at him, he had the decency to look embarrassed. "That is so beyond unprofessional. To go into my workspace for something that I would have given you freely? That's *one* thing that needs to be addressed. But to mess up my stuff because you think it's funny is something else." My whole body was fiery hot, and I could feel the flush of anger spreading up my neck. "Everything is funny to you, isn't it?"

"Who's laughing right now?" He spread his arms open. "Not me."

"I'm not either, because if you were anyone else at this company, you'd get fired for doing that."

"I grabbed a *file*, Rory. One that I have every right to look at considering I was assigned to this project too. I didn't move your pens.

I was kidding. You're acting like I went in there and lit your computer on fire."

"This is bullshit," I whispered and paced in front of his desk.

"Calm down," he said in a placating tone, but it didn't placate *shit*.

"Why? Because *you* said so?" Oh, I was good and pissed. Maybe more than was warranted, but I was beyond caring. The thought that he went into my office and searched through my things made me feel violated somehow. That he was in there laughing at the way I lined up all seven pens to the left of my laptop every night before I left, that he touched my things and probably made fun of me in his head. "I don't think so. You're the most *ridiculous* person I have ever met. So out of line, Calder."

His tone was steel when he answered and it actually drew me up short. "Remind me of my title, Aurora."

Blink. Blink. Blink, blink. Ladies and gentlemen, that was the sum total of my response to his strangely timed question.

Garrett twirled his hand in front of him. "I'm waiting."

"Chief Operating Officer," I said smoothly, masking the *WTF* from my voice even though it was spinning around my head.

He snapped his fingers. "That's it. I couldn't remember with you standing there making unprofessional statements at me."

"*I'm* unprofessional?"

"Would you go into my father's office and say this shit to him?"

"Of course not. Why would you even ask me that?"

"Thank you for proving my point." The way he said it, so genuinely, made me furrow my eyebrows. "I am still your superior at this company, and you might want to rein in your temper a bit when you think about throwing names in my direction." His dark eyes held me steady and I felt the dull thump of my heart as I processed his words.

But I shook my head. "You're not my boss. *Cal* is my boss and he'd never fire me. Neither would your father."

Garrett nodded. "You and I both know that Cal is about four seconds away from retiring. Who do you think you'll temporarily report to when that happens?"

Shit. He was right. All Cal talked about was the fishing and hiking he was going to do after he retired. He and his wife had already purchased a massive fifth wheel camper to drive across the country and visit their grandchildren.

It was like Garrett was watching me process it right in front of him. He didn't smile though, which surprised me. I'd expected full-on gloating.

"If you have to sift through the hypocrisy that you'd never speak this way to my father, but it's acceptable with me, then I can't help you. I won't be disrespected in my own office, Aurora." Then he glanced over my shoulder at the door, where there was a low hum of voices. A couple people were slowly arriving for the day, completely oblivious of the possibly career-ending grenades I was launching around me. Maybe on a different day, I'd have found it admirable that Garrett had his hackles raised for the first time since I'd known him.

But not this day.

I held Garrett's eyes for another breath and opened my mouth to apologize.

"That'll be all, Aurora."

Effectively humbled and embarrassingly dismissed, I gave him a curt nod and marched back to my office without making eye contact with anyone.

CHAPTER FIVE

GARRETT

For the first few minutes after she walked out, her head held high, I was proud of myself. Maybe Aurora wasn't the only person at the office who didn't take me seriously, but she was the only person who had the cajones to say it to my face.

"Unbelievable," I muttered under my breath while I spun my chair so that my back was facing the hallway.

My thumb tapped a furious rhythm on the arm of my chair and the pride started ebbing away. Thinking about her face when I all but said once Cal retired, I'd be able to get her fired, the pride morphed into hot shame. Thinking about the way her face had lost color and her chin notched up made my stomach curl.

I wasn't this guy. The guy who threatened an employee who was not only good at her job, she was phenomenal. Aurora knew everything about CFS. More than I did, easily. And she didn't go past her assigned duties because she was a kiss-ass, it was because the woman had the work ethic of a freaking war horse. Not only that, but when Cal *did* retire, Aurora was the logical choice for his replacement. My dad and

Cal had discussed it more than once in front of me. She was the most qualified senior manager we had, nobody in their department even coming close to her when it came to their ability to do the CFO's job.

At the end of the day, if she believed I wasn't a serious COO, it's because I wasn't one. That was a tough pill to swallow. I was in a job that I didn't really earn and definitely didn't continue holding because of my passion for the work we did. If I expected her to respect me and respect my position, then I needed to start by showing her the same courtesy. It's the only way we'd be able to work on our project, and however many more years we spent working together.

Instead of going to her office to apologize, I took a bit to review the files she'd started. Aurora was the kind of person who needed space to organize her thoughts. And probably organize her office too, making sure my grubby hands hadn't done any irreparable damage.

My eyes fell closed and I rubbed at my forehead. If someone else had done to me what I'd done to her, I'd have been livid. And instead of copping to it, I taunted her. Threatened her.

No wonder she hated me.

I stood slowly, placing all the papers back into the manila folder in the exact order that she'd had them. The only stop I made on the way to her office was the break room to grab her a fresh cup of coffee.

If she drank it. To spite me, she'd probably say she didn't and then chuck the damn thing back in my face.

"Shiiiiiit," I said as I poured the scalding hot liquid into a Styrofoam cup, imagining how it would feel if she whipped it at me.

"You okay?" Mark from IT asked from where he was doctoring a cup of his own.

"Yeah, man. Just, forgot where we keep the creamer."

"Uhh, in the drawer to your right." He peered at me over the rim of his thick black-framed glasses. Probably checking to see if I looked drunk or high.

When he left, I sagged in relief and tried to not look like a moron anymore. Before I pushed open the break room door with my free hand, I attempted to make my happy, smiling Garrett face. The one I'd normally reserve for my friends or a free beer or someone who didn't look at me and automatically want to box me in the head.

Judging from the pained grimace that I could see in the reflection, I was failing miserably. Whatever. It was no big deal. All I needed to do was humble myself before my arch-enemy and the woman who constantly made me feel like I was less.

Less intelligent.

Less driven.

Less worthy of respect.

Not necessarily even because of how she treated me. Because in the current world we shared, she was *more* than I was.

It wasn't a realization that many men would be comfortable making. But as I came to a stop just outside her door and watched her smiling while she was talking on the phone to someone, I didn't have any other option but to know how true it was.

Aurora Anderson was the kind of person who deserved the job I was in. She would do a better job than me. And I was too chicken shit to admit to my father that I hated working there.

The sound of Rory's laugh made me blink. I'd never heard it.

Maybe it should have bothered me that she wasn't sitting in her office and stewing over our conversation the way that I had been, but seeing her laugh, seeing her happy in a way that I wasn't used to, swept away any annoyance.

Her laugh was light and feminine. Her smile was wide and bright, and she wrapped the phone cord around her pointer finger in a way that was so girlish and young that I almost forgot she was the same age as me.

But she was, and I needed to get this over with. The thought of walking into her office and being honest with her made my skin prickle with nerves. Because she could laugh at me, or think I was screwing with her. Or she could see my admission for what it was: A peace offering.

Before I could talk myself out of it and back up before she saw me, I rapped lightly on her door. Even though she was still on the phone, she looked up with a smile on her face.

Then the smile was gone. Because it was me waiting for her.

"Gavin," she said into the receiver while she pinned me with that deep blue gaze that made me fidgety. "Can I call you back in a little bit on those reports? Mmhmm. Thanks."

When she set the phone into the cradle with a soft click, I cleared my throat.

"Do you have a couple minutes?"

Aurora nodded and I walked in, setting the file and cup of coffee on her black-stained desk before turning and closing the door behind me.

It was obvious that she was trying to keep a collected face, but her fingers fidgeted along the row of pencils that she had to the right of her computer. One by one, she touched each eraser, messing with the seventh pencil longer than the others. When she pulled her hands back, I heard her let out a quiet sigh.

Aurora was nervous. The way she clenched her teeth and darted her eyes away from me while we sat in silence confirmed it. It was weird, but her nerves actually made me feel better. This wasn't easy for me, and clearly not for her either. So I nodded, decision made.

"Have you ever felt like you're living someone else's plan for your life?"

Immediately, she stilled. Her eyes stopped darting and rested on mine for a heavy beat. When she blinked, it snapped the moment.

"Yes." She said it quietly, not elaborating on her answer, which was fine with me.

"It's how I feel every single day that I walk in here." I shrugged my shoulders. "It feels like, I don't know … like I'm trying to fit into someone else's skin, but it's two sizes too small."

Aurora didn't say anything, just kept watching me. Her face was blank, but her focus was so intense that I knew she was really listening. I leaned forward in the chair that I was sitting in and let my hands hang between my knees.

"Who's skin is it?"

I lifted my head at her softly spoken question. "I don't know. I haven't figured that out yet."

"So why are you telling me? No friends willing to listen to you?"

We both smiled, hers smaller than mine, like we knew it was only a matter of time before one of us tossed a barb. "Because it's incredibly difficult to admit to people that you," I swallowed and held her eyes, "that you don't love your job when it's been handed to you on a silver platter"

Her mouth popped open and she immediately started shaking her head. "*What*? How can you not love what you do?"

I held up my hand. "I get it. I'm handing ammunition to the one person who wouldn't hesitate using it against me." She lifted her eyebrows briefly in concession. "But I'm telling you because I acted like a capital A asshole this morning. I've never threatened anyone's job, especially someone who does it as well as you do."

With slightly narrowed eyes, she kept watching me. "Is that your way of apologizing? You could always start with 'I'm sorry.'"

Laughing under my breath, I settled back in the chair. "You'll never go easy on me, will you?"

"Why would I? You just admitted that you hate the job that I would kill to have. Your father built this company. Don't you take any pride in that?" She glanced over my shoulder, like the people out in the hallway could hear us somehow.

Did I feel pride about it? It was a question that I'd never really asked myself. Just another one of the fundamental differences between me and her. It was the first thing she thought of.

"Pride is a funny thing though, right?" I asked. "People talk about being a proud American or a proud parent. But on the opposite side of the coin, if you're prideful, it's a negative thing. Goes before the fall and all that. So if I felt pride in CFS, when I didn't have a single impact on its success, wouldn't that make me shallow?"

"You say that like I don't already think you're shallow," she said dryly.

"I'm trying here. Okay?"

"I know," she groaned and sank her head into her hands. "I'm saying things I don't mean because it's freaking me out."

"Sorry."

"Oh, now you say it." Aurora lifted her head and covered her mouth with one hand. The tips of her nails were a soft pink. "Fine. I accept your apology from this morning."

"Thank you," I said, meaning it.

Aurora gave me a long look while she pulled in a breath. "And I should apologize too."

"Should? Or are going to?"

Her lips lifted in a smile. "Going to. It was unprofessional of me to say that to you, so I hope you can forgive me."

I held my hand out across her desk. Grudgingly, she took it. "Consider us even in being assholes."

She nodded after letting go of my hand. "Can I ask you something though?"

"Sure."

"Why did you tell me about how you feel about working here? It's not going to help me like you. If anything," she lifted her eyebrows and gave me a meaningful look, "it's going to make it worse."

"I'm not telling you so that you like me. I'm telling you because after how I treated you this morning, you deserved to know. *And* I've wanted to talk to my dad for months about it. You're my insurance policy."

"How do you figure?"

I tilted my head. "Do you plan on keeping this a secret if I never tell him that I want to quit and do something completely different?"

"Hell no."

"Exactly."

Aurora blew out a breath and sank back in her chair. The ends of her ponytail were draped over her shoulder and she twirled the strands for a couple seconds. It shouldn't have mesmerized me, but it did. Suddenly, more than anything, I wanted to know what it felt like between my fingers.

"But you are going to be honest with him? Soon?"

"Yes. As soon we finish this project and get his approval on it."

She narrowed her eyes again and dropped the hair from her hands. "Good Lord. Did we just agree on something?"

"It would seem so."

"This really freaks me out, Garrett," she whispered.

"I can insult you real quick. Would that help?"

"Possibly."

"Your hair is ugly."

She blinked. Then a slow smile curved her lips. Her shoulders started shaking. She was laughing. I made Aurora Anderson laugh.

The feeling that puffed up in my chest was ridiculous. Ridiculous because of how happy it made me. In the eight years that we'd worked together, she'd either avoided me, ignored me or chastised me. I'd never made her smile, and I'd definitely never made her laugh. I swear, I almost stood up and pulled a Rocky Balboa on the steps.

"My hair is *not* ugly."

I smiled at her. "I know."

Her cheeks pinked and she cleared her throat. "Okay then. So you'll talk to your dad when we're done with this. That's a … that's a solid plan."

"He'll probably tell me to pack my shit and go."

"You're his son," she reminded me gently.

"And that means he'll feel *pride* when I tell him I want nothing to do with the family legacy that he's spent twenty-five years building? When I tell him that I want nothing to do with the plans he has for me? You think he'll pat me on the back and tell me he's proud of me?"

I didn't realize how badly I wanted her to say yes when her eyes shuttered and she turned her face to the side.

But she knew as well as me that I didn't have that kind of relationship with my dad. And when she turned her face back to me, there was so much in her eyes that it gave me pause.

"I think some fathers are like that," she said cautiously. "And you won't know if he's one of them until you tell him."

The way she said it and the look in her eyes right before she answered, like she'd slammed a brick wall over the visible display of her feelings, told me there was a story there. Maybe someone had daddy issues. Which was ironic considering her easy relationship with my own. But if I asked, it'd probably end with her chucking a paperweight at my face. With an unamused laugh, I swiped a hand over my mouth. "You're not exactly filling me with confidence."

"I shouldn't have to. You're a grown ass man."

I smiled at that. An actual *that-was-funny* smile. And then I noticed she was zeroed right in on my mouth. My smile grew at that and she snapped her eyes up when she realized I was watching her. The high curve of her cheekbones flamed red, but instead of calling her on it, I just stood from the chair and pushed the file toward her.

"I brought this back for you." I pointed at the cup. "And the coffee, which is probably cold."

"Oh. Thank you." Then she took a deep breath and met my eyes. The sheer force of them almost knocked me back in the chair. They were so blue, so big that it felt like they were reaching in and crawling around my brain.

Which was gross if I thought about it literally, but with what I just revealed to her, it felt appropriate. Aurora Anderson had— figuratively, at least—been given a glimpse into my brain in a way that no one in my life had ever been given before.

Yeah. I needed to leave. Stat.

My hand was on the door handle when she spoke again. "Garrett? You really don't feel invested in CFS? Not even a little?"

Shit.

I closed the door again and leaned my back against it. I hated this. Because if I gave her my honest answer, she'd probably judge me for it. And I *hated* that she might be right for doing so. The way she'd phrased it, it was the first time that thinking about leaving, about being honest to my dad felt uncomfortable. Felt wrong. Of course, she'd be the person to make me feel like this.

"It's not a trick question."

"Isn't it?"

Tapping my thumb on the door behind me, I held her eyes until she glanced away.

CHAPTER SIX

AURORA

Honestly, if Garrett was trying to devise the worst kind of torture for me, it was this. Feeling even the teeniest pang of sympathy for him felt like I was betraying myself. But of all the things that I'd expected when he walked into my office, it was not this.

But I couldn't let him leave without actually trying to understand. Because of all the things that I could empathize with, it was how difficult it was to admit, out loud, the thing that you kept the most buried.

Garrett was still leaning up against my office door, considering how to answer. The white of his dress shirt looked pristine and bright up against the dark colored wood behind his broad shoulders. The knot of his blue tie was loosened a little, like he'd pulled at it before walking down to talk to me.

"It's not that I don't care whether CFS does well or not," he said slowly, tapping his fingers against his thigh while he watched me. "I do. If it ever folded, I'd be sad. Mainly because I know that it would hurt my dad to see that happen. But this," he gestured behind him to the hallway and offices and cubicles and conference rooms that lay outside my office, "I don't think this is it for me."

"Why not?"

He lifted his eyebrows while he pulled in a deep breath, like he was surprised I was still asking.

Hell, join the club, Garrett. But as long as the door stayed shut and nothing pricked the atmosphere between us, precarious though it was, I was really, insanely curious.

But there'd have to be a pistol to my head in order for me to *ever* admit that to him. Seeing him in my space, the place that almost felt like more of my home than the place I lived, was disconcerting.

Almost as disconcerting as these snippets of honesty that he was handing my way.

"Most days, I hate being cooped up in an office, staring at a computer all day. I can't imagine how my dad can sit in that massive office of his and look out at the mountains without wanting to be out there. And it feels like if I'm here for the rest of my working life?" He shook his head, eyes serious and his mouth flat. "It feels like it'll slowly kill me."

"Not melodramatic at all, are we?"

One side of his lips curved up, and it made the side of his chiseled face do the same. "You just can't handle it when I talk to you like you're a normal person."

"I *am* a normal person, Garrett."

Then he laughed. Not the loud, amused sound that I'd heard from him so often. This was softer and lower, and I felt it tug somewhere south of my belly button. I blinked away, staring down at my desk and fidgeting my fingers along the lacquered surface.

"So why do you love it? If you can ask me why I feel like I don't belong here, I think I should be able to do the same."

"But everyone knows that I love working here. It's not a secret. They're not questions of equal value. For that to happen, I'd have to answer a question that nobody knows."

"Oh come on," he groaned.

For a split second, I almost answered. I rubbed my lips together so that I didn't, but I couldn't fathom that he actually cared to know why.

"I'd explain to you, but there's so many big words. I'd hate for you to think so hard that your hair would start on fire. You're already thinning a little bit up top." I shot a meaningful look at his hair line, which was absolutely *not* thinning. He had this thick, light brown hair that always seemed like he'd just run his hands through it.

He just smiled even more widely, showing his perfectly straight, white teeth. It was *horrifying* how much I appreciated people who took good care of their teeth. Naturally, that meant I had to stare at the wall next to the door and not at him. But I could feel his eyes on me. On my face, never wavering, and the weight of his gaze pressed on me like a hot iron.

"What?" I snapped, not looking over at him for more than a second. Unfortunately, when I *did* glance, my eyes landed directly on his wide, smiling mouth. Shit.

"You're nervous."

My eyes widened and my mouth popped open. I forgot I was supposed to not be looking at him. "I'm not nervous."

Garrett walked away from the door and shook a finger at me. "Talking to me in complete sentences that don't involve insults makes you *nervous*, Aurora. I can see it."

Damn it, I hated that he was right. Garrett was far less nerve-wracking when he stayed in his corner and I stayed in mine, when the line between us stayed firm and solid.

This … this bullshit that he was bringing to me like an offering is what made things wonky. Blurred the edges of the box that I had no problem keeping him in.

Smoothing my face, I folded my hands on my desk and peered up at him. "Maybe you're projecting your own issues on to me, Garrett, but there's absolutely nothing about you that makes me nervous. Because nerves would indicate inferiority. Or that something about you affects me so deeply that it manifests itself physically." I lifted an eyebrow, trying to look more casual than I felt inside. "So I should probably ask.

Do I make *you* nervous?"

He leaned forward and braced his hands on the back of the chair that he'd sat in. It did crazy things to his shoulders and biceps, the muscles shifting and bunching under the cotton of his shirt. "Every single day."

Cursing the tiny flutter that gave my stomach, I pursed my lips and narrowed my eyes, plucking one of the pencils from my line. "Cute. Now is it possible for you to go back to your own office and, I don't know … do some work?"

Garrett held my eyes, the traitorous warmth coating my spine making it almost impossible for me to look away. Then he looked down at my pencils, and reached to knock one from its place.

I slapped his hand when he got close, and the smug shithead laughed again. That same laugh that made me feel padded-room crazy because of how it affected me.

"You want to know why I won't go back to my office?"

Instead of answering, I sighed.

"I mean, I'd explain it to you." Then he shook his head with a sad look on his face. "But all those big words, Aurora. And you'd be too busy watching my mouth again to even understand them."

When he yanked open the door and slid out, I chucked the pencil in my hand as hard as I could, growling under my breath when it clattered against the already closed door and fell uselessly to the carpet.

CHAPTER SEVEN

GARRETT

Just as Aurora's office door clicked shut, I heard the smack of something against the wood. I laughed, imagining her throwing something at me.

Jeannie from Marketing gave me a strange look when she walked past me, which wasn't surprising. I was standing outside an office that wasn't mine and laughing my ass off. I wiped a hand under my eye and straightened my tie before I started down the hall.

Greeting everyone I passed, Aurora's words pinged around in my head like annoying little marbles. Was there something wrong with *me* that I didn't feel invested in CFS?

I didn't even particularly know what I'd want to do when I left, but I always imagined myself in a job that was different every single day. Something that wasn't stationary or dull, even if it had humbler origins.

My sister had escaped unscathed, probably because she'd been self-aware enough when she started college to know that working in finance was not for her. The interior design firm that she'd worked for the last five years was one of the best in Denver, and for that, my parents couldn't have been prouder.

It actually lit a tiny flicker of hope in me. Maybe Aurora was right.

Wait. I shook my head quickly. I'd just thought the words 'Aurora was right' and didn't immediately want to pour bleach in my brain.

When I cleared the doorway into my office, I stopped, tapping a finger on the corner of my desk. Even if I didn't tell my dad right now that I wanted to leave, maybe I could try asking him why he loved it. I glanced over at the framed family picture that I had on my bookshelf.

It was the last one we'd had done formally, after Anna had graduated from college. My parents were standing to the left of us, with my dad's arm anchored around my mom's waist. They looked nice. Respectable in khakis and church-appropriate shirts.

Anna and I had broken our pose right before the photographer clicked the button. I'd pinched her arm, and she was just turning to slug me in the stomach. My face was frozen up in an 'oh shit' expression, and Anna had her teeth bared like she was growling and her right arm swinging around to me.

When I'd ordered the picture, my mom just said, "Oh Garrett, that's so embarrassing." Anna approved, because she'd hit me with a helluva right hook. Actually made me lose my breath for a second, if memory served.

The fact that Anna was escaping the Calder legacy didn't even really piss me off, because she was one of my best friends. I'd only been four when my parents adopted her from South Korea, but I still remembered her giant shock of black hair when my mom crouched down next to me and said, "Garrett, this is your sister, Anna. You're going to have to help me take care of her."

It was one of my earliest memories, actually. If I'd gotten along with her less, maybe I would have felt resentment, had a convenient scapegoat to throw my discontent. It wasn't Anna's fault that she had the balls to go after what she wanted, to be able to define it better than I ever had. And my dad supported her, he respected her decision. Looking at our faces, theirs in photo-appropriate smiles even though their grown children were acting like toddlers, loosened a knot of tension in me. He was my dad, and even if we weren't buddy buddy the way I was with Anna or my mom, I should be able to have a normal conversation with him about why he loved the company he built so much.

If I could do that, then maybe it wouldn't be so difficult for my dad and I to talk about what I wanted to do, if I wasn't at CFS any more. But to do that, I'd have to figure out what it was that I wanted. It was the only hitch in my plans. I wanted out of there, but where did I want to exit to? What would be waiting for me if I walked out of the building that had housed the only career I'd ever had?

I didn't precisely know yet, but maybe having an honest conversation with my dad was a solid start in the right direction.

I whistled on my walk down to his office, and when I turned to corner, his administrative assistant, Marjorie, stood quickly from her L-shaped desk.

"Garrett, I've been trying to call you."

Patting my pockets for my cell, I was surprised to see how frazzled she looked. Marjorie had been at CFS as long as my dad, and basically ran his life once he walked through the doors. "Crap, sorry, I wasn't in my office and I must have left my cell sitting on my desk. Why?"

She paced behind her desk, the thin, papery skin on her hands looking almost translucent while she worried her fingers together. "Your dad. He's missed two meetings already, and he's not answering his cell phone. Neither were you. I was starting to get worried."

Okay, so that wasn't typical. "I'm sure it's not a big deal. Did you call my parents' house? Maybe my mom is sick or something, or he's sick and forgot to call." She lifted a thin, gray eyebrow at me and I held up my hands. "What? Stranger things have happened."

"No," she shook her head and folded her arms over her stomach. "I've worked for your father for twenty-five years. He's never forgotten to call in sick. And I don't have your mom's cell number, only their house number and that's going to voicemail too."

When she blinked rapidly, I walked over to her and laid my hands on her thin shoulders. Marjorie was one of the most level-headed people I'd ever met, so to see her this nervous, I started to feel a tiny pinch in my stomach. "Hey, don't freak out on me. If you lose it, then who in the entire world can I trust to stay strong?" With closed eyes, she let out a massive breath. I wrapped an arm around her shoulder and gave her a quick hug. "There's my girl."

Marjorie snorted and peered over the edge of her pink-framed glasses at me. "Girl? Honey, I wiped shit off your ass when you were a baby."

We both smiled and I gave her a confident nod. "It'll be fine, I'm sure there's a simple explanation. I'll go grab my cell and call my mom, okay?"

"Okay. Thanks, Garrett."

I winked and turned back in the direction that I'd just came from. Maybe I walked a little bit faster than normal, because it *was* strange. Visions of my mom getting in a car accident or Anna in the hospital whipped through my head and I picked up my pace, practically jogging by the time I got to my office. There was a pretty short list of reasons why my dad would flake like this, and I didn't like any of my options.

When I snagged my cell from the far side of my desk, my heart sank like a brick when the lock screen lit up.

Anna – Missed Call (7)

Mom – Missed Call (4)

"Oh holy shit," I whispered, my skin instantly freezing up. I swiped my phone open and pulling up the last missed call from Anna, just two minutes earlier.

She picked up immediately, her voice shaking and full of tears. "Garrett, you have to get to the hospital. It's Dad."

I don't remember running from my office to my car while she kept crying on the other end of the phone, telling me in disjointed sentences what happened.

The drive to UCH was one massive blur, the only thoughts registering were my hands on the wheel and the heartbeat thundering in my ears.

Because how did that work, exactly? My heart was fine. It beat, not because I asked it to, not because I thought about it in order to make it happen. It was just there, pumping blood and keeping me going.

My eyes burned hot when I tore into the parking lot. What did he feel first? A tingle in his arm? A pain in his chest?

People moved out of my way when I ran across the asphalt. My heart never changed speed, it was the same when I'd been driving as it was while I ran so fast that I felt sweat bead on my forehead. How was that *possible*?

When I skidded around the corner, I saw Anna first. She was standing up against the wall with her arms wrapped tightly around her body. She wasn't crying, at least I didn't think so. Maybe I wasn't too late. Maybe. My mom came out of the doorway that Anna was staring at.

"Mom?"

She turned to me, her face wet and her dark hair tangled around her face like she'd been running the same race that I'd just finished.

"I'm sorry, sweetie," she whispered on a broken exhale just as I wrapped her in my arms. "He's … he's gone." Quietly, she cried and I tightened my hold on her, like it would contain the rolling waves of grief threatening to pull me under. When it didn't, I pressed my chin against the crown of her head like an underwhelming anchor against everything battering against the inside layer of my skin. My eyes held with Anna, and a single tear slipped down her cheek. I opened one arm to her, and she fell into the two of us.

My sister's sobs weren't quiet when she clutched at my back. When I blinked, hot tears fell onto my face. Maybe if I kept my eyes closed, they'd stay in. Maybe.

Holding them, feeling their tears as they soaked through my shirt and onto my skin, it felt like the only part of my body I could recognize was where they had their arms wrapped around me. Everything else was just … static. White noise.

Anna lifted her head, and the tracks of moisture on her face gutted me. Like, the messy, bloody kind of gutting. I felt it spill out onto the floor.

"I didn't get to say goodbye either. I didn't get to tell him I loved him." Her eyes filled when Mom started crying even harder.

I blew out a breath and looked up at the ceiling like gravity might keep the tears in, but they simply tracked down my temples and slithered down my jaw. I blinked rapidly and pressed a kiss to Anna's forehead.

The man who clapped my back when I graduated college and said he was proud of me.

The man who taught me how to drive with a car way too expensive for me to be touching.

The man who gave me the greatest example of how to work hard and provide for your family.

Gone.

I'd never speak to him again.

"We're going to be okay. We'll be okay," I said to them. To myself.

"How?" My mom asked into my shirt, her voice wet and muffled.

I pressed them closer and let out a heavy breath. "I don't know. But I promise we will. I'll take care of everything."

They dissolved into tears again, and I set my jaw. I'd take care of my mom and my sister. I'd never let them down. Because it's what my dad would have wanted me to do.

So I stood with them in my arms for another hour. I'd have held them like that for another ten, if they had needed me to.

The next morning, I heard Kat's ringtone on my cell phone and groggily reached over to silence it. Then I rolled back under the covers to shut out the world. When my heart threatened to launch itself out of my body with thoughts of my dad, I pinched my eyes shut and forced myself back to sleep.

It was awful, but my very first thought when Anna sent me a text the day after that, saying that my mom wanted me to come over for dinner the day after my dad died was *can't I just stay in bed?*

Everything felt fuzzy, my head, my eyes, my fingers when I scrubbed at my face before getting out of the car in front of my parent's Washington Park home.

My mom's home, I guess.

Anna's car was already parked on the curb since she'd stayed there the night before and with no small amount of dread, I walked up the sidewalk to the red brick home that my parents built in 2006. I was in college at the time, and it had felt insane to me that they were having a five-bedroom home built when neither Anna or I lived under their roof outside of holidays, but my mom had just smiled at my dad and said that someday it would be perfect for all the grandkids we'd be giving them.

The memory was enough to make me stop and brace my hands on my knees so I could steady my breathing. Having kids wasn't something I put much thought into yet, what with no girlfriend and all, but knowing that any hypothetical children of mine or Anna's would never meet our dad was enough to make me feel sick to my stomach.

"Hey, Garrett," I heard from behind me. I straightened and turned, pasting a polite smile on my face when I saw Mrs. Stevens from next door walking her stupid little poodle. "I'm so sorry to hear about your dad. You tell your mother I'll bring her some food tomorrow morning, okay?"

"Yes, ma'am. I'll do that." She looked pleased by my formal response, but as soon as she walked away, the smile dropped. I wanted to tell her that she could take her food and shove it, because a mediocre casserole wouldn't do shit in making my mom feel better.

Apparently I wasn't the most gracious person when in the numbing throes of grief.

The sound of the front door opening snapped me out of my asshole-ish thoughts and I turned to see my sister on the front porch.

"Hey," I said as I walked up the three concrete steps and held my arms out. Anna swallowed roughly and then walked into me for a hug. She pressed her face into my chest and took a long, shaky breath.

"Mom looks terrible."

"So do you."

Anna snorted and pulled back, wiping the heel of her hand on her face to push away a tear that I hadn't known was there. "Thanks."

I tipped my chin at the house. "Did she really make dinner?"

"Oh yeah. Full meal. I think she needs something to do or she's going to lose her mind."

With a grimace at the cracked-open mahogany door, I scratched the side of my face. "Mrs. Stevens said she was going to bring food tomorrow."

Anna huffed. "She's such a nosy bitch. She'll probably plant a camera so she can tell everyone how horribly Mom is holding up."

I felt a sharp pang of shame that Anna had been with Mom every single minute in the last two days, and I hadn't. If my dad was sitting up on some fluffy cloud with a shiny gold harp, I'm sure he was already disappointed in me. Or maybe once you were in heaven, you didn't feel shit like that. And while my dad and I didn't usually hold conversations about faith and the afterlife, I did feel pretty certain that he'd earned a spot up there.

I'll do better, Dad, I thought with a strange sense of fervency. I could be a good son to my mom and eat whatever meal she made to keep herself busy. Then I probably would get fat and Aurora could make fun of me. I'm sure that would make Dad smile too.

I had to take a deep breath, because thinking about my father in the abstract was still such a strange feeling. He was there one minute and gone the next, but I was the one that had to remember that fact. I had to remind myself that it was the latter.

Anna must have seen it on my face, because she gave me another hug. "Come on, she still loves you even though you disappeared yesterday."

"Have you ever considered keeping those thoughts in your head?"

"Not really."

I gave her a sad smile while we walked into the long entryway of the house. The wide, sweeping staircase to the left was framed with a beautifully carved banister that matched the woodwork in the rest of the house, and led to all of the bedrooms besides my parents'.

Besides my mom's.

Blowing out a breath, I looked up at the ceiling for a second. When would I get used to doing that? Or even worse, when would I stop needing to correct myself?

"Oh, honey, you made it," my mom called from the formal dining room to the right of us. Anna had not been lying. She'd fully set the massive dining table that we only ate at three times a year. Thanksgiving, Christmas, and Easter. But I couldn't focus too long on the massive amounts of food that were placed all over the table, because my mom really did look awful. Her dark hair was pushed around her face in disarray, and the bags under her eyes were a deep purple that matched the ones under Anna's eyes. If I'd been able to look for too long in a mirror that morning, I probably would have seen the same ones.

"Yeah, I made it," I said, sharing a brief look with Anna. My mom was fidgeting with the bowl of mashed potatoes, and I stilled her hands. "Mom, are you okay?"

She didn't look at me right away, but I could feel her fingers shaking where I still had my own wrapped around them. Then she pulled in a long, hitched breath and all the busy tension left her body. "I don't know what to do with myself, Garrett."

I tugged her into my arms and held her as tightly as I dared. My eyes burned when she started to weep softly, but I clenched my teeth together to stay strong for her.

"We'll just take it one day at a time," I said into the top of her head. "Okay?"

Anna and I locked eyes, and I was acutely relieved that she wasn't crying. She nodded, and I knew we'd get Mom through this together. I didn't know how, but we would.

We'd have to.

CHAPTER EIGHT

AURORA

Why did I have so many black jackets?

My fingers coasted over sleek linen, rough corduroy, silk that felt cool on my skin. Only the slightest differences in the deep, dark color of the fabrics seeped through the fog of my brain. Every time I bought one, I thought, it's classic. You can wear a black jacket out for drinks, to a board meeting, and to a funeral.

I'd been staring into my closet for twenty minutes. Long, quiet, heavy twenty minutes. Every minute for the past four days had felt like that.

In my eight years at CFS, I'd never experienced it that way it had been since Rich died.

Smiles were fleeting and disappeared just as quickly, like they were forbidden. Like if someone caught you doing it, you'd have to defend yourself for feeling even the briefest moment of levity while the dank cloud of grief coated every wall in the building.

Shaking my head, I moved past the jackets; it was too hot out anyway. Pulling my black sheath dress off its ivory padded hanger, I let out a deep breath before stepping into it and slipping it up my body.

When I reached my hand over my shoulder to yank the zipper up the rest of the way, and couldn't reach it, I felt the inexplicable tingle at the bridge of my nose that always preceded my tears. The hot ball of emotion stopped dead in my throat, right where I couldn't swallow it down. There was no one around to help me, no one to walk in behind me and pull my stupid zipper the rest of the way up.

I dashed a hand under my eye, furious that this would make me cry for the first time all week.

"Come on, you son of a bitch," I whispered, hating the full sound of my voice, and reached my hand so far back that I felt a twinge of pain in my neck at the awkward angle. The zipper slid up in a smooth movement and I sighed, feeling the yucky weight of tears abating.

Turning to the side so I could see my profile in the massive floor to ceiling mirror that I'd had custom made for my bedroom, I cocked one foot back at a time, trying to decide which shoes to wear.

The nude sling backs with the three-inch heels.

While I was setting the black peep toes back on their shelf on the far side of my closet, I heard the faint buzzing of my cell phone from the hard lacquered surface of the white nightstand next to my bed.

When I saw my cousin Mia's name on the screen, I smiled.

"Hey," I said while I tucked the phone in between my cheek and my shoulder.

"Dude, you sounded legit horrible on your voicemail last night. Sorry I didn't call you back, I was working late and didn't want to risk waking you up."

Perching on the edge of my bed so I could pull my other shoe on the back of my foot, I rolled my eyes. "You can't possibly say that I sounded horrible. My entire voicemail was made up of about eight syllables."

"Mi-a, call me when you get a chance. Love you." She made a considering sound. "I'm no smarty pants like you, but that's like, a lot more than eight. And it's way more than I need to know that you're Mopey-Pants Rory."

It was so tempting to fall back on my bed, let the fluffy white duvet puff up around my head and forget that I needed to leave in ten minutes to watch them bury the man who singlehandedly influenced my career.

"It's eleven," I argued for no other reason than that I was pissy. "That's not a lot."

"Are you on the rag or what? We're usually pretty synced up, and I'm not due for another week."

"That's so crass, Mia," I said on a sigh. "I've never once told you when I'm … when I'm…"

When she cackled in my ear, I couldn't help but grin.

"Say it. Say it, Rory. Saaaaaaaaaaay it."

"On the rag," I said and then huffed. The sound was pure exasperation, but in reality, it was the lightest I'd felt all week. Like she'd managed to pluck something spiked and heavy off my shoulders by the simple act of making me laugh. Grief wasn't a cloak that I'd really had to don often in my life. It felt cold and overpowering. I couldn't sift through it when I would have random flashes of conversations with Rich from the last eight years.

"So if that's not it, what's your prob?"

I gave the clock on my nightstand a quick glance to make sure I wasn't running late before I answered. "So you know Rich from work?"

"Boss man with the douche son. Sure."

My brows furrowed when she said it. I hadn't seen Garrett once since he ran from my office, and in all the times I'd thought about him and wondered how he and his mom and sister were doing, I'd never thought of him that way. "He died a few days ago."

"Oh shit, Rory," Mia said on a heavy exhale, like I'd socked her in the stomach. Fairly close to how I felt when Mark called a mandatory staff meeting about two hours after I'd last seen Garrett. "I'm so sorry. I know he meant a lot to you."

There were so many trivial sayings, so many clichés when you'd try to describe someone who had a significant impact on your life. Usually simple words and phrases that had been recycled a trillion times on sympathy cards and in conversations about death, about loss. They all fell woefully short.

I nodded and then cleared my throat when I realized she couldn't see me. "He did. Rich was so kind to me from day one. He never showed me anything but patience and unending support. There was no questioning from him that I was cut out for my job, that I couldn't handle whatever they threw my way." That mother effing tingle was back and I used my free hand to pinch the bridge of my nose with my thumb and my forefinger. "The first time I met with him after my internship was done, he told me that I had the same look in my eye that he did when he finished his MBA. That there was a drive in me that made him sit up and take notice. He barely even knew me and he believed in me. Instantly."

The burn spread across my face and I blinked rapidly, imagining the last time I'd spoken to him. Nothing of importance was talked about, just the simple conversation between two people who saw each other five days a week for years. Maybe the fact that nothing of significance passed between us was bothering me.

"You okay?"

"I'm fine."

Mia clicked her tongue and it set my teeth on edge. I pressed my molars together before standing off the bed and smoothing down the front of my dress.

"The General isn't here, Rory. It's okay for you to cry about losing someone important to you."

"It's not about that."

"Isn't it?" she asked gently. Mia was two years my junior and my only cousin. Even though we'd moved from state to state my entire childhood when my dad would get reassigned, she was the one person that never slipped away from me. And she'd spent enough time with us during summer break to know exactly what kind of conditioning I had working against me. Through every deployment my dad went on, I never once saw my mother cry.

She never even faltered in her day to day activities.

"Crying won't change anything." They were her words, not mine. But I'd heard them enough in my life that I could actually recognize the truth in them. Me crying over Rich's absence in my life, over the abrupt hole that he left for so many people, wouldn't change a single thing.

"Crying is cathartic, yo. Sometimes I just put on *A Fault in Our Stars* or the mother effing *Notebook* because it feels so good just to let it all out, you know?"

I breathed out a laugh, imagining Mia curled up around a pint of Half Baked and sobbing into her spoon. "No, I don't know. I've never seen either of them."

"Shut. Your. Mouth." I heard a sharp smack in the background. "I just hurt my hand smacking the wall because I am so incensed for you!"

"It can't be for me because it was my choice. Maybe *at* me is a better way to say it."

While she bemoaned my complete lack of entertainment knowledge, I grabbed my car keys and small black clutch from the table by the door leading into the garage.

"You haven't seen *The Notebook*," Mia said sadly.

My car started with a gentle purr and I hit some buttons on my steering wheel to switch our call over to Bluetooth. "Am I really missing that much?"

"I mean, only the greatest love story *ever*. That Nicholas Sparks, man. He knows his shit."

When I saw the thin sliver of my reflection in my rearview mirror, the slightly crinkled skin around my eyes that only did that when I laughed, I knew what she was doing.

"Maybe you should come visit me. Be able to distract me in person."

"Dude. I'm so there. Let me put in for some PTO and I'll come spend the week. Could you take some time off too?"

I hummed, turning onto the freeway toward the church where the funeral was being held. "Maybe. I'm not sure what will happen now that Rich is gone. It might be harder for me to disappear."

Another call flashed on the screen of my sound system, a number I didn't recognize. "Mia, I've got another call. We'll talk soon."

"Okay! Love you, Rory-balory."

I was still laughing a little when I picked up the other call. "This is Aurora."

"Ahh, yes. Miss Anderson, my name is Graham Caldwell and I'm Richard Calder's attorney."

Tilting my head while I took my exit, I lifted my eyebrows. "Is there something I can help you with?"

"Yes, actually. I'm assuming you'll be attending the funeral here shortly."

"I am."

"Wonderful. After the service, there will be a reading of Richard's last will and testament, and he had instructions that you be in attendance along with his family."

My jaw popped open, heart immediately thump-thumping in a twitchy rhythm. "*What?* Are you sure?"

"Very. Rich was very clear the last time we updated his will."

His voice was kind and patient, and it sent a shooting pang through my ribs at how similar his tone was to that of Rich's. "And umm, when was that?"

"I'll answer all your questions, I promise. Because I'm sure you'll have more later. There will be a time for the family to greet everyone after the funeral for about an hour, as they've chosen not to have a separate visitation, so if you could wait until after that and we'll find a quiet spot to meet at the church."

"Yes, of course," I said quietly. When my car eased to a stop at a red light, I said my goodbyes to Graham and propped my elbow up on the door next to me so I could brace my forehead with my hand. My brain whizzed around so many possibilities that it was impossible to settle on one. Maybe he left me some money, which was preposterous. We were close, but not inheritance close.

When I parked my car in front of the tall brick church, I sat for a few minutes to collect myself. The soaring white columns that held up the front of the building led up to the sharp steeple that was topped with a simple spire.

I hadn't been in a church in fifteen years. From the quiet interior of my car, I watched a steady stream of people walk through the wide double glass doors that sat behind the columns. With their dark clothes and somber expressions, they all looked completely incongruous to the spectacular summer day. The sky was almost painfully blue and dotted with puffy white clouds.

Waxing poetic about the sky, I thought ruefully. It was a stalling technique that I'd never tried before. But going into to say goodbye to Richard was hard enough before that phone call. Now it would be pressing at the back of my grief the entire service.

Instead of sliding my black sunglasses over my face, I stepped out of my car and let the full force of the sun hit my eyes. It hurt at first, but I blinked right up into it.

I didn't know whether I believed Rich could see what we were doing, but on the off chance that he could, I stared straight up into the brightness.

"You better not have pulled something crazy," I said under my breath. Sure, speaking out loud to the recently deceased person as I walked into their funeral was the picture of sanity.

By the time I walked through the doors, there was already a minister at the front of the church, standing behind a wood pulpit. I didn't really hear much of what he said, because the casket behind him that was covered in an obnoxious spray of lilies and roses held every speck of my attention.

I couldn't even bring myself to look at the photo of Rich that was propped on an easel next to the pulpit.

When the minister was done, someone else walked up and said things about Rich. The words were simple and kind, which made me happy. There were no overblown sentiments about the person that Rich Calder was. Just the truth. That he was a hardworking man who loved his family, loved what he did, and had earned the respect of everyone who knew him.

My eyes wandered the front pew, and in between the bowed heads of the people sitting between me and the Calders, I could see the back of Garrett's head and his left shoulder. Wearing a black suit over his broad frame and staring straight ahead, I had to breathe through a momentary swell of sympathy for him. The last conversation we'd had about his father had been whether his dad loved him enough to want him to be happy, even if that meant leaving the company that Rich had built with his own two hands.

From what Marjorie had told me through her hiccupping sobs and quiet tears, neither Garrett or his sister Anna had been at the hospital in time to say their goodbyes. Without even feeling the warning signs, I sucked in a breath of surprise when a single tear splashed down my cheek and dropped onto my lap, trying to imagine what that might have felt like.

Despite the fact that I hadn't spoken to the General since the day I walked out of the house, it still was impossible to try to imagine racing to be by his side, only to have that last moment already gone. The last chance to say something, even if it's not perfect.

My brain rolled that around while I stood with the everyone else. They sang a hymn that I didn't know, so I clasped my hands in front of me and kept my eyes trained on my feet. If I knew the General— my father— was dying, what would I want to say to him? Would he say anything to me?

Knowing him, and I'd wager a year's salary that I still did, he'd wait me out just to prove he was more stubborn.

Through a few stilted conversations with my mom each year, I knew they were aware of what I did, when I was promoted and how I was doing exactly what I'd set about doing when I left. Not only was it the opposite of what he'd raised me for, he thought it was shallow. To help people make more money that they didn't earn, that they didn't work for, was unacceptable. I wasn't serving my country or raising children or being a teacher or a nurse. I wasn't contributing to society in a way that made a tangible difference.

So maybe what I'd tell him, if I had a few stolen moments right near the end, was that I was proud of what I did. That, even if he didn't see it, what we *did* made a tangible difference to the people who trusted us with the dollars that they earned.

That the money they'd paid into life insurance or a 401k was the difference between having nothing, and being able to provide for their families when something awful happened. When tragedy pushed their lives to the edge of the cliff, we were able to help pull them back. He didn't see it, and he might never. But one of the things that Rich Calder taught me was how important it was, what we did.

I lifted my head and looked at the front of the church with watery eyes.

People started exiting the rows in hushed groups, nobody speaking much above a whisper. Marjorie caught my eye from the other side of the church and she gave me a sad smile while she kept a tight hold of her husband's arm. The way she leaned into him, his tall, thin frame that didn't look like it was much sturdier than hers, made something ache inside of me.

Instead of looking away from the picture they made, I smiled back before leaving my row. People milled around the back of the church where there were a few small stands holding pictures of Rich. One in particular made me smile.

The sepia tone of the picture in its enlarged size, the cut of his hair and the shirt that he wore made it look like a classic late 80s shot. He was sitting behind his desk with his arms spread open. Anna was perched on one of his legs with a perfectly adorable smile on her face. And Garrett.

Without thinking, I stepped closer and almost lifted my hand to touch the print, but pulled back before I did. He was sitting on the edge of Rich's desk wearing scuffed jeans and a dirty t-shirt. He couldn't have been more than six or seven, with the ridiculous bowl haircut and missing front tooth that showed in his mischievous grin. Mischievous because he was dumping out a box of pens right as the picture was snapped.

Making a mess of his father's office when he couldn't have possibly known where he'd find himself not quite a couple decades later. But they all looked so happy.

Suzanne, Garrett's mother, must have snapped the shot, but I couldn't help but wish I'd been able to see them all together in it. That thought snapped me out of my own head. There were still people waiting to give their condolences to Garrett, Suzanne and Anna, and even though I'd be sitting in a room with them all too soon, I went to get in line while I could.

With each hug and tearfully given sentiment, I felt increasingly nervous. I'd only met Anna twice, and Suzanne and I had never had much more than pleasant, surface conversations. Would they need a reminder of who I was, with Garrett off to the side probably hating that I was even standing in front of him?

Before the last person moved past them, I took a deep breath and smoothed a hand over the end of my ponytail. Suzanne blinked over to me first and I braced myself for her blank, polite look. But her eyes welled up and she opened her arms for a hug instead.

"Oh, Rory," she said quietly, her casual use of my nickname slicing straight through my heart. When she wrapped her arms around me, I pressed my eyes shut. "He may have never been able to say it to you, dear, but he loved you very much. He was so proud of you."

I squeezed my arms around her shaking back and let two more tears slip down my face. "I'm so sorry, Suzanne. He was a wonderful man."

She let me go with a smile, nodding her thanks before moving on to the next person. Anna, who was beautiful and stoic in a dress very similar to mine, gave me a cautious smile. "I've heard a lot about you, Rory."

Going with the swell of emotion that still hadn't ebbed, I leaned in to hug her too. "I'm sorry for your loss, Anna. He talked about you all the time."

She rolled her eyes a little when she pulled back, but the dark brownish black of her irises were bright with tears. "Yeah, that sounds like him." Anna had to take a second to compose herself and she reached forward to clasp my hands while she did. Her eyes were direct and clear, and I noted absently that I wanted her to show me how she kept her eyeliner so perfect when she was probably crying all day. "He talked about you a lot too, Rory. I used to joke with him that you were his work daughter, because you followed in his footsteps in a way that I never could. Go figure, right? His Asian daughter didn't want the finance math job."

I couldn't help but laugh with how good-naturedly she said it. My eyes flicked to Garrett, who was watching me with an unreadable expression on his handsome face. He was pale and had smudges under his eyes like he hadn't slept well.

Anna squeezed my hands and let go to greet the person behind me.

Just me and Garrett.

His hands were shoved in his pants pockets, and the knot of his bright red tie was perfectly centered underneath the starched collar of his white dress shirt.

We both held there, waiting for the other to make the first move when I finally met his eyes. The aching that I saw there almost knocked me back. I blinked a few times and then cleared my throat before holding my hand out to him.

"I'm very sorry for your loss, Garrett. He was a good man."

His chest heaved on a couple deep breaths, but he didn't so much as blink while he stared at me. Right before I was going to drop my hand, he reached out to clasp it. The warm, dry skin of his palm was rough against my fingers. He tightened his grip, but not in a way that was uncomfortable or presumptuous.

It felt like a tether. Like I was holding him down, or he was holding me down, I didn't know. But something in his eyes screamed at me that he was on the edge of losing it completely.

"It'll be okay," I said quietly before giving his fingers a gentle squeeze.

Garrett blinked when I said it, and the moment snapped and then broke.

When he turned to the person behind me, effectively dismissing me, I had to wonder if I'd imagined the entire exchange.

CHAPTER NINE

GARRETT

There was such a tight lid on my emotions that when my mom came and stood behind me, laying a gentle hand on my back to let me know that my father's attorney, Graham, was ready for us, I had to take a second to remind myself that her easy touch wasn't some surface level, well-meaning sympathizer who wanted me to make them feel better.

Even my friends, to an extent, who'd taken their time to give me their condolences before the funeral started. He had been *our* family, but almost everyone coming through the line wanted us to hug them and tell them that we'd be okay because it would make them feel better in their grief.

Except Aurora, I thought as I followed my mom and sister into a small library down the hallway from the sanctuary. There had been one split second where she squeezed my hand and looked in my eyes, and I felt her.

I felt how sorry she was for me. For my mother. For Anna. But I also felt how little she judged me for acting toward her the way I'd wanted to act toward every single other person approaching me.

In fact, I don't think she'd judged me at all.

Wasn't that a friggin' head trip? That she of all people would give me the most crystal clear moment of reality all damn day. That the feel of her hand in mine, her cool fingers and smooth skin, grounded me for a long, relief-filled moment.

That hammered through my head while I numbly sat down into a chair that was hard and cold. Then, like I conjured her, Aurora slid into a chair across the wooden table from me. My eyebrows probably hit my hairline, I raised them so quickly.

"Garrett, Anna, Suzanne," Graham said from his seat at the head of the table before I could question Aurora's presence in the room. "In the most recent update to Rich's last will and testament, he included a change that required Miss Anderson's presence here today, which is why I invited her."

Aurora dropped her chin to her chest and folded her hands on the table in between us. With narrowed eyes, I stared at the top of her head, the different shades of gold that made up her sleek, smooth hair.

"I'm sorry if this is awkward," she said quietly and raised her face, her deep blue eyes leveling me with her sincerity. There was no pity there, thank God, because I'd probably have wanted to break something.

"Nonsense," my mom said from next to me. "You being here certainly doesn't make me feel awkward."

Anna, who was seated to Aurora's right, gave her forearm and quick pat. "Me neither. Unless he's giving you all his money and leaving us destitute. Then maybe I'd change my mind."

It was so inappropriately timed that I snorted. Graham, who had the sense of humor of a broomstick, looked at my sister in shock. Glancing at my mom, she had a tiny smile on her face while she looked across the table. I shook my head at Anna and she gave me a look like, *what? You know I'm right.*

When I rolled my eyes a little, I got a stern look from Graham. I didn't give a shit, because that break in the stagnant, grief-coated day was the first taste of normalcy that I'd had since waking.

"And you're sure my husband doesn't need to be here for this?" Anna asked and gave my mom a quick look. I mean, we all hated him.

Mainly because he was a douche who thought of my sister more like a lamp or something that was pretty and decorative, but not completely necessary to have around.

For the first time since we sat down, Graham looked uncomfortable. "Ah, no. It isn't necessary."

Interesting.

"Okay," Graham said and opened up a dark green folder in front of him. "This is the last will and testament of Richard Wallace Calder. I, Richard Wallace Calder, being of sound mind, revoke any former will or codicil and declare that this as my last will and testament. I am married to Suzanne Marie Calder, and all references in this will to 'spouse'— "

"Graham," I interjected wearily, already wanting a drink, "can we cut the legalese? We'll get copies. Just tell us what he wanted."

Graham lifted his eyebrows and looked to my mom for confirmation, and when she nodded, he cleared his throat.

"Okay. Any debts, funeral expenses or expenses incurred by illness are to be paid first from the estate. Suzanne, you'll have sole discretion when it comes to Rich's estate, possession and/or sale of your home in Washington Park and the rental property in Breckinridge. His retirement pension from Calder Financial Services is yours as well." He took a deep breath and glanced at my sister. "Garrett and Anna, you will equally split the first of your father's life insurance policies. The second will go to you in its entirety, Suzanne."

I took a deep breath, a strange disconnect in my gut, talking policies when my father's dead body was still encased in wood under the same roof as us. This all felt wrong. So wrong. Anna and I locked eyes, and hers were bright with tears again. She was right there with me.

"But there are caveats for both of you," Graham said. I snapped my head in his direction, sensing Aurora shift in her seat.

"What kind of caveats?"

Graham cleared his throat. "Anna, you will be given your share of the two-million dollar policy upon the signed divorce decree from your husband, one Marcus Callahan."

"What?" she gasped. My mom covered her mouth with her hand.

Me? I grinned. I grinned so widely that I thought my cheeks would split. Aurora gave me a wide-eyed look, clearly assuming that I'd lost my mind. Oh, I had to fight not to pump my fist in the air.

"Can he really do that?" Anna asked Graham, who nodded slowly and pushed a folded piece of paper across the table to her. With shaking hands, she picked it up, her face losing color while she read it.

"What does it say?" I asked her, smiling like a loon. She ignored me, still staring at the paper, which held CFS letterhead. "Anna, come on, what does it say?"

My mom elbowed me in the side.

Slicking her tongue over her top teeth, Anna handed the letter to my mom, who only quickly glanced at it before she handed it to me. When Mom covered her mouth with one hand again, I knew it had to be good.

Most fathers think no man in the world is good enough for their daughter, but that's not what this is. You are smart and beautiful and kind, I couldn't be prouder of the woman you've become. But Anna, your husband is a giant asshole and you can do better. I love you.

I rolled my lips in between my teeth, trying to kill the laugh before it came up my throat. This was, by far, the best thing my dad had ever done. Maybe better than marrying Mom, conceiving me, or adopting Anna. This kind of high-handed trick was so perfectly him, that I had to turn my face away from Anna before I burst out laughing.

"This isn't funny, Garrett," Anna hissed.

"Oh," I tossed the letter back in her direction. "It is. It really, really is."

"I am not divorcing my husband so I can cash a check from dad." She said it to all of us, even though she was looking straight at me. If we hadn't been in the presence of our mom, an attorney and under the roof of church, I had a feeling she'd be giving me double middle fingers and throwing lots of F-words at me.

"Maybe you should divorce your husband because he's a giant

douche-bag," I said with a tilt of my head. "Dad's just saying what we've all thought since day one. He's not even at your father's funeral, Anna. What kind of husband *does* that?"

I could see Anna clench her teeth, and when she finally looked away, a tear slipped down her face.

"Shit, Anna. I'm sorry."

She folded her arms over her chest and wouldn't look at me. So I said her name again.

"What's Garrett's caveat?" she said with a sharp edge to her voice, lasering her dark eyes on the lawyer.

With puffed out cheeks, Graham blew out a slow breath and muttered something that sounded like, *oh boy*.

I could feel Aurora's eyes on me, but I kept my eyes on the attorney. Oh Lord, what if he was going to make me marry Rory or something? What if that was it? Before anything came out of Graham's mouth, I was shaking my head. I couldn't do it. I couldn't fricken do this.

"Garrett will receive half of his inheritance now, and half upon completing twelve months as interim CEO of Calder Financial Services. Aurora Anderson is to be promoted to Chief Operating Officer for that same time period." Rory and I locked eyes, my heart thundering in my ears while Graham paused. Her cheeks flushed and I could see complete and utter confusion stamped on her face. It probably looked a whole helluva lot like mine. This was almost worse than if he'd made me marry her.

Because I was stuck.

I was *stuck* in the one place that I wanted to leave.

That meddling, know-it-all asshole of a father must have known that I wanted out.

My mom jabbed me in the arm and I blinked back over to Graham. "Sorry, what did you say?"

"If at the end of the twelve months, you decide to abdicate your role of CEO, Miss Anderson is to step into the position indefinitely, while you'll retain your shares in the business. If you walk away before the twelve months are up, your ownership shares will be dispersed equally between your mother, sister and Aurora."

My sister started laughing under her breath while I swiped a hand over my mouth. Yeah. My father had known.

Graham slipped me a letter of my own, but I didn't read it. I tucked it into the inner pocket of my suit jacket and looked back at Aurora while she took a letter of her own. Her slender hands were shaking while she picked it up. They were shaking so badly, in fact, that the thin silver bracelet on her wrist rattled against the large-faced silver and diamond watch that she always wore.

The fact that I had no desire to see what my father wrote on my letter didn't surprise me. But what did surprise me was how closely I was watching Aurora's face. She blinked rapidly, her breath coming in shallow jerks. The long, curved black lashes that framed her remarkable eyes swept her skin when she pinched her eyes closed.

I peered at her. Wait. Was she going to cry?

Half tempted to ask her if she was okay, I shifted my gaze from her so that I didn't look like a creep.

My sister was glaring at me from across the table.

"What?" I snapped.

"I just don't understand why you get half for doing absolutely nothing, and if I don't divorce my husband, I get jack shit."

"Anna, please," my mom admonished. "This is hard on all of us, okay?"

Anna's face smoothed out as soon as she heard the wobble in Mom's voice.

"If I may?" Graham asked, but none of us looked at him. When we didn't interrupt, he continued. "Rich knew exactly what he was doing when he did all this. I can't tell you how seriously he weighed every decision that he made. I've dealt with a lot of clients and seen some strange requests when preparing these documents, but I know when decisions are being made out of love and when they're not."

I closed my eyes while he talked, imagining the annoyed look on my father's face when he constantly admonished me to take things seriously. A thick band of emotion clogged my throat when I heard my mom sniffle.

"Rich loved you. All of you at this table."

When I opened my eyes, Aurora was pressing a hand to her mouth and staring straight at me. Neither one of us blinked for a long, charged moment. There weren't any tears in her eyes, but there was so much rolling around the purplish blue of her irises that I had to remind myself that her reaction wasn't really my problem.

Graham stood and shook my mother's hand before saying his goodbyes to the rest of us. Neither Aurora or I moved from our chairs. Anna stormed out and slammed the door shut behind her.

"I love you, son," my mom said before she dropped a kiss on the top of my head. But it made me feel like a little kid, so I stood and gave her a tight hug. "Your sister will be fine."

"I know."

"And so will you." She gave me a meaningful look when she pulled back. "Bye, Rory."

Aurora smiled at my mom while she walked out, but when the door clicked shut, leaving us in the room alone, her soft pink lips flattened into a line.

The silence crackled between us, but I didn't speak yet. Mainly because I couldn't get a handle on my emotions.

The first thing that I could nail down was anger. And look at that, I was three feet away from the person who took my anger in the best possible way.

"So," I said slowly, enjoying the way she watched my mouth form the word. "Looks like I'm your boss, after all."

CHAPTER TEN

AURORA

Breathe. Breathe in, let it out slowly.

Must not have a panic attack when the only person in the room would likely let me pass out due to oxygen deprivation.

There were two things at war in my head. Complete and utter elation that Rich was trusting me to be COO. That at the end of twelve months, I might actually run the entire company.

But that particular thought was shoved out of the running for dominance by the reminder of who I would have to answer to for that particular period of time.

My skin tingled while I struggled to calm my breathing, struggled to form words when Garrett was watching me so steadily from across the table.

I opened my mouth to say something, but then closed it again.

What? It's not like I could say, well this effing blows, because your dad just sabotaged the one thing you were looking forward to and shackled us together for at least a year by inconveniently dying. When my mouth opened and closed for a second time, Garrett burst out laughing.

His head fell back and he laughed, long and loud. The column of his throat, tanned and smooth, drew my eye first. I'd never noticed his Adam's apple before, because why the hell would I have?

One stupid notch of bone on Garrett Calder's body shouldn't register. Nothing about him should register except his ability to do his job, which now directly affected how my future would play out.

That ushered in the third emotion: Annoyance.

Yet again, Garrett was handed something that he didn't want and would most likely take for granted. Cal retiring and Rich passing away left the administration of CFS with a gaping hole. Garrett and I were the two most qualified to fill the gaps.

But the fact that he was currently wiping tears of laughter off his stupid face didn't exactly leave me reeling with belief in his abilities.

"I don't get what's so funny about this," I finally snapped.

His laughter trailed off, leaving abject misery all over his face. "Yeah. I know it's not funny, Aurora. I'm laughing because I don't know what the hell I'm supposed to do otherwise. I'm laughing because the sight of you biting your tongue in my presence is the only thing that feels normal right now. I am laughing because I don't want to be sitting here, in this damn room, where my father essentially just shoved his boot up my ass and my sister's ass so that he could tell us how he wants us to live."

By the time he was done, his voice was raw and his eyes were red. Shame flooded me, because I wasn't this person who snapped at the person who just finished up with his father's funeral, no matter how much I disliked him.

The part of me, of my life, that was easy and uncomplicated—my dislike of Garrett—was seriously unnerved at the moment. This passionate outburst from him, the wounded confusion that he was hurling at me because I was the only person to catch it, that didn't feel easy or uncomplicated.

It felt electric. It lifted the hair on my arms and made me shift in my seat.

It felt real.

And I hated that.

"Garrett," I started, still not sure of what I was going to say.

"I am laughing, Aurora, because there is no part of me that wants this." His dark brown eyes trapped me, locked me right where I was. Like he was begging me to understand something. "I don't want this."

"And I'd take it in a heartbeat if I could," I said slowly, nodding in understanding.

He dropped his head into his hands and I could see the flex of his muscles underneath the custom lines of his suit. "I know you would."

My heart ached at how miserable he sounded, so deep in the throes of grief and confusion.

I stood from my chair and walked to the back wall where there was a coffee pot, drinking fountain and a stack of white Styrofoam cups. Using the tip of my shoe, I held down the foot pedal and filled two cups before walking back to the table.

Such a small thing, but inactivity was making me feel useless with all the raw emotions bouncing around the room. When I went to set his cup of water down, he'd just uncapped a small silver flask.

"Were you drunk at the funeral?" I asked carefully, instead of yelling it at him like I so desperately wanted to. Maybe a yell and a slap on the back of his head.

"I forget sometimes how little you think of me."

"Garrett," I said wearily. It was never my intention to pick a fight with him on the day he said his goodbyes to his father. "Stupid question. Sorry."

His eyes tracked me when I took the seat that Graham had used instead of going back to the opposite side of the table. "This was just an emergency stash that my friend gave me before I left."

I considered that while I took a slow sip of the cold tap water. When I set the cup down, I licked at a drop of water on my lip, and Garrett never took his eyes off my mouth while I did.

Okay. I was watching his mouth and he was watching mine.

What even right now? I screamed in my head. Maybe I was drunk and didn't know it. Maybe this whole thing was a hangover-induced dream that I'd wake up from any minute.

Except I didn't really drink. And no way would any dream that I could conjure involve me and Garrett Calder running the company together.

Garrett took a pull from the flask, sucking in a breath. "I wish I'd been drunk."

"No, you don't."

He held my stare when I said that and finally grimaced. "How in the ever-loving hell are we going to run a company together? You *hate* me."

I smiled a little. "Maybe I do." When his eyebrows lifted, I could tell he was surprised I actually said it out loud. But then I pointed a finger at him. "Probably about as much as you hate me."

After taking another drink from the flask, he offered it to me when he was done but I declined with a shake of my head. "I don't know if *hate* is the right word, exactly."

His words hung there like a frayed rope that I could have easily grabbed on to if I wanted, pull on it to see where it went. I even opened my mouth to do it when he beat me to the punch.

"You know what I did hate? Your relationship with my dad." With an efficient twist of his hand, he capped the flask and laid it flat on the table before looking at me again. The stark emotion from before was gone, a tempered version of the man that I'd seen so briefly.

"I know you did," I said quietly, opting for truth. This was an opportunity for us, for me and Garrett. An opportunity to build something that was tangible and strong. No matter how we felt about each other, neither of us were the kind of people to willingly run an established company into the ground. "I hope you know that's not why I had it. To spite you," I clarified when his brows pinched down.

"I know. You can't really fake that kind of relationship. Everyone saw it."

Taking a deep breath, I leaned forward to grasp at the corner of the flask with my fingers. He watched me while I pulled it across the surface of the table toward me. Once I had it, I curved it into my palm, felt the metal where it was still warm from his hands, from being tucked against his body somewhere throughout the day.

I didn't open it right away, just ran my thumb along the top edge. "The first time I screwed up, I was still an intern. I'd entered the wrong formula into one of the spreadsheets that I was supposed to be maintaining. It was just one number that was off. One of many, but it altered the monthly report enough that Cal knew something was wrong." I smiled, still following the trail of my finger over the metal. Garrett was watching me, though, I could feel the weight of his eyes on my face. "He told me that the report had already been passed along to your dad and it would be a good lesson for me to have to walk down there myself and let him know what had happened. No email, no interoffice memo. I had to face the boss and tell him that I messed up."

With a shake of my head, I unscrewed the cap and paused before wrapping my lips around the mouth of the flask. Garrett had just drank from this same place. Without looking at him, though I wanted to see if he was thinking the same thing I was, I took a tiny sip. Fire shot down my throat, but I didn't cough. Instead, I welcomed the flames as they settled in my belly.

"When I walked into your dad's office, he was finishing up a phone call, but he waved me in. I'd only talked to him once or twice at that point, so I was still a little intimidated by him. Looking back on it, I think he must have known what I'd messed up already. Maybe Cal told him. Maybe he knew enough to notice the error in the report. When I admitted what I'd done and apologized for it, he smiled at me. Then he asked me if I'd ever make a mistake like that again. When I looked him in the eye and said, 'never again', he immediately said, 'I believe you.'"

Garrett hummed and I risked a glance at him. When the naked hurt in his eyes became too much to look at, I blinked away. It was awful to imagine that Garrett might not have ever heard his dad say something like that to him.

But that wasn't the point of the story.

"Your father believed in me from the very beginning. It was like," I shook my head and searched for the right way to say it, "like he saw exactly who I was, right away. He never treated me differently for being a female in a place that was dominated by men. Never expected me to perform differently. Held me to the same standards. That respect, it … it meant everything to me. I don't know that I can ever put into words how important it was to me. At the end, of course, but especially at that point in my life."

"Why is that?"

I laughed under my breath, not really prepared to answer that kind of question. Maybe someday Garrett would know why proving myself at work was so important to me, why proving myself was so hard, but it wouldn't be today. "It's a long story."

He was quiet for a minute while I stared at the table. When he finally spoke again, it almost made me jump after sitting in the silence. "Well, thank you for telling me the other one."

Surprised by the soft tone in his low voice, I looked at him. "I don't want you to hate my relationship with your dad. It was important to me, valuable in who I've become. And if we're going to work together, I can't have you hating something that put me where I am today."

Garrett inhaled through his nose, considering that. Then he held out his hand for the flask and I handed it over. When he brought it to his mouth, I couldn't tear my eyes away. It tightened my stomach in an unfamiliar way, watching him linger there.

"I'll try my best," he said after he'd swallowed. "Just like we're both going to have to try not to kill each other for the next twelve months."

My lips curved in a smile. "Piece of cake."

Garrett smiled back, but it did nothing to settle the flutters in my stomach. If anything, they increased. "Piece of cake," he repeated.

"And what happens after the twelve months?" I asked before I could stop myself. Maybe a tiny sip of whatever lighter fluid was in that flask had loosened my tongue a little.

"After that?" He shrugged his shoulders and held my eyes. "I have no fucking clue."

CHAPTER ELEVEN

GARRETT

Honestly, it was amazing how little you could get done when you weren't motivated to do it. The first time I walked into my dad's … *my* office, I stared at the room for a solid five minutes before turning around walking right the hell back out.

Marjorie had given me this look when I stormed past. Full of pity and heavy with grief. It made me want to rip my hair out.

Nothing felt the same, walking through the halls of work. People still acted a little subdued for about ten days after the funeral. Cal's retirement party had been postponed for a week, so he could help Aurora and I get our feet under us.

I laughed from where I was slumped in the massive leather chair behind my desk.

But it didn't feel like mine. Nothing in that room did. Probably because the only thing I'd moved was the framed photo from my parents' wedding that he'd had perched on the corner of his desk.

I'd brought it home to my mom that day, watched her clutch it to her chest and try not to cry. Try and fail, ultimately. Her tears, so quietly released, did nothing to soothe the wild beast of guilt and anger that was boiling and bubbling up inside of me.

In two weeks of being CEO, I'd missed three morning meetings. I think that's about how many times I'd showered in the same time frame too.

And the best part? I didn't even care.

I didn't want this. I didn't want to be sitting in that chair, behind that desk, because my dad had some misplaced idea that if he all but chained me to it, I'd sprout some glittery rainbow of love for a company that had sucked out eight years of my life. Maybe the extreme anger I was feeling was a byproduct of grief, but it was there all the same and I wasn't entirely positive how to move past it.

Marjorie tapped on the door before coming in, a concerned look on her face. "Garrett, aren't you supposed to be down in the west conference room with Max right now? The meeting started almost an hour ago."

Blinking at her a couple times before what she said registered, I sat up in the chair and tapped the keyboard of my computer to bring the screen back to life. My calendar was flashing an alert at me.

"Huh. Yeah, I guess so."

When she pursed her lips, I braced for her anger. "He won't be happy."

"Well, he can join the club then."

She let out a disappointed sigh before turning and walking out. "This can't keep happening, Garrett."

"Wanna bet?" I muttered under my breath after she pulled the door shut behind her. It was already late afternoon, and I wasn't entirely positive what I'd accomplished all day. Other than the epic rubber band ball that I started with the box that I found in the bottom right drawer.

Who really cared if I sucked at this?

I had cashed a check for half a million dollars the week after my father's funeral. It sat in my savings account like a stain, bleeding into everything around it, and there was nothing I could do to stop it.

That's how my whole body felt, actually. Like the life was seeping out from my pores and I didn't have it in me to give a single, solitary shit.

My dad was six feet under ground? Well, he'd made me a coffin right along with him. The four walls of his office, no matter how amazing the view was, felt an awful lot like a tomb to me.

Feeling claustrophobic at the thought, I scrubbed a hand over my face and sank deeper in the chair. While I was pinching the bridge of my nose, the door to my office flew open so hard that it banged into the wall.

Aurora stormed in with color high in her face and rage flashing in her eyes. "What the *hell* is the matter with you?"

"You're going to have be more specific," I drawled.

She clenched her jaw and narrowed her eyes.

Inconvenient. It was *terribly* inconvenient how beautiful she looked when she was pissed. It's not like it was the first time I noticed that Aurora was a ten, with her sharp featured face and long, lithe body, but as I sat like a bump on a log in my office chair, it felt like the worst possible timing in the world.

"I just spent an *hour* trying to convince Max King to not bring his business elsewhere." She lifted her eyebrows. "And why did I have to do that?"

"Beeeeeecause you were bored?"

Her jaw dropped open while she stared at me. "What is the matter with you?"

"I feel like we've been here before." I rubbed the tips of my fingers against the sides of my head. "So many questions."

Aurora stared at me with an intense focus in her eyes that unnerved me. Especially when she made a sharp pivot and dragged one of the side chairs over so that she was facing me across my desk. Today she was wearing light blue. Some wrap shirt thingy that made her eyes look like they were lit from the inside. It did weird things to my head.

"Garrett, I get it. You're mourning." She shook her head. "And it's okay to mourn, but you are self-destructing and bringing CFS down with you. I am not okay with that."

I shrugged. "It's not really your call, is it?"

When she slammed a fist on my desk, I actually sat up straight. "Knock it off. If you want to throw a temper tantrum, you go right ahead. But do it on your own time. Not here. Not when there are millions of dollars at stake at any given time. Not when your actions reflect on the people who are working their asses off for you."

Her words dug under my skin, like little worms seeking out my blood. There was guilt at knowing she was right, but the embarrassment was so much worse than the guilt.

And the petulant child in me didn't feel like making it easy on her. Not yet.

"And you're here to, what?"

With a huff, Aurora pushed up from the chair and dug her hands into the hair at her scalp. "I am here to try to talk some sense into you. This isn't you, Garrett. I know it's not."

Seeing her on the edge of her sanity, because of my actions, made me pause.

"You don't know me." Naturally, that's what I said instead. Instead of admitting to her that when she was losing it for justifiable reasons, reasons that I was causing, it made me feel like a dick.

When she flung her arms out to the side, it loosened her ponytail, giving her a harried, wild look that I'd never seen. I swallowed, trying to stay focused on the reason she was in my office. Which was not to look like some sexy, crazed goddess that I'd very much want to muss up some more.

"No, I don't know you very well, but what I do know is that you are the person that has to keep everything stable right now. He was your father, and those people out there," she pointed at the door that was still wide open, "they loved him. They respected him."

"I know that," I said in a dangerous tone, standing up from my chair.

"Do you? Because you're not acting like it. No one is asking you to be exactly like him. But for crying out loud, don't check out on us. *You* are the one who has to let them know that everything will be okay. I can't do that on my own."

"I didn't check out." She gave me an incredulous look, so I held up my hands. "I'm still ... processing, okay? I didn't know it would be this hard to step into his place."

Her face softened slightly, but her voice still held the steel edge. "Processing is good. But look at this office, Garrett. You've kept it *his* because you refuse to accept that it's yours now."

"For at least the next eleven-ish months." I said it lightly, hoping it would make her smile, lighten the mood. I walked out from behind the desk and scratched my scalp.

"If you have no intention of pulling yourself out of this selfish little tantrum, then leave."

I drew up short, only an arm's length away from her. "Excuse me?"

"You're being selfish. And if you can't manage to get your shit together and attempt to run this company the way it needs to be run, then get out of my hair and let me do it for you. Quit, Garrett. That's what I'm saying." She leaned in to me, and my skin tightened at the smell of something soft and sweet. "If you can't man the hell up, get out of my way."

Her words, so quietly spoken, raked like nails down my back. Her porcelain carved face, so close to mine, might have been a temptation. But given the gauntlet that she just threw down? It really wasn't.

"Get out of my office, Rory."

If I expected her to be pissed at my softly spoken command, I was wrong. The side of her lips curved up for just a moment and she gave me this satisfied look that made me want to curse.

Right before she closed the door, she looked at me over her shoulder. "You might want to take a shower tomorrow morning. You smell like shit."

I sank onto the corner of my desk, heart hammering at the exchange. She'd just tossed the equivalent of a massive bucket of ice-cold water at my face.

What was I doing?

Missing meetings? Almost losing important clients?

With shaking hands, I pulled at the lapel of my jacket and yanked out the letter from my dad, the one I hadn't read yet.

I'm sure you hate me for what I've done, but I love you, Garrett. CFS is our family, too, and they'll need you right now. There's a greatness in you that I wish you could see more clearly, and as you grew up, I didn't do a good job of letting you know that I did see it. My hope in doing this is that you can find it, let it out, and figure out what you want to do with it.

"Well, shit," I said into the empty office and fought against the hot weight of tears in my eyes. It took four deep breaths to do it. So deep, in fact, that the edges of my vision turned black. But it worked. When the emotion cleared, I leaned back to hit the button on my phone that rang directly to Marjorie's desk.

"Yes?"

"Marjorie, what's my morning like tomorrow?"

"Oh," her surprised reply almost made me smile, if I still didn't feel like such an ass. "You're open, actually."

"Good. Can you keep it that way, please? I've got some stuff to get caught up on around here. And in the afternoon, can you schedule an all-staff meeting for four? Anyone who can make it."

"Of course," she said, sounding pleased.

"Thanks, Marjorie."

"Good to have you back, son."

I ended the call with a smile, wishing I could have heard my dad say the exact same thing.

CHAPTER TWELVE

AURORA

Déjà vu.

It was the story of my life now.

Go to work at dawn, console people, hire people, read reports, take a brief pause to think about how much I loved my new job, yell at Garrett, go home and fall face first into bed. Though I was yelling at Garrett less since our Come to Jesus talk in his office two weeks earlier, I was still boiling by the time I shoved open his half-open office door.

"I'm going to *kill* you," I said the moment I could see him, the simple sight of his handsome face sending a fresh surge of anger through me at his blatant disrespect for my position.

Marjorie was standing to the side of his desk, and they shared a look at my dramatic entrance. But he never paused what he was reading when he pulled out his wallet, snagged a bill and handed it to her. Her pale ivory skin wrinkled even more than normal when she smiled so widely.

"Wha," my voice trailed off. Marjorie winked at me when she tucked the money into the pocket of her pants.

"Thanks, sweetheart. I bet him I'd hear you say that in less than a month, and mister know-it-all here figured he had two months before death threats occurred."

The entire time she walked across the large office, my jaw hung open. She gave me a soft pat on my shoulder when she passed me, closing the door quietly on her way out.

"You made a bet about that?"

Garrett finally glanced up at me, and I hated how good he looked. Hated it. With all the fiery suns that could possibly be behind the kind of hate that was coursing through me.

He'd had a haircut recently, the top a little bit longer than the sides, but he hadn't shaved that morning, according to the stubble he had over his sharp jaw. And his eyes. They were clear and bright, despite the dark brown color, the way they'd been looking more and more lately.

"Of course I made a bet about that. Marjorie and I bet on everything. Which recent hire will get canned first, though I have a leg up on her in that department now." When he grinned, I crunched my molars together so tightly, I could not believe they didn't crack.

"Yeah." I marched up to his desk and slapped some papers down. "About that."

Apparently he was expecting this, because he didn't so much as glance down at them, just leaned back in his chair and braced his hands behind his head.

"Garrett," I said, striving for an even tone, "you cannot fire the new CFO after two weeks without discussing it with me first."

"You were in a meeting and I was told you couldn't be disturbed."

What was that throbbing in my forehead? Maybe a vein popping under my skin?

"He was my hire. You were still sulking under your desk when he started. You do not get to do something like this without discussing it with me first."

"Yes," he said simply. "I do."

My left eye started twitching as I stared at him. A big twitch, too.

"That's not how this organizational structure works, Calder. You may be the CEO, but *I* am in charge of operations. He reported to *me*."

"Your meeting? It ran for two and a half hours."

"What does that have to do with anything?" I snapped, enunciating the words so crisply that I may have spit at him. When Garrett clucked his tongue, I swear, I almost had an aneurysm.

"Temper, Anderson. Did you happen to check your voicemail after your meeting?"

"No," I shouted. "I did not have time to check my voicemail because the first thing I noticed on my desk was the paperwork from HR that you fired our new CFO the second my back was turned." Oh, I was seething. And he must have seen it, because he stood from his chair, unfolding his tall, broad frame with ease. His charcoal gray jacket was unbuttoned, and he took his time fixing it back up. "You're just pissed that I was forced to make that decision about hiring him without you."

But Garrett didn't respond, that ass. He pulled his chair out and gestured for me to sit.

"No," I said immediately. "I'm not in the mood for your games. And I'm not in the mood because you had a member of the administration team escorted out of the building without discussing with me!"

"I'd like you to sit down so you can be more comfortable while you're checking your voicemail. Please, feel free to use my phone."

His calm tone of voice scratched across my skin, leaving smoke in its wake because I was still so damn hot. But fine, if he wanted to play this out, I walked around his desk. He didn't really move out of my way, and thanks to the four inch red stilettos I was wearing, my shoulder brushed the top part of his chest.

I so obviously did not notice how he drew in a quick breath at the accidental touch. And I so obviously did not notice that goosebumps popped up on my arms under the black silk of my shirt at how warm and firm he was.

When I sat in his chair, I took a second to look around his office. He'd moved some things around, swapping the brass lamps that his dad favored to more contemporary looking ones with dark wood bases and linen drums. The way he tapped his fingers against the top of his computer screen snapped my eyes up to his.

He wasn't smiling, but the look in his dark brown eyes was happy. Not mocking, but genuinely amused. With that sinking feeling in my gut, I picked up the receiver and tapped out the numbers for our voicemail system.

I may have hit the buttons harder than necessary when the commands prompted me to put in my password.

"Oh good," he whispered from right above me. "I can hack your voicemail now."

I rolled my eyes while his voice filled the speaker in my ear. His stupid, low, sexy voice.

Rory, it's Garrett. I know you're in a meeting and can't be disturbed, but we've got a problem. Ross just got flagged by IT. You know that new monitoring system we put into place right before my dad died? Well, apparently our new money guy likes his porn. And he likes watching it at work. I slapped a hand over my mouth and heard Garrett chuckle behind me. "Shit," I whispered behind my fingers while the message kept playing. *So as much as I hate to do this without talking to you first, or letting you be in on the meeting with him, I'm going to go take care of it now and make sure he's out of the building ASAP. Oh, also? You should probably tell HR to post for the position. Again. Thanks, Rory.*

Very, very slowly, I lowered the receiver back onto the cradle. Embarrassment made my skin hot and without needing the assistance of a mirror, I could tell my face was a lovely shade of pink.

We've got a problem. That's how he'd said it. We do. Not *I.* Not *you. We've* got a problem.

Using the balls of my feet, I twisted his chair to the side so I was facing where he'd hitched a hip on the corner of his desk and was still watching me.

"So," I started, fiddling my fingers on the seam of my white and black-striped pencil skirt. "It appears that I owe you an apology."

"It does appear that way."

Looking up at him through my lashes, I tilted my head to the side and groaned. Maybe he'd take that for how I meant it. *I really don't want to have to grovel because my righteous indignation was so righteous and now I feel like a shit and this sucks.*

But he nodded. "I know. I'd hate it if it were me too. But please, do continue."

"Garrett, would you please accept my apology for coming in here and yelling at you?"

"So gracious of you to say that," he said with a magnanimous nod of his head. "Of course, I forgive you."

I gestured my hand to him. Your turn, buddy.

"What?"

"Aren't you going to say you're sorry?"

He narrowed his eyes at me.

"I just admitted that my reaction was … dramatic. But I felt like you'd sidestepped me. That you didn't respect me enough to include me in the conversation. That throws up every red flag in my arsenal, and I don't always react well when that happens." I paused when he flashed a quick smile. "Do you see why I did though?"

"I can," he said grudgingly. "I didn't intend any disrespect, I promise. I'm sorry it came off that way." He held out his hand like I'd done moments before. "And? Anything else you'd like to add while we're communicating in such a healthy way?"

I lifted my eyebrows. "And? And *what*?"

He adopted a wounded expression. "You said you wanted to *kill* me. That's not very nice."

"I'm sorry I said I wanted to kill you," I ground out.

"But you don't anymore?"

I lifted my eyebrows in answer and he tilted his head back to laugh. Yeah. On that note, I needed to not be sitting in his chair when he was being so funny and understanding. But I stood at the same time that he stopped laughing and pushed off the desk.

My chest brushed up against him and I jerked backwards so fast that I almost fell right back into the chair.

"Whoa," he said, holding a hand around my waist to keep me from stumbling. "You okay?"

The spread of his hand was so big that it stretched almost the entire width of my rib cage. When his fingers pressed against the silk of my shirt, I stared up at him.

One of my hands must have gripped the lapel of his jacket when I started falling and I instantly let it go. His smell was everywhere.

Clean and masculine, nothing overpowering. Like the only thing he used was soap.

Soap. Shower. Garrett.

His eyes bored into mine, a searing intensity that I'd never seen on his face before. When his attention dipped to my mouth, I jumped backwards, making his chair roll back about a foot.

"Sorry," I said hurriedly, smoothing the top of my hair and returning to the opposite side of his desk.

Maybe I imagined it; that he'd just been about to kiss me. Unfortunately, the thing that wasn't as easy to dismiss was the rapid thrumming of my heart, the instant fluttering in my belly at the feel of his strong hand wrapped around my waist.

"I accept your apology." One side of his mouth lifted in a self-deprecating smile. "I can't really blame you for immediately jumping to homicidal tendencies. I haven't exactly been the picture of a solid employee since we started this whole … thing."

Even if I had imagined it, the almost kiss, this side of Garrett was worth anything I'd hallucinated. The side of him that put forth an effort when he needed to. That stepped up because I had asked. Screamed. Whatever.

"You've been trying. We all see it." I took a deep breath, willing my heart to settle back into rhythm. "And that's all I can ask, is that you try."

"I can do that."

"Try, and effectively communicate with you when an employee is storing his personal spank bank on company equipment."

I grinned, turning my face away in hopes that he didn't see it. "That too. But please, don't ever call it that in front of me."

Garrett lifted his chin in acknowledgement, a deep dimple still carved into his stubbled cheek from his smile.

Yeah. I needed to get the hell out of there.

"I'll let you know if HR has some people for us to interview," he called to me while I practically sprinted to the door. I think I gave him a wave. I don't really know.

But I do know that I heard a low laugh from him just before the door closed behind me.

CHAPTER THIRTEEN

AURORA

Walking down the quiet hallway after locking my office door, I glanced at my watch. 5:32pm. But the place was a ghost town. Usually there were a few stragglers after five, but on a beautiful Friday in September when the heat finally dipped a little bit?

Not a soul in sight.

Some small part of me wanted to stay in my office, which was still the same as the one I'd used under a different job title. It suited me fine, actually, because the twelve by twelve room with a moderately-sized window felt like an extension of me. Even though my responsibilities had changed and my stress level had certainly risen, behind my black desk in the black leather chair was the place that I felt the most comfortable in my own skin. It was the moments that I left it where I struggled.

Thankfully for me, my new job suited me even better than my last one had. So much so, in fact, that I'd stopped numerous times in the last few weeks to question whether I'd feel that much happier in the CEO position. The operations side of CFS was fascinating, not in that I learned new things about the company, but being the person who studied everything to see the patterns of what worked and what didn't, to be the person who got to step in with the employees to make sure everything was delegated correctly and clients were kept happy, it suited me.

Every part of my new job suited me.

Which threw the question around my head of how I would feel if Garrett chose to walk away at the end of his twelve months. It wasn't something I obsessed over, because there was still such a substantial amount of time before that decision would be made, and I knew how time could smooth out the rough edges.

Once, Garrett had told me that being at CFS made him feel like he was living in someone else's skin. How did he feel now that he'd stepped straight into his father's?

Right before I pressed the button on the wall panel next to the elevator, I heard a noise come from Garrett's office.

Then another one. Then a muffled curse.

"Shit," I said, finding myself walking quietly just in case I decided I didn't want him to know that I was still here. Just beyond the door, I paused and tried to crane my neck to see through the open sliver. His legs were visible, and he was sitting on the floor.

I found myself smiling when he tossed something and it hit the wall with a smack. What on earth?

"I can see you, Rory."

Slapping a hand to my chest, I jumped back. "You scared me."

"Really? Imagine how I felt when, all of a sudden, I see someone peering into the crack of the door trying to spy on me."

I rounded the door and he was grinning up at me from the ground, looking pleased as punch. "How did you see me?"

Squinting at the door beyond my shoulder, he pointed. "The light in the hallway. You blocked it when you turned into Peeping Tom."

"What are you doing?" Deflection. It was a solid choice in my current predicament. But he knew. He shook his head and gave me that smug grin that I used to hate.

Used to? Well, that was new.

"I'm taking someone's very smart advice. Finally cleaning out my dad's office." Garrett looked around, his smile dropping and eyes losing a little bit of that sparkle that he got when he hassled me. "Seeing his things around after this long, it was making it feel … I don't know, weird."

Carefully stepping over his legs so I could sit in one of the arm chairs, I let that settle in, the question from just a few moments ago gaining steam and swirling faster and faster. If Garrett finally felt like he could get comfortable in this office, how did that reflect in the rest of his twelve-month commitment? For the first two weeks, he'd been such a basket case, that I'd started thinking of CFS as mine. That it was only a matter of time before he imploded and I'd be forced to step in.

But this new motivated Garrett? The one who ran meetings with efficiency and an easy smile on his face? Who never challenged or undermined me in public?

This Garrett made me feel like I was walking a tightrope with no net. Not only did I not have a net, I couldn't even tell which way was up and which way was down. That swooping pit in my stomach? I couldn't pinpoint where it came from.

That was a lie. When he scraped a hand along his jaw, I knew.

It came from him.

And I didn't even know if I hated it.

"Do you need any help?"

The shock on his face absolutely mirrored the shock in my head. I mean, I'd thought it, *maybe I should offer to help*. But the filter between my brain and my mouth was on hiatus, apparently.

"You don't have plans?"

"Only if you call leftover takeout and *How to Make a Murderer* on Netflix having plans."

He nodded, letting the subtext of my answer settle in. No, Garrett, I didn't have a boyfriend waiting for me at home.

"Doesn't sound like a horrible night to me. Though I guess that depends on the leftovers."

"Pizza."

"From where?" he asked with narrowed eyes, like he was testing me.

"Benny Blancos."

He groaned, clutching at his heart. "Stop. I'll cry."

When I laughed at his theatrics, he fixed me with a strange look.

"What?" I shifted in my seat, unnerved by his focus.

"You're beautiful when you laugh."

And with that, folks? My heart stopped. Altogether. I could not afford to have Garrett Calder say things that made my heart gallop. If I thought I was confused before, moments like that launched me into an entirely different stratosphere.

I was up out of my chair before I knew it, and he held up a hand to stop me. "Wait. I'm sorry, I shouldn't have said that. I just…" he blew out a breath and pinched his eyes shut. "It was in my head one second and I had no intention of saying it out loud. I'm not trying to make you uncomfortable."

Given my earlier offer of help that I hadn't precisely meant to say out loud, I felt myself soften. He didn't mean to say his thing any more than I'd meant to say mine. And it wasn't the first time a man had told me I was beautiful. It wasn't even the first time that I man I found attractive had said it. Even though I sometimes felt like my chin was too sharp and my body wasn't curvy enough, when Garrett looked at me and said it, I felt beautiful.

Maybe he'd have gained more favor with me by saying I was smarter than him, or that I was the hardest worker he'd ever seen. But the fact that he said something so simple and kind, it lanced through my heart with ease.

"I'm not uncomfortable." I tossed my purse onto the floor next to the chair that I'd just been in and gestured to a box. "Want me to start here?"

"That would be great," he said after a beat.

We worked quietly for a while, shifting through files and books. Occasionally, I'd ask him if he wanted to keep or toss something, and for the most part, he said toss. Only pictures and books went into the box that was destined for his mom.

"How are they holding up?" I asked after setting a gold-edged frame that held a picture of his parents down on the corner of his desk

"My mom is doing okay. She's been going to a grief support group that one of the nurses at the hospital told her about. I think she'll move though. That house is too big for just her, and I think all the memories of them make it hard for her."

I hummed, trying to picture it. I'd only been to Rich and Suzanne's house once, for a company Christmas party. Large and stately, in an established neighborhood in Wash Park that boasted homes of all different styles, it felt like such a foreign concept from the humble houses that my parents and I had lived in with every new station for my dad.

"And Anna?" I gave him an apologetic smile. "I'm not trying to pry, but that was pretty intense at the church."

Garrett smiled while he tossed some files into the trash bin. "She's still processing."

"Well hopefully she's showering more than you did when you were processing."

"Ouch." He lifted an eyebrow and held his arms out. "I think I'm doing okay with my personal hygiene."

Yes. He was doing okay. The way his crisp white shirt stretched across his chest, setting off the tan of his face made me feel … warm. Very, very warm.

"But she's not mad at you anymore?" I asked, wishing I could fan at my face without being obvious.

"No," he said thoughtfully. "But it was never really about me anyway. Anna married Marc too young, and she knew going into in that she should have called off the wedding. He's not the right guy for her."

"So she doesn't love him at all?" It was hard to imagine someone as beautiful and sweet as Anna being stuck in a loveless marriage that had been that way since day one.

Garrett took a few seconds to choose his words before answering. "We don't talk about it much, because she knows that I can't stand the guy. But I think Anna feels obligated. Because she made the choice to go through with the wedding, she needs to stick it out. But honestly? I don't think he'd even notice if she just packed her shit and left."

"That's awful."

"Yeah." He laughed, but it was dry and not very amused sounding. "It would almost be easier if he cheated on her or something. Give her a clear cut reason to leave. But, he's just oblivious and neglectful. He doesn't even see her. Makes me want to dick punch him."

I smothered a laugh, but Garrett caught it, giving me an easy smile.

"You want a drink?" he asked, standing up off the floor with a groan. "I'm getting too old to sit on the floor like that."

"Tell me about it." I stretched my legs out while he walked to the cabinet behind his desk. About a half an hour earlier, I'd kicked my heels off and didn't miss the way he stared when I did. "What do you have back there? A full bar?"

"Believe it or not," he said as he took the chair closest to me, the one I was resting my back against. His legs brushed against my shoulder and I fought my initial instinct to flee to the other side of the room. "This was my dad's whiskey."

"What?" I smiled. "He drank in the office?"

Garrett leaned forward and set two glass tumblers on the coffee table, pouring a couple fingers of the amber liquid into each one. "Not sure. I certainly never saw it."

"Wow, I absolutely would have thought this was yours."

"Because I'm the type to drink on the job?" His voice had a slight edge to it and I looked up in surprise. He handed me a glass and knocked his back in one swallow.

"That's not what I said."

"But it's what you implied," he tossed back, still holding his empty glass.

When I set my drink back down with a sharp clink, I shifted to the side so I could see him better. "Why are you getting so defensive? I didn't mean anything by it. I'm just ... I don't know, surprised that your dad had a stash in here."

"Ahh," he tipped the edge of his glass to me like I'd just proven his point. "But you wouldn't have been surprised if it was mine."

My head was spinning, and I hadn't taken a single sip. "No, I guess not, but— "

Garrett let out a harsh laugh, pouring himself another drink. "Unbelievable."

"You're overreacting," I said, standing up and wiping my hands on my pants.

"Am I? I've been working my ass off trying to prove myself to you, and you're still so quick to think the worst of me." His eyes flashed and I felt like I was drowning. For once, I wasn't accusing or thinking ill of him. For once, I felt like we were just being Garrett and Rory. And for *once*, it felt really good.

"You don't need to prove yourself to *me,* Garrett. You needed to prove yourself to them." I pointed at his door even though no one was out there. "I can't even believe we're arguing about this."

"You're right," he said, standing and brushing past me. "I can't believe it either. I don't know why I thought we'd be able to figure out how to do this in peace when you still don't take me seriously. I think I'd like to finish this by myself."

To my horror, tears burned in my throat and in my nose. "Not a problem."

I snatched up my purse and walked briskly to the elevators, not pausing to walk through the doors, even when I heard the sound of his shouted curse.

CHAPTER FOURTEEN

GARRETT

The knocking didn't stop.

No matter how loud I turned up my music, they just kept banging on the door.

"Garrett, open the damn door," Cole shouted when there was a break between songs. As soon as the transition was done, I jabbed the remote to my sound system from where I was laying on my couch.

Closing my eyes so the angry guitar and violent drum beat was the only thing that I could focus on, I couldn't even bring myself to care that they were practically staging an intervention.

I'd barely seen my friends since my dad died. They all came to give their condolences, sent me texts to make sure I was alive, but I hadn't hung out with them in a solid month. When they had guy's night, reserved for drinking beer and playing cards, I'd either been working, at the gym, or passing the hell out in my bed from the effects of the previous two things.

But this last argument with Rory?

Yeah, the one where I lashed out for no reason because I'm a sensitive little bitch? That sent me spiraling, and I couldn't pinpoint why.

The tickle at the back of my subconscious that was screaming something about Rory being under my skin abruptly stopped when my music shut off.

"What the..." I sat up and about fell off the couch when I saw Tristan looming at my feet with a scowl on his face. "How did you get in here?"

"Picked the lock," he deadpanned.

"And this felt appropriate to you because?"

"Because Cole and my brother thought you might have accidentally fallen and died or something." The look on my face was incredulous and he rolled his eyes. "Just come over and have a beer so they can sleep better tonight. You've been MIA for a while, man."

Without waiting for my answer, Tristan made an unhurried turn to stare at the framed pictures on my dining room wall. When I'd bought this place, Anna went crazy, turning it into something that looked like a model home. While it may have had a few too many throw pillows for my taste, I loved it. The dark blue accents went with the bright white trim and crown molding that she'd insisted I add, and set off starkly from the mahogany wood floor that spread through the family room, dining room and into my open kitchen.

I didn't immediately get off the couch, since I was too busy thinking about my house so as to avoid the grumpy man in the room, and Tristan speared me with a dark look. "One beer. That's it."

"You're annoying," I said, but rolled so that my feet hit the floor.

"So I've been told."

"So why didn't Cole bust down the door?" I asked while I walked to the kitchen to grab two longneck bottles from the middle shelf of my fridge. "I'm surprised no one called the cops with how long he was banging on it."

"How do you know they didn't?"

I paused before using my key to lock the door behind us. "Are you serious?"

"No." And he kept walking.

By the time I crossed the street separating my house from Michael and Tristan's, I already felt better. Time with my buddies was just what I needed. The weight of my new responsibilities, of trying to be there for my mom and sister as much as possible and this thing with Rory all felt like they were tumbling around in my brain on an endless loop. I couldn't even tell anymore which felt like the biggest bother, which was troubling.

Rory should have been the clear choice for what bothered me the most. Except she wasn't.

The way each of our interactions felt like the strike of a match against my skin, the lick of fire that remained, wasn't troubling at all.

It was the thing I was starting to look forward to every day, even if I was genuinely pissed off like I had been earlier.

"Your sister doing okay?" Tristan asked. He'd waited to go in the house, bracing his shoulder against the column on the front porch.

My eyebrows lifted in surprise. Tristan knew Anna, of course. I'd been friends with him and Michael for almost six years at that point. Anna hadn't even been dating Marc yet, but I didn't think I'd ever seen them exchange more than pleasantries.

"Uhh, yeah." I scratched my jaw with the hand not holding my beer. "I mean, she has good days and bad days. Same as my mom."

The only thing I got in terms of a response was a hard look followed with a miniscule jerk of his chin. Seriously, a caveman would probably communicate better than Tristan.

With a sigh, I followed him into the house and was met with a rib-crushing hug from Cole. Cole was a big dude, taller than all of us, and as I had discovered when my lungs deflated of oxygen, he was friggin strong.

"Air," I croaked and he let me go. "What is it with you guys? Can't let a guy properly wallow without breaking and entering *and* assault?"

But he laughed, shoving at my shoulder. "I'm man enough to be able to admit that I missed your ugly face."

I sniffed. "My face is not ugly."

"Yeah," Michael said, socking me in the stomach when he walked past me, "that's why you have so many girls around all the time?" He paused thoughtfully. "Oh wait, you don't."

A bright, vivid flashback of Rory fisting the lapel of my jacket when I held her waist swept through my head. She was tall, and if I'd just dipped my mouth down…

Right. Not the time.

"Michael, if we're all meant to keep up with your number of women, there wouldn't any left in the greater Denver area by the end of the year," Cole said while he took a seat at the massive wood dining table that Tristan had built.

"True." Michael took the seat across from him with an unrepentant grin.

"Where's Dylan and Kat?" I asked, cracking my first beer.

"Visiting his family in Michigan," Cole answered without looking up from the cards that he was shuffling.

"Huh. Didn't know that." An uncomfortable feeling settled into my chest. Grief was consuming, sure, but I'd been so out of touch with my friends that I didn't even know when they were out of town? "Wait, who's watching Leonidas?"

"Someone that Kat works with."

"They could have asked me," I grumbled, studying the shit cards that Cole dealt to me.

"Because you've been so present lately?"

I shot Michael a look at his casually spoken question. "I'm still getting my feet under me. It hasn't been an easy transition."

All three of them shifted in their chairs. Well, maybe not Tristan. He probably wasn't bothered by my absence the last couple months. It's quite possible he didn't even notice until Cole made him break into my house.

"So," I continued, determined not to make this whole night about my current shit-show of a life. "Have I missed anything good? Nobody got married or anything?"

Michael made a fake gagging sound that caused Tristan to give his brother a slow shake of his head. Cole smiled at them but didn't answer me. Didn't even look at me.

"What's *that* look for, Mallinson?"

After taking a second to toss a card down, Cole glanced at me. "It was my anniversary yesterday. Guess I've been thinking about weddings."

Ahh. The never-ending torch he carried for his ex-wife Julia. "Former anniversary, you mean?"

"I suppose," he answered, his voice resigned. "Would've been twelve years."

"Good Lord," Michael said in horrified awe. "How young were you when you got married?"

"Twenty. And married for five. Separated for two of those years before she sent me the papers."

"And she won't speak to you?" Tristan asked.

Man, it probably made me a douche, but I'd ask questions about Cole and his ex-wife *all night* if it kept the spotlight off of me. His hands curled into fists on the surface of the table and his face was so tortured that I felt bad. So maybe I wouldn't ask questions all night. But for like, a solid hour, minimum.

Truth was that Cole hadn't given us many specifics about his relationship with her. Just that he had been the one in the wrong, and she'd left. Considering that the man lived the most monk-like existence I'd ever seen, given the number of women that threw themselves at him, I knew he was serious about still being in love with Julia.

She'd cut him off and all but disappeared.

"Not one word, call or text since the day she mailed me the divorce papers." Cole pushed his tongue against the inside of his cheek while that hung in the air. Seven years he'd been thinking about this. About one woman that had sucked something out of his chest and never returned it.

Michael cleared his throat in the awkward silence. "Well. That's enough to keep me celibate for a solid month. Just in case I accidentally find myself married."

Cole actually smiled when Michael shivered at the thought. "A whole month?"

"I know," he said gravely.

We all laughed, and the dark cloud of a moment was gone. For the first time since before my dad died, I felt like me again. Laughing with my friends and talking about preseason football and the crap that the crazy lady at the end of our street always pulled. There was a comfort glowing inside of me sitting at that table, and it pushed my equilibrium back to rights. Maybe that's what the oddest thing is about a single event setting off a chain of massive changes in your life. When they happen so rapidly, your brain can't even register the ripples in the water until they're so far beyond you that you can barely even detect them anymore.

And oh my hell, I was turning philosophical.

"Garrett," Cole said my name and I blinked at him.

"Did you ask me something?"

He laughed under his breath. "Yeah, I asked about work. You doing okay?"

"Fine. Who's turn is it?"

"It's okay if you're thrown, man," he continued as if I hadn't completely brushed him off. But I really didn't want to talk about work. There was a still a festering sore over what had happened in my office with Rory. Her face when she realized I was pissed and the way that I couldn't drop it, it just ran on a loop, and with each pass I felt more and more unsettled.

"I'm not thrown, I'd just like to not talk about work bullshit and hang out with my friends." I gave them all a hard look. "Or can we not manage that?"

"Take it easy, Garrett," Michael said mildly. "He's just asking a simple question."

Heat flushed my face, temper swelling like a tide. "And what makes it simple? The fact that I don't have a choice in what I'm doing right now? That the only person who should be helping me on a daily basis is the one person who expects me to screw up? That my dad felt it was necessary to play puppet master with his will and my sister and I are paying the price? What part of that is fucking simple?"

"Easy," Tristan said quietly, but his eyes bored into me in a way that I couldn't look away. "None of it is simple. But don't expect your friends to ignore it just because it's hard and you can't joke it away."

I shoved back from the table, embarrassment making my skin hot. First Rory, now my friends all but calling me a clown like she had. "And you wonder why I didn't want to hang out with you guys? You're completely incapable of keeping your nose out of each other's business. Every damn time we hang out, it turns into counseling hour."

"Don't be a dick, Garrett," Cole called out while I stomped to the front door. "If your go-to response to anyone questioning your life is anger, then you've got bigger problems than your dad's will."

My hand was on the doorknob, and I paused for a brief second to let that settle in. So much emotion pumped furiously through my veins, like if I didn't find an outlet for it and soon, I'd explode through my skin.

So I didn't look back. Not when I slammed the door or when I only stopped inside of my house to throw on some gym shorts and snatch my keys off the kitchen counter.

There was a whole wall of punching bags at the gym, and when my tires squealed down my quiet street, I knew I was going to do my best to rip the damn things apart.

Except my plan was a failure from the second I wrenched open the doors, because Aurora *bane of my existence* Anderson was the very first person I saw.

Perfect.

CHAPTER FIFTEEN

AURORA

Just as I pulled my arm back to do another rep, someone gripped my upper arm. Hard.

I was so caught up in what I was doing on the punching bag in front of me that I couldn't stop myself from whipping around with a solid right hook into their stomach.

Garrett sidestepped with a shocked expression, so I barely glanced at the hard midsection of his body.

"What the hell?"

"You scared the shit out of me, Calder," I whisper-yelled. "And would you quit stalking me? I started coming later because *you* weren't here."

"Get over yourself, Miss Narcissist. Not everything is about you."

"Oh, I am well aware that you don't make all your decisions with my best interest at heart."

His burst of laughter drew the eyes of people around us, and I crossed my arms tightly. The sweat on my stomach should have been cooling after my stretching, but my temper flared so bright and so hot that I felt a drip slide down my neck and into my bra.

"Be quiet," I hissed. "People don't need to be privy to our … issues."

"Issues," he repeated, raking a rough hand through his hair. The disheveled strands stayed up, like he was already sweating. "Such an innocuous word for what you put me through."

"Me?" I scoffed. "The fact that I haven't kicked you in the balls every single day that I see you is a mother-effing miracle. You snapped at me for absolutely *no* reason earlier."

Someone cleared their throat and Garrett cast a look around the room. With a gentler touch than he'd started with, he wrapped his fingers around my upper arm and led me through the main workout area and took a right.

My breath was whooshing through my ears so loudly that even the clang of weights being dropped onto the floor didn't register. Absently, I pressed a hand to the skin above my heart to make sure it was staying in place underneath my skin and bone and muscle.

Garrett paused by a door that led to a room used for classes, but it was dark inside.

Warning bells clashed horribly under my rampant excitement. Because all of this, every word we spat at each other felt like the best kind of foreplay in the world. The feel of his hand on mine, the searing heat of his palm and fingers gripping me almost made me lightheaded.

Over his shoulder, Garrett gave me a heated look before pushing the door open with a hard shove. The full glass pane in the door let in a square of fluorescent light from the hallway, and it cast ominous shadows along his face and neck, making him look like a chiseled, handsome villain.

And wasn't he? In the story of Aurora, he was the bad guy. At least, I had thought so.

"Garrett," I said, poking a finger into the solid wall of muscle of his chest. "This is where I come to work out all the bullshit that you put me through fifty hours a week. And when you show up here manhandling me and acting like it's okay that you jumped down my damn throat earlier? It makes me really, really not like you."

He stared at me for beat before he started laughing. I popped a hip out and rolled my eyes.

"Of course, you'd find this funny," I said under my breath, not expecting that he'd be able to hear me.

But then he straightened to his full height and took a step closer. "I am laughing because I don't know what else to do right now. Because I don't know how the hell I thought we'd be able to make this work."

"That makes two of us," I threw back, fisting my hands on my hips. His eyes darted down my frame, and I was fully, uncomfortably aware of the amount of skin that I was showing him. I had been so hot under my own skin from our argument earlier that I'd only thrown on my black running shorts and a pink sports bra. "But I tell you what? You show up here one more time and ruin my workout, and I'll— "

"You'll what?" He spread his arms open, the dark stretch of floor that separated our feet steadily growing smaller until I could smell the slight tang of beer on his breath.

All around me, it was Garrett. Sweaty and mad and muscular Garrett.

So I did the only thing I could. I growled and pushed at his chest with two hands. "You're so aggravating."

"Me?" He hooted, pointing a finger at me. "I can't do this. I cannot handle another ten months with a harpy breathing down my neck, just waiting for me to make a mistake."

"Better a harpy than a screwup, don't you think?"

Garrett's exhales made his chest heave and he gave me wild eyes. "I am no screwup."

"And I am not a harpy," I yelled, stepping up into him so that my breasts brushed his shirt. "I've said it before and I will say it again. Just quit. Walk away if you can't handle it. I did nothing wrong today, Garrett. Nothing. And you flipped out on me. But there is such an easy solution to our problems." My tone went soft, taunting. "Just quit. You'd get what you always wanted. And so would I."

"You never stop, do you?" he ground out, frantic eyes searching my face. "You never cut me even a tiny bit of slack."

"Why would I?" I said, my voice thready and weak, a direct contradiction to the pulse that was thundering along every inch of my skin.

"Just shut up." His hands gripped the sides of my face and we held there for a slow, elastic moment.

Then he kissed me.

My arms were around his neck in the next breath, and our tongues fought. It wasn't sweet and it wasn't soft. His teeth clacked against mine while I wrapped a leg around his hip.

But when I moaned, he took it. I felt him breathe it in, felt how his arms wound around my back and his hands dug painfully into my sweat-slicked skin, like the sound from deep within the pit of my stomach flooded his fingertips with strength.

With only one foot on the ground, I pushed up on my tiptoes so I could shove my fingers through his hair. It was damp by the scalp and I tightened my grip far beyond what I'd normally do.

Because I felt crazed.

He'd slipped something in my veins, electricity pooling through all the blood that ran through my body. His lips pushed and pulled over mine, like he was punishing me for how good it was.

So, so good.

I broke away to gasp for breath, and he wrapped a hand around my ponytail.

"Why do you feel so good?" he whispered, his lips tracing the skin of my neck.

My voice, any backbone I may have had at this momentary blip of insanity fled at the ragged, tortured question. *We shouldn't*, it was such a fleeting, whispy thought. Nothing that I could have grabbed onto or solidified into action.

Because his teeth grazed the tendon in my neck and I lost my ever-loving mind.

"Garrett," I groaned, slipping one hand from his hair, down his back and up underneath the thin, worn cotton of his shirt. His skin was so hot, so firm. The cords of his muscles bunched under my hand and we both turned so that our mouths melded again.

Over and over, until I thought he'd drown me.

Right then, I'd have gone down without a fight.

CHAPTER SIXTEEN

GARRETT

I'd lost my mind.

It was the only plausible explanation. Because nothing, nothing in my life had ever felt as good as Rory in my arms. Her lips were firm and sweet and she almost brought me to my knees when she slipped her tongue against mine.

Stumbling forward, I pushed her against the wall, groaning when she bit my lower lip in answer.

"This is insane," she said, dropping her head back and baring her long, graceful neck for me.

"It is."

"We should stop."

"Absolutely not," I said firmly, stamping my lips over hers again. She whimpered, such a sweet, mewling sound that completely contradicted the fierce competitor that I'd come to respect.

She hummed when I started kissing down her neck, and the vibration of the sound against my lips lifted goosebumps on my arms. So I caught the edge of her throat with my teeth, just to see if I could taste it too. Rory moaned, pushing her hands into my hair and grabbing on so tightly that I hissed.

When had she become the perfect woman? I'd blinked and missed it.

But I wasn't blinking anymore.

I'd sleep with my eyes open if it meant seeing her clearly from there on out.

"We're fighting about whether we should kiss or not. Do you realize how ludicrous that is?"

"Nope." I licked the edge of her jaw, grinning against her skin when she slumped down a few inches. Then I pulled back so I could see her, see the effect of this explosion on her face.

It was worth the distance, because in the dim light of the room, her cheeks were pinked and her lips were red from my own. Her hair was as mussed as I'd ever seen it and her eyelids were heavy, the blue of her irises dark with passion.

I pressed my forehead against hers, relishing the way she stared at my mouth when I spoke. "The only thing that's ludicrous is that we waited this long to do it. It's too good, Rory." Our lips brushed after I said it, and I held there to see what she'd do. Her breath passed from her lips to mine and I greedily sucked it in, taking that little piece of her into myself.

Then she tilted her chin and pressed her mouth more firmly onto my own.

Hallelujah.

Tilting my head to the side so I could sweep my tongue into her mouth, I finally allowed my hands to wander. The fact that I'd waited this long with her entire body, her beautiful, strong body up against mine was a freaking miracle. Up her side, feeling each sweeping line of her ribs underneath her sweat-sticky skin, the edge of her sports bra and the warm rounded shape of her breast with my thumb.

I slid my other hand down the curved line of her toned back and almost wept. She was wearing shorts. Tiny, miniscule shorts.

With one thumb, I played with the elastic band wrapping around her slim hips. "I'd like to take this moment to thank you for wearing these."

She laughed, a breathy, satisfied sound and it tightened my skin. "I certainly wasn't thinking about you when I put them on. Mainly I just wanted to get here to work out all the shit you put me through on a daily basis."

"I assure you," I said into her ear, causing her to shiver, "you give as good as you get, sweetheart. Now it'll feel like you're teasing me though."

Alert. Warning. Her body froze against me, and I knew it was the wrong thing to say. Her hands braced on my chest, not pushing me away, just stopping me from the way we'd been plastered together.

"Garrett," she whispered and I dropped my head onto her shoulder in defeat. "We can't."

"Incorrect phrasing. Can't means we're not physically capable." I rocked my hips and she curled her fingers into my shirt, gripping the cotton. "Shouldn't is something different, but I'd argue that we're in the perfect situation where we can and we *should*."

"How do you figure that?"

Her voice sounded naked and vulnerable, a questioning Rory that I'd never heard before. I lifted my head from her shoulder and met her eyes. They looked so deeply into me that I couldn't lie even if I'd wanted to.

"Are you asking about the current moment we're in or once we walk out the door?"

She exhaled through her nose. "Both, I guess. *Can't* still feels like an accurate word choice to me, especially outside of this room. We've barely just figured out a good balancing act at work, and this?" She motioned between us and gave a sad shrug of her shoulders. "It's a major complication that we can't afford to pursue."

"I wouldn't agree to that," I said quickly.

"Sure," she snorted, an indelicate sound that was completely incongruous with what I'd ever heard from her before. "You say that because you're a guy. Guys never think sex complicates things."

"Hey, don't lump me in with the men you've known before. I don't treat women casually, and I don't sleep around."

Rory narrowed her eyes at my tone, probably trying to figure out if I was being serious.

"Have I paraded a hundred women around over the last eight years? Or even brought a single one to office parties?" I asked when she didn't say anything.

"No," she answered slowly. Her hands pressed on my chest again and I backed up instantly. I may have wanted to kiss her for the next twenty-four hours straight, but I wasn't the kind of guy who pressured a woman. Especially Rory. She'd rip my nutsack off if I tried. "So then what are you saying, Garrett? You want to, what? Date me? Besides the work issue, you don't even like me."

"Patently untrue." When she arched an eyebrow in disbelief, I laughed under my breath. "Okay, fine, there may have been times when I wanted to strangle you."

"And now…"

Knowing it was a risk, I stepped up to her again and kept my movements slow so that she had plenty of time to push me away again. It would have been easy to make some declaration to her about the fact that I hadn't actually kissed anyone in the last year. Hadn't slept with anyone in almost two. Maybe she'd think I was pathetic. Sometimes I felt like it, considering my friends didn't even know about my dry spell. And maybe the fact that my apathy toward finding a woman to spend time with was so rooted in the fact that I was afraid to fail, afraid to have someone not look at me and see a man that was worth investing time in, that I'd become unable to even try. That fear— the one that wouldn't dislodge from the back of my skull— that a woman that I was genuinely interested in wouldn't see me as anything other than the funny guy or the casual guy, was a fear that I'd never admitted to myself. Rory was the first woman in years that made me want to risk it. Who made me want to rip open my rib cage so she could see what was inside of me. I hadn't dared think about that for so long.

Until now.

Until she kissed me back with the kind of passion that I'd never come close to touching before with my bare hands.

But if I told her those things? That kissing her made something click inside of me. That her hands in my hair almost brought me to my knees? She'd run so far and so fast that I'd never see her again. At least, I thought she would. But even if it was a possibility, I didn't want to push my luck.

Even the slightest possibility that she'd clam up and lock me out … that was unacceptable.

So I kept it light. I cupped the side of her neck, using my thumb to tilt her chin up so that she was forced to look me in the eye. "And now I think I'd like to kiss you again."

"That's not what I was asking, and you know it."

"Doesn't make it any less true." I held her eyes and dropped my mouth to suck her top lip in between mine. She didn't kiss back, but she didn't slap me either, so that was good. "Come on, Rory. We're alone. We're in a dark, quiet room where no one can hear us."

"Wait, oh please wait, I can hear you," a random voice popped up from the corner of the room. "Please don't have sex right now."

Rory shrieked, pressing into me, and I cursed, fumbling my hand along the wall to find a light switch. When I found one and flipped it up, the room was suddenly so bright that I pinched my eyes shut. Rory's face was tucked into my shoulder, which was just about as disorienting as the painful flood of light.

I looked behind me and there was a woman about our age sitting up against the wall holding a bottle of water and wearing an embarrassed smile.

"You've been here the whole time?" I accused her with narrowed eyes.

I think maybe she was attempting to smile at me, but it looked like a grimace. "I'm sorry, I just hide in here a couple times a week to have peace and quiet. My husband thinks I come to work out, but really, I just want an hour without any kids asking me for something."

Rory was shaking, and it took me a second to realize she was laughing.

The sheer absurdity of our first kiss, the most exciting thing to happen to me in years, being witnessed by a random stranger in a dark exercise room, made me smile too. Rory lifted her head, and there was so much in her eyes.

She looked happy, albeit slightly embarrassed. And so beautiful that it made me hurt.

Despite the fact that it was the very last thing I wanted to do, I stepped back from her. The space between us felt like a vacuum, sucking everything into it that I just felt. The residual emptiness turned my stomach into a heavy brick.

Rory turned to leave the room and I followed.

"You guys are really cute together," the woman called after us, and I gave her a small smile over my shoulder.

Rory ducked into the woman's locker room, and like a chump, I paced the hallway while I waited. Maybe she didn't want me to, but I was walking that woman to her car. When she came back out with her purse, I couldn't decipher the look on her face, but the blankness in her eyes made the brick in my stomach drop down to my feet.

"I'll walk you out," I said unnecessarily. And this, ladies and gentlemen, is why I didn't date. It all felt uncomfortable. The courtesies that you were supposed to show, even if she didn't want them. Maybe they'd always felt uncomfortable to me because I hadn't found a woman that I could be myself with.

And walking Rory through the gym and out into the hot, dry air wasn't exactly *comfortable*, but it didn't make me want to stab my eyes out either. Even though I kept pace with her, she didn't look over at me until we got to her car.

With a sinking feeling, I knew that I was up the proverbial shit creek without a paddle. Because I was searching for the tiniest flicker of hope in Rory's eyes, and I would only have been doing that for one reason.

I wanted her.

Like, *take her on a date and spoon her in bed and buy her birthday presents and rip her clothes after doing it* wanted her. Girlfriend and boyfriend wanted her. Wanted her to keep pushing me and testing me and making me crazy like she'd always done, because now it felt like the most perfect form of foreplay that I'd ever experienced.

With my head spinning in circles on my shoulders and my heart attempting to escape through the crack in my ribs, I watched her give me a forced smile and hop into her car without another word. While she drove away, I stayed exactly like that. Only after her taillights disappeared did I stumble back and rest up against the car that had been parked next to her.

"Well, shit," I said. "Now what do I do?"

CHAPTER SEVENTEEN

AURORA

When I was twelve, my dad was reassigned to Luke AFB in Phoenix, and we'd had to move during the school year. We would have another move before ending up in Colorado Springs, which started my love affair with Colorado, but the move to Arizona was undoubtedly the hardest of all of them. I came home crying from my last day, after saying goodbye to the two friends that I'd made in the year and a half prior. And as hard as it was for me in my thirties to make new friends, it had started about two decades earlier from the constant moves. Having two friends in that place had felt like an embarrassment of riches for me.

Even at that young age, I'd known to be careful with my emotional outbursts in front of my parents. I had no siblings to distract them, so when I acted out, I had to bear the full brunt of their disapproval. And considering that I'd never seen my mom cry when my dad was gone for months at a time, I remembered furiously wiping my tears before I walked through the front door of our house in Youngstown, Ohio.

Unfortunately for me, the General had been outside detailing his car and caught me.

"You're not crying, are you?" He'd muttered from where he circled a white rag over the back fender.

"No, sir." But my immediate sniffle earned me a sharp-eyed look.

He'd sighed then, like my sadness was the most inconvenient thing in his life. "Does it help?"

That had made me pause, because when he unfolded to his full height and stared down at me, I wondered if he was actually caring about why I was sad.

"Crying?" I'd asked.

"Yeah. Does it make it better? Make it easier to say goodbye to people?"

"No, sir," I'd said quietly, lifting my chin. "It doesn't make it easier." He nodded like I gave a correct answer, but something had bubbled up in my chest. Something I didn't normally indulge because I'd known it was pointless. "But sometimes it feels good to let them out anyway."

My dad, as I still had thought of him then, leaned down and gave me a stern look. "Letting them out gives those weak feelings power. If you give them power, they'll take over your life. You'll make new friends, just like you do every time we move. And we're moving for a good reason, an important reason. You'll be fine, because you're an Anderson. That's what we do."

Why that particular memory was burned on my brain on that particular morning while I dressed for work, I didn't really know.

A lie.

I did know. I hadn't slept the whole night before, staring up at the ceiling of my bedroom and replaying every moment of Garrett's kiss, of the hushed words that he'd whispered into my skin, which burned with every replay.

And I'd cried. Just one tear, because in the dark exercise room, he made me feel something that no man had ever made me feel, and that was horribly inconvenient.

Because at the end of his twelve months, he'd either be my boss and I'd have to reconcile how those stolen moments shifted something inside of me, or I'd be taking over his family's company while I watched him walk away.

See earlier statement about inconvenience.

So when I stood in front of my closet doors and had to decide what to wear, I felt like I was trying to pick my strongest shield for battle. What would leave the least number of weak spots for Garrett to pick at? What would cover me with the most confidence in my ability to stay strong against him? Because even if I very much wanted to feel him pressed along the entire length of my body again, it probably wasn't the smartest thing to indulge in. So armor it was.

Black three-piece suit. Skinny, fitted pants, trim, double lapel blazer, black vest and my white silk shell underneath. Red shoes. No jewelry. The only accessory was my lipstick, which matched the blood-red patent of my stilettos. It was completely over the top for work, and I couldn't even care.

When I stared at my reflection in the full-length mirror in my bedroom, I looked like a warrior with wild eyes and a perfectly pressed suit of armor.

"Perfect," I breathed.

Unfortunately, I didn't see him on my walk in, even though his office was lit up and open. And I didn't see him for the first few hours.

So I lost myself in work, not giving myself permission to delve too deeply into why that pissed me off so much. He was the one who'd done this me. Made me feel so wildly out of control, so completely unsure of my footing.

An alert popped up on my computer, reminding me of a finance meeting, so I took a few moments to touch up my lipstick before walking down to the west conference room. Garrett only attended when his presence was necessary, and I couldn't remember the agenda items off the top of my head to know whether he'd be there.

I was about to print off my copy when I saw someone pause outside of my office.

A short, blonde someone. With a dog.

Tilting my head while I walked around my desk, I called out to her. "Can I help you?"

She turned, greeting me with a massive smile. "Oh yay. A person. I was about to start yodeling to see if someone would pop their head up and tell me where to go."

"Umm, well then I'm glad I saw you before that had to happen" I said with a tiny smile, while side-stepping where her dog was sniffing at my pants. If that thing got hair on my black pants, I would not be a happy camper. "Can I help you find anyone?"

"Garrett Calder," she answered with a happy smile when my head snapped up. She was pretty. Short, with slight curves and messy blonde hair that barely reached her shoulders. Big brown eyes and a wide smile. "Man, I'm so rude. I'm Kat and this is Leonidas. I'm training him to be a therapy dog, so I'm taking him everywhere with me. I mean, except like, restaurants and stuff. They don't really like that much."

"I'm sure they don't." I glanced down at the dog, who was medium-sized with golden brown fur and a long, shaggy tail. Then he pranced sideways and I saw a plastic sleeve strapped around one of his front legs. "He's missing a leg."

"Yup. Birth defect. He's been wearing that for about ten months, and he's such a badass, right?"

I didn't care about the dog. I'd never had a pet, because the General thought they were a waste of money. And a dog like this one would've had no sympathy with my father. A physical weakness like that was strongly frowned upon at our house. It's still why I found myself at the gym five days a week, because he'd drilled that into my head so deeply that I couldn't dig it out. Strong body, strong mind.

"Right, sure," I answered belatedly, shifting on my feet. "Well, I'm not sure where Garrett is. I haven't seen him this morning."

Kat watched me while I talked, and I saw something shift in her eyes. "Are you … umm, are you Aurora?"

"Yes," I said cautiously, not at all liking the way she said my name. "He's talked about me?"

"Once or twice," Kat said with a gleeful smile covering her pixie face. "Oh my gosh, I'm *so* glad to meet you!"

"Are you his girlfriend?" I blurted out. I knew the answer, I did. He'd just talked the day before about not having anyone, but clearly I'd lost my damn mind. Garrett and his stupid lips and tongue had actually made me *lose my mind.* So much for my freaking armor. Apparently it didn't bar my mouth from saying completely idiotic, embarrassing things.

Kat stared at me for a beat before she hunched over in hysterics. Her dog licked at her face while she laughed, his body wiggling in delight. I rolled my eyes, mostly at myself, and very much wished I could rewind this entire conversation over.

Had I seen Garrett? No. Great, moving on.

But the kernel that had been planted the first time I thought he was going to kiss me had bloomed into an oak tree inside of me, each branch that slithered through my body consumed with him and me and what was happening between us. It was so big and sturdy, that I didn't know how to get it out without spilling my organs everywhere.

And it was all *his* fault.

Kat finally straightened and wiped underneath her eyes with both hands. "Oh man, that's the funniest thing I've ever heard. No," she shook her head vigorously, "I am happily taken with someone that is not Garrett. My boyfriend, Dylan, is one of Garrett's best friends, actually."

"Oh." I wanted to go away. Just be far, far away from this entire situation that was unfortunately, of my own making. "That's … nice."

"Speak of the devil," Kat said, smiling over my shoulder. "I was looking for you."

"Oh, and you brought my favorite guy," Garrett said from right next to me. Not that I was going to look. No freaking way was I giving him that satisfaction.

Garrett kneeled on the floor and greeted the dog with ridiculous baby talk, allowing it to lick his face. His face. The same face that I'd been intimately familiar with less than twenty-four hours earlier.

"What are you doing here, Kat? Miss me that much?"

"I've cried myself to sleep every night for the last week," she said sweetly. "I was just down the street with Leonidas getting in some practice for his therapy dog certification and thought we'd stop by and say hi. We got back late last night and figured you'd like to see Leonidas."

I could feel Garrett looking at me and I managed two full seconds before I glanced down at him. The warmth in his eyes was what surprised me the most. Damn near knocked me backwards, actually. He looked happy to see me. He was wearing a white shirt, charcoal slacks and a deep silver tie that I'd seen once before. That instant cataloging of what he was wearing is how I knew that he'd gotten way too deep under my skin. Oh, it was bad. And I had no clue how to stop it.

"Yeah," he said, still holding my gaze for a breath before smiling at Kat. "I've missed you guys."

"Did you even notice we were gone?"

"Hey, don't get crazy. You know I've been busy here," he said in a warning tone, but it was obvious that it was friendly and affectionate. This stuff was so easy for Garrett. It was one of the things I'd used to hate about him. He could walk into any room and immediately have people eating out of his hands. A few smiles and questions, and he had a roomful of new friends.

I wasn't like that. Even though I'd been in one place for college and my MBA, friends hadn't come easily for me.

Watching their easy banter stuck like barbed wire in my throat, so I coughed, bringing their attention to me. "I need to get to a meeting. It was nice to meet you, Kat."

"Likewise," she said with a genuine smile. "Hopefully I'll see you again soon."

Garrett pinned her with a glare, but instead of wanting to push her on that just to see him squirm, I turned and all but fled down the hallway.

And I'd thought a few pieces of clothing and stellar lipstick could toughen me up around him. What a joke. I was starting to think that nothing short of a ten-foot cement wall could protect me from what Garrett Calder was doing to me.

CHAPTER EIGHTEEN

GARRETT

"Ohhhhhh my gosh," Kat breathed while Rory practically sprinted down the hallway.

I pointed a finger at her. "Shut up. Whatever you're going to say, shut up."

"You had literal heart eyes." She shook her head and started following me when I pivoted to head to my office, not at all needing Kat's ribbing to be within ear shot of anyone. "I mean, right in front of me, I saw you become an emoji."

"That's insane."

"I agree. It's insane that we heard you mention her once or twice with a string of expletives behind her name, and I just watched you become a steaming pile of goo while you kneeled at her feet." Then she started cackling.

With a muttered curse, I shut my office door and then plopped in an arm chair so I could scratch Leonidas' head. "Ignore her, dude. She thinks she knows what she's talking about."

His tail thumped against the front of my legs and I smiled.

"Oh, I know what I'm talking about," Kat said once she'd calmed down. "I know all the things about all the things. And that?" She tipped her forehead at the door. "That was a thing like I've never seen from you."

"Because you see me so much lately?" I asked with only the slightest edge.

"Not my fault. I haven't seen you because you've turned into workaholic Garrett." Then she grinned. "And I think I know why."

"You know? I wish I had something to throw at you. Because I'd do it."

Kat tapped a finger on her chin. "I see, I see. Deflection. A solid tactic, my friend."

"Why are you here, Perry?" I asked. Even if her line of observations annoyed the shit out of me, it was an excellent distraction for how quickly Rory had fled from me. Like the hounds of hell were nipping at her insanely hot shoes. Oh no, it was just me. Just the man that kissed the hell out of her and felt his heart fall into bloody mess at her feet.

"Well, I really was down the street. And when I talked to Cole, he said you were one giant ball of PMS last night." She shrugged. "Figured I'd ambush you to see how you're doing."

My annoyance receded slowly. Even though she pretended like I was an inconvenience every time I dropped by her and Dylan's house, Kat had become one of my closest friends in the year that she'd been with my friend. And when my dad died, throwing my life into complete upheaval personally and professionally, I'd shut them out in the blink of an eye.

Because who would want to sit and listen to me bemoan my ridiculous first world problems? *Oh, poor baby, you have to run a successful company that your dad entrusted you with when he died and make really good money doing it. And the woman who is running it with you is smart and beautiful and strong, who pushes you like no one ever has before.* Poor Garrett.

I snorted, imagining how that conversation might have gone. "I'm fine, Katherina."

"Not my name," she said dryly, like she did every time I called her that. "And you're not fine. You're hiding from us. We're your friends, yo. Let us just … I don't know, hang out with you again."

My eyes fell shut, unable to see the soft, concerned look on her face. "Yeah, we can do that."

Kat clapped and Leonidas flipped to his feet from where he was lying next to my shoes. "Yay! Okay, let's do a barbecue at Dylan's. He'll cook. And maybe," she cleared her throat and gave me a long look, "maaaaaaaybe you can invite Aurora."

I hooted a laugh. "Kat, were you just out in the hallway? She could barely converse with you because she was so uncomfortable."

"Yeah, who did she remind you of?" she asked quietly.

I thought about that for a second, and then lifted my eyebrows in concession. "Fine, you were awkward when you first started coming around."

"Awkward? Garrett, the first time I met you, I wanted to *die* because Dylan made me come over to his house and you were there. You were so nice. It freaked me out."

Instead of answering, because she didn't need me to verbalize the fact that she was right. She knew it as well as I did.

"It's complicated with her, Kat."

"So un-complicate it. You like her. Ask her over for a barbecue. Tell her she can bring a friend if you think it'll help." Kat gave me a little smile. "But I know what it's like to feel uncomfortable around new people. I'm the queen of it. She probably likes you as much as you like her and doesn't know what to do with it. So let us be the buffer. Aurora can see how awesome you are with all your friends, and we'll be able to get to know her. Make sure she's kosher and all that."

"You make it sound like we're in high school or something," I grumbled. Grumbled, even though I was all but vibrating with excitement over the thought of seeing her in that kind of situation. With my friends, maybe at my house. My heart would probably seize. "Fine. I'll ask her. But let's do it at my place. I don't want to throw too much at her if she says yes."

Kat squealed, and I rolled my eyes. "She'll totally say yes. Women don't ignore a man the way she just ignored you if he means nothing to her."

That made me pause. I'd never thought of it like that before. I must have affected Rory as much as she affected me, she just didn't know how to channel it now that we were at the office.

I glanced at the clock hanging on the wall behind Kat's head. Rory would be in a meeting for another thirty or so minutes, so I'd have time to psyche myself out.

To ask her over for a barbecue. And hope that she didn't laugh at me outright.

Truthfully, while I said goodbye to Kat, I knew that was as likely a response as any.

"So I was thinking," I said from the doorway of Rory's office, watching her freeze at the sound of my voice and then take a second before turning around in her chair to face me, "that you should come over to a barbecue that I'm having at my place."

"No," she said firmly, practically before the last word was out of my mouth, turning back to her computer.

I narrowed my eyes at her profile. "You could pretend that you're contemplating it, just for the sake of my ego."

"Your ego does not need help from me," she said, not taking her eyes away from the screen.

"You'd be surprised," I said under my breath.

"What was that?"

"Nothing." I tapped the folder I was holding against my leg. "So beyond the invite, which still stands until I can convince you to come," I paused when she snorted, "I also wanted to apologize to you."

Turning her chair slightly, Rory watched me with a carefully blank face. "For what? The fact that you practically mauled me in the gym?"

I laughed. "No, definitely not apologizing for that completely two-sided kiss. It was phenomenal, and you know it."

"Eh."

My smile widened, because even though she sounded completely bored, the curve of her cheekbones pinked immediately. I'd leave that alone. For now, at least. "I'm apologizing for snapping at you in my office the other day. You made an innocent comment and I overreacted. I'm sorry."

Rory took a deep breath while she watched me. "Thank you. I appreciate that."

"Are you so appreciative that you want to come over to my house and eat some hamburgers that I'll probably over-cook? You might even be able to see my friends make fun of me for it."

She laughed under her breath at that, immediately smoothing out her face like she hadn't meant to do it. "I don't know if that's a good idea, Garrett."

"Why not?" I asked, tamping down my excitement at the fact that it wasn't another no. "I've all but promised that you'll see me be publicly humiliated. How could you possibly turn down that opportunity?"

"A tempting offer, to be sure."

"Name-calling, too. That happens a lot. We're a fun group," I said, then hesitated. Or at least we would be once I apologized to them too.

If Rory noticed me trailing off, she didn't say anything. She was too deep in thought, processing through something in a similar way that I probably just had. "I'm not saying yes, but when are you having it?"

"Not sure yet," I admitted. "Kat and I talked about throwing something together next weekend maybe. I haven't done much with my friends lately."

"How come?" Her voice was steadier and she had her professional mask slipped firmly into place now.

I shrugged, walking into her office and bracing a shoulder on the wall beyond her door. She had two chairs opposite her desk, but sitting might have made her more uncomfortable if she thought I was planning on staying a while. "Busy here, I guess. And after my dad died, I didn't want people to feel weird around me. Like they needed to console me."

A brief picture of my dad laughing in the middle of a staff meeting punched the breath from my lungs. I'm sure some day I'd be able to talk about him dying without feeling that way, but apparently it wasn't happening yet. Rory had never acted that way toward me —like I needed to console her— which is maybe why despite our differences, she'd become the person I felt most comfortable around since he'd died.

Rory nodded slowly, searching my face with her evening sky blue eyes. "That makes sense."

"So you'll come?" Look at me. No begging or pleading. I could absolutely do this.

"Next weekend?" She bit the edge of her bottom lip, and I wavered. Maybe there would be pleading. Like, *please let me touch your lip with my tongue again* kind of pleading. Then she shook her head. "I can't. My cousin is going to be in town."

"Bring your cousin along," I said easily.

She blinked at me, clearly not expecting me to say that. "Really?"

"Absolutely. The more the merrier. I'm sure Anna will come too, so you'll know another person besides me and Kat."

Rory scoffed, but had a self-deprecating smile on her face. "I don't know Kat. I met her for a completely awkward thirty seconds and her dog got hair on my pants. That does not constitute knowing someone."

I held up my hands. "Wait. You don't like dogs?" Oh shit, depending on her answer, I may have to rethink everything.

"I don't dislike them," she answered carefully. "I just don't have much experience with them. We were never allowed to have them while I was growing up."

"Well that's stupid."

Her lips curved at the edges in a tiny smile and I wanted to fist-pump. "You'll have to tell the General that if you ever meet him."

"The what who?"

Her face dropped. "Ah. That's my father. He's in the Air Force, Chief Master Sergeant, and I call him the General because it would drive him crazy if he knew." She must have seen the confusion on my face. "General is an Army rank, not Air Force."

I smiled while I processed that. Another tiny piece of the Rory puzzle clicked into place. This time, it was big and foundational, telling me so much about who she was.

"Military brat, huh?" I asked lightly. No need scaring her off when she was finally pulling back the curtain a little.

"Does that surprise you?"

"No," I said honestly. "Without sounding weird, that explains a lot, actually."

Her fingers fidgeted on the surface of her desk. "Okay. Well, good."

I smiled. This was, by far, my favorite side of Rory. It wasn't the smooth business woman, it wasn't the fiery opponent who lashed out at me, and it wasn't the woman that melted in my arms at the gym. This unsure Rory, the one who'd met Kat in the hallway, made me feel like I had a chance with her.

Don't ask me why, but it did.

Maybe because I got the feeling that not too many people saw this side of her. It was an admission for her, one that probably cost her a lot. And that sunk into my heart like tiny claws.

"Aurora?" Our IT manager popped his head in and smiled when he saw me. "Oh, sorry if I'm interrupting."

"It's no problem, Gary" she said with a small smile. "What can I do for you?"

He waved some papers and started to hand them to her. "I just need you to sign off on hiring that guy I told you about earlier. It's fast, I know, and he doesn't have all the educational requirements that we'd asked for in the job posting, but I think he'd be fantastic." Gary paused, flicking his eyes to me. "I mean, if you're okay with it too."

I held up my hands to Gary and then tipped my chin at Rory. "I don't need to see it. I trust her judgement."

Gary nodded and got Rory's approval before she scrawled a quick signature on the bottom of the last page. When he left, she stared at me for a few loaded breaths.

"Why didn't you need to look at it?"

Lifting my eyebrows, I took a deep breath. "Because I meant what I said. I trust your call on stuff like that."

"And if he'd ran into you in the hallway and had asked you the same question?"

"I would have told him to come talk to you. You're the COO. Gary answers to you, not me. I'd never question your decision on hiring."

Rory pulled in a deep breath, the bright red of her lips drawing my eyes like a siren. If I kissed her now, it would smear over her face, leave a stain on my skin.

"Thank you," she said simply. "That means a lot to me."

I swallowed against the rush of emotion when she said it. Another admission that probably felt like she was drawing knives over her skin to say it. And say it to me, of all people. But she'd done it all the same.

"You're welcome." My voice was rough when I answered and I could tell she noticed by her quick inhale.

"I have another meeting soon."

"Right. Sorry, I'll let you get back to work." I smiled and turned toward the door.

"Let me know what time for next weekend."

Pausing in the doorway, I turned slightly and nodded at her. "I will."

If I'd left even a millisecond sooner, I'd have missed the quick smile on her face when she looked back at her computer.

Next weekend wouldn't get here soon enough.

CHAPTER NINETEEN

AURORA

"Gawd, you need more color in this house," Mia groaned when I let her walk into the front door of my condo after picking her up from the airport.

"Says you." I set her massive purple suitcase next to the dining room table, but still cast a critical eye over my family room, dining area, and kitchen. I favored whites, creams and browns in my décor because it felt soft and sumptuous to me. Only my artwork on the wall— contemporary pieces with simple statements— added anything different. "Too much color in my living space feels chaotic. This calms me."

When Mia didn't respond, I looked over to where she was slouched against the wall, pretending to be asleep. We hadn't seen each other in two years, and I'd been living somewhere else the last time she visited. She was thinner and leaner, like she'd been working out regularly since the last time I'd seen her. Her mother was my mom's sister, and since I favored the General when it came to my height and coloring, Mia and I didn't even look like we were related.

Her petite build, deep brown hair, which currently sported dark blue ends, and olive skin looked more like the Italian roots that our mothers shared. I was all Viking. Our personalities were even further apart than that, but given that I'd moved about a dozen times before I turned eighteen, Mia was the person that stuck. And because she was from the non-Anderson side, she took no offense when I railed against the military strict upbringing that still stuck under my skin like a burr.

"Oh," she stretched and yawned, "sorry, dozed off from the calming colors."

I rolled my eyes and she laughed, which made me smile. A childhood like mine, and the adulthood that I'd chased in order to avoid said childhood, didn't lend itself to deep, solid friendships. Mia was it for me, the person that I had never to explain myself to or apologize for being the way that I was.

"Chinese for dinner?" I asked while I slipped my heels off with a satisfied groan.

"Honey, as much I dig those," Mia peered down at my purple slingback Jimmy Choos with a lifted eyebrow, "I do not understand how you can wear them all day long at work."

"Are you kidding? My feet are frozen like Barbie feet now. When I try to walk in flat shoes, I practically have to break them off to make them fit." I lifted up on the balls of my feet and waltzed toward her like I was still wearing my shoes and she snickered.

"You look like Barbie, so that's appropriate." Mia wandered down the hallway and tossed her carryon bags in the guest room across from my bedroom. "And yes, Chinese sounds delish. Can we eat from the cartons and drink wine straight from the bottle and watch a chick flick?"

"Yes, yes and no," I called down the hallway while I pulled open my drawer full of takeout menus. "I haven't seen you in almost two years. I'm not spending our first night watching a movie."

While I ordered the food, Mia flopped onto the couch and started flipping through her cell phone. I hung up and motioned for her to move her feet so I could sit on the opposite side of her.

"So," she drawled when I tucked my feet up underneath me. "What are we going to do this weekend?"

Ahh. The moment I'd been dreading for the last week, since Garrett stood in my office door with a genuinely kind expression on his face and invited me to a party. At his house.

After he'd kissed the bejeesus out of me, and then we didn't speak about it. And I'd been horribly awkward with his friend with the three-legged dog.

My heart did an impressive back flip and somehow lodged itself in my throat. And considering that I'd only ever spoken harshly about Garrett to Mia, this may have been turning into the most interesting conversation that Mia and I would have during her four-day visit.

"Well, actually, we got invited to a barbecue thing tomorrow night."

There. I managed to sound mildly interested and not at all like the thought of it made my skin hum and my pulse race to dangerous levels. Go Rory.

"Barbecue thing?" Mia shifted to face me, tucking her hair behind her ears. "Details, please."

Her prim posture and clipped words made me smile a little. Just enough to chop up my nerves into manageable levels. "It's at a coworker's house."

"Coworker?" Mia prodded, narrowing her eyes at my caginess.

I slicked my tongue over my front teeth and narrowed my eyes right back. "Garrett's."

"What?" she shrieked so loudly that I winced. "Is this a mother-effing April Fools' Day joke?'

"Unlikely, since it's August."

"The slacker? We're going to the slacker's house? On purpose?"

"He's not a slacker," I found myself saying instantly, and quite vehemently, then slapped a hand over my mouth when Mia's jaw popped open. Shit. Shit, shit, shit.

"You *like* him."

"I, umm, I don't precisely know," I hedged, feeling a traitorous flush sweep up my neck at her accusatory statement that I, unfortunately, could not deny anymore. Not to Mia. And even more importantly, to myself.

When Mia started chuckling under her breath, I picked up an ivory silk pillow and buried my face in it to hide my embarrassed groan. This entire exchange smacked of middle school, back when I still cared what the boys thought of me.

"Oh, this is so awesome," Mia said on a sigh. Then she yanked the pillow away from my face. Her entirely amused, entirely thrilled smile actually helped soothe my rankled nerves.

"I'm so out of my element, Mia." The delicate beading on the edge of the pillow made for a perfect distraction, so I traced the pattern with the edge of my thumbnail. "The last guy I dated was three years ago. I barely even remember how to do any of this, without the added complication of us working together."

"And he's your boss," she quite unhelpfully pointed out. When I glared at her, she cackled. "So he invited you to a party? That's not exactly a romantic date. Maybe he's just trying to be friendly."

Something in my expression must have given me away. Most likely because Garrett's idea of being friendly with me had involved palming my ass through my shorts and sucking on my tongue so hard that I saw stars.

The good kind.

"You filthy little liar," Mia said, shaking her head. "What haven't you told me?"

Pulling my face up in apologetic grimace, I hugged the pillow to my chest so that maybe she wouldn't hurt me when I told her the truth. "We kissed. Last week."

"Peck, tongue action, or tongue *and* hands action?"

"Number three," I answered quietly, waiting for her to smack me. So when she whooped and pumped both fists in the air, imagine my surprise.

"Rory, why do you look like I'm going to punch you in the boob? This is amazing! You haven't gotten any action in forever."

"But he's so inconvenient," I groaned. "Going to this party is not smart."

"Is there a rule against interoffice dating?"

"No," I admitted, ignoring her smug smile.

"Did he give you tingles in all the good places when he kissed you?"

"Yes."

She held out her hands like, *see?*

"It's not that simple, Mia."

"Yes, it is. You haven't dated for so long, because why?"

I pulled in a deep breath and then let it out in a harsh puff. "Because none of the men made me want to spend any more time with them. I'm busy. And for the most part, their idea of romance is completely manufactured. They bring roses because they think it's what they're supposed to do. They ask you surface level questions that they don't really even care to hear the answers to. Or worse, they see your picture and immediately make a judgement about you. Nothing surprised me or felt genuine. And if there's no spark, then it's not worth my time."

"Yeah," Mia said after a second, sounding thoughtful and serious. "I just … I want a man who makes my toes curl. Repeatedly." We both laughed. "For real though, what you're saying? That's what most women want. It has to feel real, even if it's inconvenient sometimes."

"So I'm not crazy?"

"No way," she insisted. "Why do you think *The Notebook* is so popular? We want a Noah. Preferably one that looks like Ryan Gosling."

"Uh huh."

She rolled her eyes. "Ugh, that's right. I think I blocked out the fact that you're related to me and haven't watched it yet."

"That's not overly dramatic at all."

"So since we last talked about it, you didn't decide you loved me enough to rent the damn thing?"

"No." She opened her mouth to argue but I held up a hand. "All those movies seem so cheesy, Mia. And predictable. Why would I want to spend my precious free time watching something predictable about romance when I'm actively trying to avoid that in my dating life?"

Her mouth hung open so long, I couldn't believe she wasn't drooling.

"Don't you have to swallow by now?" I asked.

"I … I don't even know how to speak to you right now. How are we related? How are you *female* and not want to watch it for the Gosling action?"

"Oh come on, he's not *that* hot."

Mia screwed her lips up and gave me the dirtiest look I'd ever seen from her. "You're speaking heresy, cousin. You don't rag on my Ryan. *Ever.*"

"Fine. I recant as long as you don't make me watch it." Flipping my wrist over, I tapped the face of my watch. "We need to go otherwise our eggrolls will be mushy."

She stood, but still gave me a look like I was crazy. Over a movie.

"So," she started while we walked four blocks over to the restaurant, "I'll get to meet some hot Colorado boys tomorrow night, right?"

"Honestly, Mia? I have no idea. But if his friends are even close to as handsome as Garrett?" I glanced over at her with a wry smile. "The odds are definitely in your favor."

"Perfect."

"I can't do it."

"Yes you can," Mia said soothingly. "You look amazing, okay?"

"I know I look good," I said miserably, glancing down at the ombre maxi dress that she'd convinced me to buy earlier in the day. The straps that held the dress up were impossibly thin and the way it was white on top and gradually turned to a pale aqua at the hem made me look tan and strong. The skirt flowed down my hips and brushed the floor, making me feel like a queen. Mia had curled my hair and convinced me to leave it down, something I didn't do often, and it fell over my bare shoulders while we sat in my car.

We were still sitting there because I couldn't find it in myself to push open the door. In front of Garrett's very nice house in a very nice neighborhood. The landscaping was tasteful and clean, letting the simple beauty of his house go unobstructed. Maybe it shouldn't have surprised me, that his place looked so grown up, but it did. And I felt no small prick of shame about it. It was exactly the kind of thing that I knew bothered him so much.

"Well, maybe try to sound a little bit more humble about it if someone compliments you, mmmkay?"

That made me smile. "I will. I just mean, that's not what I'm nervous about. What if it's awkward? What if I can't relax and it's one giant ball of terrible and we can't leave without it being obvious?"

"Ahh, social anxiety." She clucked her tongue and gave me a soft pat on my forearm where I still gripped the steering wheel. "It won't be awkward because I'm fun. And if you're ready to jet, we can have a code or something."

I furrowed my brow and looked at her. "Like what?"

Mia bit her lip while she considered it. She'd slicked her hair into a high bun, the blue ends of it forming the rounded shape and somehow not looking cheap. "The blackbird flies at midnight. If either of us says that?" She snapped her fingers. "Boom. We out, bitches."

"That's the worst code word I've ever heard."

"I was under pressure from your puppy dog eyes. Sue me." Mia was about to keep talking when she trailed off, her eyes trained out her window. "Ohhhhhhhhh, we need to go inside."

Angling so I could see what she was looking at, I laughed. Two tall, muscular guys were walking up Garrett's driveway. They both had dark hair, though the one on the left had his tied back into a sloppy bun at his nape. Even though one was slightly taller— the one with short hair— they moved the same.

"*Brothers*, Rory. They're totally brothers." She clasped her hands to her chest and bounced in place. "Come on, cupcake. Get your shit together. I need to call dibs. Unless they're married, then never mind."

While she slipped out of the passenger door, I let out a deep breath and caught my reflection in my rearview mirror. The wide-eyed person who stared back didn't resemble me in the slightest. Because buried underneath the fear of what was waiting past Garrett's solid wood front door with craftsman details was visible excitement.

The flush-cheeked person couldn't be me, could it?

Either way, I was about to find out, because Mia was standing in front of my car with a hand fisted on her hip. "Come on, Anderson," she yelled. Both guys in the driveway stopped when she did, glancing over at us.

"Great," I mumbled under my breath and reluctantly pushed my door open. "We're already a sideshow."

With shaking hands, I tucked my keys into the small purse I'd taken with me. Mia didn't wait. She was already chatting with the, yup, definitely brothers. The one with short hair was grinning broadly at my cousin. The other one though, he was standing back, visibly removing himself from their conversation.

Mia turned when I approached them. "Rory, this is Michael and Tristan. They live across the street. Gentleman, my beautiful cousin is the one who works with Garrett."

At the meaningful way she said Garrett's name, I narrowed my eyes at her.

The one with short hair stepped forward and held his hand out. His greenish brown eyes assessed me quickly and I did my best to give him a friendly smile while I shook his hand. "Michael. Nice to meet you, Rory. *Really* nice to meet you." He winked while he pulled his hand back and jerked his chin at the other one. "Tristan is the friendly one between the two of us."

Tristan grimaced at his brother, but softened his face slightly when he turned to me. Not quite a smile, but enough that I wasn't completely wary of him. "Nice to meet you."

"You too," I replied and then cleared my throat. "Are we the first ones here?"

"Dylan and Kat are probably inside," Michael said, gesturing to the front porch for us to go up first. "I heard you already met Kat, right, Rory?"

Clearing the last step onto the porch, I nodded even though I wasn't sure if he could see me. I could just about imagine what Kat had told them about me. Hadn't precisely been a shining moment for me. The ability to maintain my professionalism was important to me, something I was incredibly proud of. But stumbling through that first introduction with one of Garrett's friends had been the polar opposite of professional. Not even that, I'd been borderline unfriendly.

"She seems nice," I said, fully aware of how lame that sounded.

The front door loomed in front of me, and beyond it, I could hear the muffled sounds of laughter, both male and female.

My breath stuttered in my chest when I recognized Garrett's voice among the chatter. Clearing that threshold would change something. This wasn't an unintentional run-in at the gym or a casual conversation in the office after a meeting.

"You can go on in," Michael said from behind me.

My cheeks burned when I thought about the fact that they were all waiting behind me on the front porch. Amazingly, my hand stayed steady when I turned the knob and pushed it open.

He was the first person I saw, standing behind a massive granite island in the middle of an open kitchen with tasteful, subdued colors. The bright white of his cotton polo shirt stretched across his chest and wrapped around his biceps. And he was laughing. His lips were wide over his face, the easy smile that I hadn't seen as often in the last two months making my heart tighten around the edges.

Then he saw me, and impossibly, his smile grew wider. And I didn't miss the way his eyes dipped over my frame and took in my dress and my hair, sparking something warm and gooey in my stomach. Mia, Michael and Tristan entered behind me, but I stayed just inside the entryway, holding Garrett's eyes while he came from around the island.

He only looked away once, when Michael introduced Mia. The grin he gave her was dangerous, but she was already flitting her lashes at Michael, so I wasn't jealous.

Even though, I reminded myself firmly, there was nothing for me to be jealous over. We'd kissed once.

Okay. One long kiss that couldn't really be chopped up into a concrete number.

Garrett clapped Michael and Tristan on their shoulders, and made his way to me, stopping just out of my reach. "Rory."

"Thank you for having us." Dork. Giant, massive dork.

He fought his smile valiantly at my wooden response, tilting his face down when he lost the battle. "You're welcome. Can I get you a drink? We've got a few different kinds of beer, and some white wine in the fridge." Garrett hooked his chin over his shoulder. "And if you're lucky, Kat might share some of her sangria with you."

"Oh, just water for me."

All that I needed in this situation was alcohol as a crutch. With the anxiety coursing through me, I'd end up hiding in the bathroom with the entire pitcher of that sangria just to make myself feel calmer. Not a pretty picture. If Garrett judged me for my choice, he didn't show it, simply nodded and went to get me a glass of ice water.

Insanely curious about the place that he called home, I wandered through the beautifully appointed kitchen that led into an open dining area and family room beyond it. The colors were muted, but rich, with dark leather couch and matching chairs angled toward a large glass slider that led into a backyard with thick, lush grass and various trees.

The whole place felt masculine, but comfortable. Nothing stark or under-decorated, like I'd assumed. A cool hand touched my arm, and I turned to find Kat smiling up at me. Her wide grin set me at ease, given what a tool I'd been with her at the office.

"Hi, Rory. It's good to see you again."

She opened her arms to give me a hug, and I returned it, stunned at her easy affection. "Umm, thank you. It's good to see you too."

"That dress." She clucked her tongue and then gave me a rueful smile. "I cannot pull those things off because I look like a little kid playing dress-up."

Short though she was, there's no way Kat could have been mistaken for a child. A tall man with dark hair and striking blue eyes stepped up and wrapped an arm around Kat's shoulders.

"Oh, Dylan, this is Rory."

"Ah," he said with a meaningful lift of his eyebrows. Kat elbowed him and gave me an apologetic smile. "Sorry, didn't mean it like that. It's nice to meet the person who gives Garrett as much shit as we do."

I laughed, ducking my head down for a moment. "I don't know about that. But hello, Dylan. It's a pleasure to meet you, too."

"Are you being nice, Steadman?" Garrett asked, joining us and handing me a tall glass full of ice water.

"I'm always nice," Dylan said to Garrett, winking at me.

"It's true," Kat said to me in such an earnest way that I smiled. "He really is always nice."

"Bullshit," Garrett said, shoving at Dylan's shoulder. "I've never told you about some of the crap he pulled in middle school."

Dylan laughed, an easy, rich sound that made Kat snuggle into his side. Their love was obvious, and it tugged on a string of yearning that I hadn't felt in years. It felt thin and fragile, like if it was pulled too hard or too fast, it would snap.

I breathed through it while they talked around me. Garrett leaned in and spoke into my ear. "You okay?"

Swallowing at the concern in his voice, I gave him a tiny nod. "Fine."

He wanted to ask me more, I could tell, but the front door opened again and a tall, handsome man walked in with Anna.

"Is that her husband?" I asked Garret quietly, not sure who might know about the contingency in their father's will.

But he laughed easily. "No. He'd never come to something like this. That's our buddy, Cole. He lives one street over."

Anna stopped briefly to grab a beer out of the fridge before she came over to us. It was clear, to me at least, that she'd lost a little weight since I'd seen her at the church. Her silky dark hair was pulled back into a long braid that came over her shoulder. Instead of hugging Garrett, she punched him in the stomach and hugged me instead.

"Hey," she said warmly. "I didn't know you'd be here."

The confusion was clear in her voice, and I couldn't blame her. "Yeah, Garrett was kind enough to invite me."

"A truce of sorts," he added, giving me a brief look with smiling eyes.

"Of sorts," I agreed, taking a sip of my water.

Anna hummed, watching us over the rim of her beer. "Well that's good. Have you gotten a tour of Garrett's place, Rory?"

"No, but it seems very nice from what I've seen."

She perked up, a satisfied smile covering her beautiful face. "That's because he let me have carte blanche with the décor when he moved in."

"Yes," Garrett interjected. "No man would have this many throw pillows otherwise."

I laughed. His eyes zeroed in on my lips and then flicked away in the next breath. "Well you did a great job, Anna. You're very talented."

The way she beamed at my compliment warmed my heart. She'd been so upset the last time I saw her, justifiably, of course. From the corner of my eye, I saw Tristan shift over from where he'd been leaning up against the wall in the dining area. His eyes were lasered in on Anna.

He didn't see me, and I didn't think anyone saw him, but my eyes narrowed at him all the same. The way he was looking at Anna was pure tortured aching.

Interesting. Very, very interesting.

I smiled back at Garrett and Anna, then shook hands with Cole when he made his way over. Mia was settled on the couch laughing at something Michael was saying. Everyone was nice. And Garrett was being sweet.

Maybe I'd survive this thing.

"Anybody ready to eat?" Garrett called out amongst the chatter. Everyone said yes, and he winked at me before heading back into the kitchen. That wink did strange things to me, especially in the vicinity of that string of yearning. It tightened it, strengthened it and looped it around my heart.

Or, maybe my survival wasn't so certain after all.

As long as I stayed away from Garrett, didn't sit by him at dinner, I could probably get away unscathed.

CHAPTER TWENTY

GARRETT

One thing I was starting to seriously admire about Rory was her ability to separate herself when necessary. I wasn't entirely certain what had precipitated it right before I went outside to cook the burgers and brats, but she'd done it all the same.

Admire may have been a strong word, because it laced so strongly with frustration. There'd been that suspended moment when she walked through my front door and we just … connected. Her nerves had blanketed her, but there was something else in her eyes that I'd never seen before.

An anticipation that was probably mirrored in my own face. The entire day leading up to everyone's arrival, I had an underlying hum of excitement to everything that I did. Cleaning my house and prepping food was welcome, a way to keep myself busy and not worry about whether she'd bail at the last minute.

Not only did she not bail, she walked through the door like a damn queen, looking so beautiful that it almost ripped the breath from my lungs.

During dinner, she'd sat at the opposite end of my picnic table, but on the same side, so I didn't even have the privilege of watching her. Instead, I was stuck with Dylan's ugly mug across from me. Him and the gooey looks he regularly traded with Kat, who'd sat next to me.

Once dinner was done, Cole had left because a call from one of his clients came in. It broke the meal, so I started clearing some plates with Kat's help. Once they were stacked next to the sink, she scurried back outside to plant next to Dylan. Rory had her back to me, only the long blanket of her hair on her back for me to study. It was a poor substitute for her face, the subdued smiles and quiet laughs that I'd wanted to dissect during the meal.

In fact, she seemed to be doing just fine giving those to everyone but me.

While I was washing off the platter that had held the burgers, the slider door opened and Michael and Mia walked in, heads tilted toward each other while they talked.

"Need any help, man?" Michael asked, but I could tell it was an empty offer.

"Nah, it's fine."

Mia took a seat at the island and gave me a considering look. Nothing about her reminded me of Rory, but their bond was obvious. Maybe only to me, because I'd never seen her so casual with anyone as she was with her cousin.

"So if I leave with Michael to go grab a drink somewhere, will you be nice to my cousin?"

"I'm always nice to her," I said defensively. Mia slowly lifted an eyebrow and I rolled my eyes. "Okay, fine. I'm nice to her now. But does she know you're leaving?"

"Rory won't be surprised."

"Surprised about what?" Rory said and I had to grip the platter so as not to drop it into the soapy water. She only let her eyes rest on me briefly before focusing on Mia.

Her cousin waved a hand. "Just telling Garrett you wouldn't need to give me permission to go grab a drink with Michael."

Rory turned her gaze to Michael, and I grinned when it turned hard. "Just get her home safely, or you'll have me to deal with."

Michael nodded. "Understood."

Mia giggled while they practically ran out the front door.

"That doesn't bother you?" I asked before she could turn and bolt in the same direction.

"What?"

"That they're leaving together."

"Is he a serial killer?"

I laughed, setting the platter on the drying rack next to the sink. "No. A notorious womanizer, maybe."

Rory shrugged, leaning a hip on one of the chairs that was tucked under the dining table. "Mia's an adult. And probably the female equivalent of Michael. She's safe, and that's all I care about."

"So your threat was empty?"

"No," she said decisively and I smiled. "If I wake up tomorrow and have to start worrying about her, I'll castrate him."

That made me wince, and I could see Rory relax a touch at my reaction. Of *course,* the threat of violence against the male species would be the thing to get her to loosen up a little bit around me.

"You having fun?"

"Mmmhmm." She glanced at the slider, where Kat and Dylan were sitting across from Tristan and Anna. "They look good together."

"Kat and Dylan?"

"Sure. I meant Anna and Tristan though."

I barked out a laugh. "That's not her husband either."

"I know that." Rory paused and gave me a considering look. "But he's in love with her."

"What?" I gaped at her. "You're crazy."

"No, I'm not," she said gently. "You've never seen how he looks at her? It's so obvious."

"No way." But I didn't sound as certain this time. The hard edge of the counter caught me when I sank backwards. My hands were still wet and soapy, dripping onto the tile floor, but I didn't care. Peering at the backyard, where Tristan was next to Anna and angled toward her enough that he could occasionally look at her when she was talking. "Holy shit, Rory."

"You really didn't see it?"

"*Hell* no."

She snorted. "Such a guy. The whole meal, he could barely take his eyes off of her."

My head was spinning, and forgetting that they were still wet, I pushed both hands through my hair. "I … I don't even know how I'm supposed to feel about this. Tristan is so, he's so— "

"Self-contained?" she added helpfully.

"Pretty much." I shook my head and glanced over at her. It probably should have bothered me that the only reason she probably felt comfortable conversing with me was because we were focused on other people. Something to distract her from the fact that it was the most alone we'd been since we kissed. And so I had no problem dragging out the conversation if it kept her in the kitchen with me. "It's not like I don't think Tristan is capable of," I swallowed, feeling a little pukey over the fact that I was saying this in regards to my little sister, "loving someone. If he's dated since I met him, then he's never mentioned it to us."

"When was that?"

I blew out a breath. "Six years. Cole was my realtor, Michael and Tristan hadn't lived here long before I bought the place and moved in."

Rory moved toward the kitchen island, the flowy fabric of her dress molding to her legs when she walked. Normally, I thought dresses like that were pointless. So much fabric covering them that they couldn't possibly be cool in the hot weather. But on her, I was officially a convert. It made her look taller and leaner than normal, and so casual with her hair down that I couldn't believe I was looking at the same woman who wore power suits like she'd been born in them.

"I guess it's possible I'm wrong," she admitted and laid her folded hands on the granite that stood between us. "I'm certainly no expert on love, but I know desire when I see it."

So many questions zipped through my mind. Rory wasn't an expert on love. Because she'd never experienced it? Because she'd had her heart broken? Or was it possible that, in this way, we were similar. That making yourself vulnerable to love was the scariest possible thing you could imagine, and so you avoided it at all costs. Instead of blurting all of that out in hopes of shedding some light on what made her so hesitant, I pushed my tongue against my cheek and snatched the dish towel off the counter to dry my hands.

"Can I get you a drink?"

"Does it make you uncomfortable to talk about your sister like that?"

I laughed under my breath, because if she only knew why I was changing the subject, all I'd see was a flutter of aqua as she sprinted out the door. "Maybe. Not just my sister, who happens to still be married, but one of my best friends. I guess yeah, it's a little strange to try to wrap my mind around it."

She hummed. "I can see that. If it makes you feel better, I don't pick up on anything reciprocal from her."

"So my sister isn't contemplating cheating on her husband? How comforting," I said dryly.

"I didn't mean it like that," she said primly. "Besides, I thought you hated him."

With a groan, I turned to the fridge and opened it to grab another beer. "I don't think I can handle all this light party conversation without more alcohol." Glancing over my shoulder at her, I cracked the bottle with the opener that always hung on the side of my fridge. "You sure I can't get you anything?"

Rory gestured toward the backyard. "I think I'll go back out there. But thanks."

"Wait," I said quickly, hating the bolt of panic that I felt when she turned to go. That powerless feeling when the person you wanted couldn't move fast enough to be anywhere else was friggin awful. I'd never experienced it so strongly before. Actually, anything I'd felt for a woman before felt like muted off-white splashes of color on a white canvas compared to the bold, bright sweeps of *everything* that Rory made me feel. "What about a cupcake?"

Smooth. Oh, so smooth, Garrett. At her confused expression, an adorable crinkling of her forehead that I'd never noticed before, I pointed at the platter of white-frosted cupcakes that Kat had brought with them.

"Kat made them," I managed without stumbling over the words in an effort to cover my acute sense of embarrassment that I was acting like a twelve-year-old who'd never spoken to a beautiful woman before. "You should have one."

"She told me that too. This is her first foray into baking and we're her guinea pigs."

Yup, I was right. As soon as she started talking about someone else, her entire body relaxed and she'd make eye contact with me again. The tiny glimpses of her blue-purple eyes weren't enough. If anything, it made me feel jittery, like I was close to gripping the sides of her face just so I could force her to look at me. Which sounded creepier than I imagined when the thought crossed my mind.

But apparently, my frustration was enough to loosen my tongue. "So, if I wanted you to stay in here and talk to me, will we have to talk about other people? Or will you eventually move past your nerves in being alone with me?"

"What?" Confusion was thick in her question, but her cheeks pinked immediately.

"Yeah, see that right there?" I walked around the island, which made her back up a few steps like she was planning on keeping it between us at all costs. "You're blushing because you know I'm right."

"I'm blushing because I'm annoyed," Rory protested, but the slight hitch in her voice made me smile. "Oh, don't you look at me like that, Calder."

"Relax, Rory. It's a party."

"I'm completely relaxed," she scoffed.

When I lifted an eyebrow and gave her a disbelieving look, she shook her head at me.

"I am!"

"You've barely looked at me all afternoon."

"Patently untrue," she said, throwing one of my own phrases back at me. "I'm looking at you right now."

I leaned closer, and I could see how hard she was trying not to back away again. But her spine straightened and she lifted her chin. There she was. The Aurora Anderson I'd known for the last eight years. The one who'd never back down because I pushed her. But the kiss had changed something in both of us.

For me, all it did was make things clearer and sharper. I knew what I wanted. For the first time in my adult life, I knew exactly what I wanted.

Her. Just her.

"So what do you see?" I said quietly, letting my eyes bore into hers so she had no chance of missing what I was trying to convey. "Come on, miss reader-of-body-language. What do you see?"

Her breathing picked up and the tip of her tongue darted out to lick at her bottom lip.

"I don't know what game you're trying to play, Garett, but I'm not joining in."

The words rolled right off my back. She was playing, all right. The fact that she was still here and not running to the safety of the rest of the group told me she was playing. This was familiar territory to us, and I would not be the one to squander the opportunity in front of me.

No office, no coworkers, no CEO or COO roles to define us in the quiet space of my kitchen.

Just Rory and Garrett.

"No games. Just telling you that you can loosen up a little bit, Anderson. It's a party, not the Spanish Inquisition."

I saw the instant that my verbal challenge sparked something in her eyes.

"Says the person who's interrogating me in his kitchen. If I'm not loosened up, it's because of you."

"Prove it." I stepped into her, the sharp intake of her breath hitting my skin like a lit match.

"I don't have to prove anything to you. I'm quite *obviously* having fun."

My head tilted back and I boomed out a laugh. When I saw her narrow-eyed expression, I laughed even harder.

Then something cold hit the side of my face.

I blinked and straightened, feeling it slide down my neck. Rory's mouth was hanging open, her hand still up in the air from when she threw the fruit salad at me. Her eyes were as wide as dinner plates in her face when I reached up and plucked a strawberry from my shoulder.

"Oh shit," she breathed when I twisted up my lips and looked over the food offerings on the island with deliberate slowness.

"You started this, Rory," I said while I used my fingers to scoop a generous amount of that weird fluffy jello salad that I'd made the mistake of buying. No one had touched it.

Lucky me.

I flung it at her, catching her shoulder when she shrieked and ran to the opposite side of the island. Pausing when she did on the opposite end of the island from me, I waited for her to yell at me about not ruining her dress or something.

But then she smiled. A flawless, wide, sparkling smile.

Right as she grabbed the serving spoon full of potato salad and whipped it at me. It caught me in the chest, and her answering, breathless laughter made it completely worth it.

Not that I could let her win, of course.

Oh no, it was on now.

CHAPTER TWENTY-ONE

AURORA

If there were over twelve thousand days in the lifetime of a thirty-four year old woman, then I was finally able to take one moment, one small space in those dozens of thousands of days, to make a memory so fun that I'd probably remember it on my death bed.

Tears of laughter mixed on my face with strawberry jello when Garrett slipped on potato salad in his attempt to chase me around the island.

My last handful of food —a roll because I didn't look close enough— had smacked him in the eye and lit a fire in his eyes that made my skin tingle.

"Did you break your hip?" I asked in between peals of laughter when one of his hands reached up to the island so he could try to stand.

"Come and find out."

I lifted up on my tiptoes so I could peer over the edge of the granite. At this point, I didn't trust him not to fake being injured to throw me off. "No way, Calder. I'm not that stupid."

His hand disappeared and I stepped back, my heart speeding with excitement. This was childish and juvenile, and it felt amazing. Something in his eyes flipped a switch in me. Suddenly I didn't care about any of things waiting for us outside of his house.

Not work, or how wrong he might be for me, or vice versa. I'd spent two hours doing my best to pretend he wasn't sitting at the same table as me, and it was exhausting. The challenge arcing from him to me stoked the flames that had been banked since our kiss.

Nothing was banked or smoldering now. It was a full-fledge bonfire over my entire body. The ends of my hair were probably smoking from all the tension surrounding us. It was perfectly quiet in the kitchen, and I wrapped my hand around one of Kat's cupcakes. Just in case.

With a roar, Garrett stood and charged around the island. With a breathless laugh, I took off running, only for him to change directions a second later and wrap his arm around my waist when he caught me.

I smashed the cupcake into the side of his face, rubbing it in with the flat of my hand when he gripped me even tighter.

"Give up," I giggled. "You just got your ass kicked."

Garrett paused, licking at the white frosting at the edge of his lip and my stomach tensed. His eyes searched my face when I did it. With only the strength of his arm, he shifted me so was I facing him. The muscles from his bicep burned through the thin fabric of my dress at my back.

I could have pulled back. He would have let me. But the reckless energy coursing through my body never would have allowed it, had I tried. In the same breath that I realized it, that I didn't want to back up, his mouth was on mine.

Moaning at the sweetness of the frosting and the strong line of his lips, I wrapped my arms around his neck. *This* was a kiss. A man's kiss that every woman should be able to experience at least once.

Not because I didn't want to be in control sometimes, but to feel his hand splayed open on my back and pushing me further into him, the other burrowing into my hair to hold my head in place, made me feel wild and powerful. His tongue swept against mine and he pushed me up against the island. It was messy and graceless, with tongues and teeth and frosting.

It was perfect.

The sound of laughter in the backyard filtered through and our lips broke apart. His breath hit my neck when he ducked his face down, tucking his body into mine while we stood there. With his arms wrapped tightly around me and his hips bracketing mine, I didn't want this to end. I didn't want one of us to pull back and make excuses or apologies for the most carefree, fun moment of my entire life.

Garrett lifted his head and met my eyes, a question locking every muscle of his face.

In answer, I lifted my chin and touched my lips to his. He breathed out in relief, tilting his head to fit our mouths together more securely. From the sugary sweetness of the frosting to Garrett's spicy, masculine scent, I felt like I was having sensory overload. My brain couldn't decipher what I liked best from all the senses fighting for dominance.

The skin at the back of his neck, under the soft, prickly line of his hair, or the heat of his breath on my face, the slickness of his tongue when it traced mine, they all wanted my attention and I couldn't decide where it should be.

Despite not having a single drop of alcohol, I felt drunk on him. He was making my head spin and my center shift underneath my feet.

But then he pulled back. We were both breathing hard, and I prayed he wasn't about to kick me out of his house. It wasn't even a logical thought, since he was the one who wanted me there.

"I'll be right back," he assured, like he could tap into my thoughts. Still covered in frosting and potato salad, he marched to the slider and yanked it open. "Nobody is allowed in the house. If you want to keep socializing, take it across the street."

I slapped a hand over my mouth, praying none of them had witnessed our unintentional show. But before I could let the mortification seep in, Garrett was back in front of me, cupping my face with both of his strong, capable hands.

"Stay with me," he whispered, letting his lips brush against mine when he spoke. "Just like this. I don't want to lose this side of you."

The quiet passion in his voice was my undoing. I pushed my hands up under his shirt, felt the muscles rippling under my fingers and met him kiss for kiss.

"This is crazy," I said when he wrapped my hair around his hands and used it to tilt my head back.

Garrett paused, his mouth hovering over the skin of my neck. "Crazy how? Like, so crazy amazing that I never want to leave? Or crazy get me out of here crazy?"

I laughed, shivering when he dropped a kiss on the side of my throat. "Probably the first."

Instead of a teasing response, which was what I expected, Garrett paused. In the bright light of his kitchen, with his eyes locked onto mine and his hands gently threading through my hair, I felt a strange lightness in my soul. And when he smiled, I felt the tug of it behind my belly button. "I like this Rory."

I fought to answer while he swept my hair behind my shoulders with careful hands, like he couldn't stop touching it. "Better than the other Rory?"

"No," he said quietly, sliding his thumb along the edge of my jaw and dipping his knees so he met my eyes more directly. "That other Rory is smart and sexy and terrifying."

I laughed and he swept me up in another kiss, sliding his tongue along my lips and his hands down to cup my backside. While I let myself wind around him again, there was no small part of me that marveled over how well all the pieces fit. I was tall, but Garrett was taller, and it only took small shifts of our head and hips for us to match up perfectly.

So perfectly, in fact, that any arguments that had been stewing in my head for the last week were completely mute. For the first time in my life, all I cared about was how he was making me feel in that moment, how I was making him feel in return. And it wasn't naïve for me feel that way either. It wasn't irrational or illogical. Because even the deep-seeded cynic inside of me knew that moments like that weren't meant to be ignored.

A spark caught low inside of me, and I pushed against him harder, wanting to feel every inch of him on me, over me, and in me. And that cynicism faded completely, swept away with the white-hot rush of skin-tingling passion that he was covering me with.

"Garrett," I whispered, cupping the sides of his face and tracing the edges of his beautifully masculine mouth with my thumbs. "I really like this kind of crazy."

"Good," he said in a rough voice, tightening his hands on me. My eyes fell shut and I dragged my nose up the front of his throat, forcing him to tilt his chin up. I dropped a sucking kiss on his Adam's apple and he hissed in a breath. "Really good."

"Do you know how crazy I felt the first time I noticed this?"

"Is that a rhetorical question, because I'm not sure I'm supposed to be able to think properly right now."

Against the hot skin of his throat, I laughed and then pulled in as deep of a breath as my lungs could hold. It'd be so easy to get high off his scent, and I'd never done a drug in my life. But with him, and the way his desire thickened my veins, I'd be flying in no time. And nothing had ever sounded so good. The rough pads of his fingers traced along the thin straps of my dress and I pressed into him even further.

"Please, Garrett," I begged in a voice so low and sultry that I couldn't believe it came from my throat. It was wanton and wild, belonging to the kind of woman who'd never had to plead for a single scrap. It wasn't even really a request.

"Rory, Rory," Garrett groaned after my imploring but I didn't like the way it fell past his lips.

Immediately, I started shaking my head as if it could change the hesitation that I could hear coming from him. My hands pushed up the front of his shirt so I could trace the lines of his abs. His breath sawed in and out of his chest.

"I don't want to leave," I said, pulling my head up so that he'd be forced to look me in the eye. If he liked the smart and sexy and terrifying Rory, then he'd get her. There was so much heated affection in his dark brown eyes when I said it, so much warmth, that I knew this wasn't something casual or sudden for him.

"I'm not asking you to."

"But," I paused, searching his face, "you're hitting pause. Not me."

Garrett dropped his forehead to mine and sighed. "Two reasons. One is that I don't want to rush into something you might not be ready for."

"Presumptuous much?" I softened it with a smile. "I'm thirty-three, not sixteen. I'm well aware what I'm ready for."

He laughed, smoothing some of the hair that had fallen forward. "Two is that we smell like potato salad and frosting."

"Oh, yeah. That's a better reason." In fact, I reached up and scraped at a dried chunk of said frosting on his cheekbone. "So then what? I go home and shower so I can be presentable?"

Garrett growled and yanked me to him again, which made me laugh breathlessly. "You're so *presentable* it frightens me. But if you want, you can use the shower in the guest bathroom. I'll clean up a little in here and then do the same." Then his eyes widened. "But in my room. Don't worry."

"I wasn't," I said, completely and utterly charmed by his gentlemanly desire to do this the right way. Even three months ago, I would've pegged Garrett as the kind of man who could remove a woman's bra without using his hands and wouldn't have hesitated in the slightest.

"Go shower. Towels are clean."

I held his eyes as I stepped back, feeling as if all of our movements were suspended in thick, tangible anticipation. "And then what?"

"I don't know," he admitted slowly. "Just stay here with me, and we'll find out together."

His words played over and over in my head while I slipped my dress over my body behind the closed door of his second bathroom. Every inch of my skin felt tight and hot when I stepped under the spray, working all of his words until I couldn't understand why I was where I was and he was somewhere else.

With absent movements of my hands, I scrubbed away the remnants of our fight, but every brush of my fingers just made me angry. Or maybe not angry, but unfulfilled. And there was no reason for it. The mania in my head from wishing I was feeling him against me was jumbled and twitchy. Could we do this? Could we take a leap of faith and not worry about all the things that might go wrong and just follow the things that felt so *right*?

It was apparent now that neither of us did casual. And I liked that. I liked that Garrett surprised me in that way. It soothed the frantic energy of my mind, replacing it with a determination that felt familiar. Maybe the fighting and the yelling, the fierce competition did nothing but burn away any reserve I might have had in that moment. All that was left in its place was trust in him and a desire so potent that my fingers shook when I raked my hair back from my face. Two components that I'd been missing in any other limp attempt at a relationship.

Trust and desire. Was it really that simple?

The shower curtain was yanked back before the next breath left my lungs and I wrapped the fluffy white towel around my damp body with a smile on my face. Because yes, it was.

The kitchen was empty when I walked through. The door to his room was slightly ajar and I didn't hesitate for a second before pushing it open. Giving only a cursory glance to the king-size bed that was covered in a simple dark blue duvet, I narrowed my eyes at his bathroom door.

I knew it was his bathroom because the sound of his running shower came from behind it. I let out a slow breath when I turned the handle.

Trust and desire. Trust and desire. Over and over, the words came out as a whispered entreaty into the steamed-up bathroom. Garrett wasn't in the shower yet. No, he was staring in the mirror, staring right at my reflection from where I stood behind him, gripping the knot on my towel above my breasts. His shirt was gone, his face was clean, and in the misty, humid air I could only get a hazy picture of the stacks of muscles I'd briefly felt against my fingers. There was so much solid strength to his broad frame, which I'd only seen hints of under his perfectly tailored clothes. But even all of that couldn't hold my attention from the rawness of his eyes on mine.

Mean it, his fierce gaze screamed at me. But he didn't turn around. Maybe he was waiting for me to answer it, to show him that I did.

I dropped my towel, never blinking as I held his gaze in the mirror.

He was around me in the next beat, gripping the sides of my face and stamping his mouth on mine.

"You're so beautiful," he said in between kisses. "So beautiful, Rory."

My hands swept over him, greedy in how much skin I wanted to feel at once. I couldn't cover everything I wanted with two palms and ten fingers, so I plastered against him, moaning at the feel of my slick skin against his.

He boosted me up and I easily wrapped my legs around his trim waist, my mouth never leaving his while he fumbled with the door and walked us into his bedroom. We fell with an ungraceful bounce, but our limbs were too wound around each other for it to faze us in the slightest.

All of a sudden, Garrett pulled back, his chest heaving as he stared down at me.

"What?" I asked, fighting a wave of self-consciousness. Then I saw his eyes narrow at my tattoo. The one he'd teased me so mercilessly about at the gym. His thumb brushed against the line of script and my breath hitched.

Garrett leaned down, saying the words in a hushed, almost reverent tone as he read them. "By the strength within, I shall succeed."

I opened my mouth to say something, I wasn't sure what, when he dragged his lips over them, over the rib underneath the skin.

"Did it hurt?" he asked in between kisses, spreading one hand over the opposite rib cage.

"Umm," I paused to gasp when he circled his tongue around my belly button, "yeah. Some parts more than … ahh, others."

Garrett settled in between my legs and propped his chin on my stomach to pin me with a serious look. Unable to stop myself, I ran my fingers through his hair, smiling when he sighed.

"What were you going to say?" I teased when he pushed his head further into my hands, like a cat.

"No clue, devil woman. You're bewitching me with your magic fingers."

"Good," I laughed.

When Garrett growled and surged forward to take my mouth again, I hugged him to me. My laughing stopped, fading into heavy breaths and the sounds of deep, deep kisses. The line of his back under my hands was smooth and strong while he reached into the nightstand next to the bed for protection, the muscles of his arms banded around me were unyielding when he pushed inside of me.

My back arched and I whispered his name, hot sweeps of emotion pulling me under again and again with him while we moved.

We fit. *We fit so perfectly*, I thought over and over, the words inking over the curves of my heart, as deeply imbedded as the black marks on my side.

When I fell over the edge, minutes, hours, days later, I wasn't sure because I never wanted it to end, Garrett came with me in the same breath. His arms pulled me to him as he rolled to his side on the bed and I tucked my legs in between his.

The early evening light covered us in soft yellow, and I traced a shadow from his window where it crossed the bridge of his nose.

"You're not going to leave, are you?" he whispered.

I shook my head and tilted my chin up to give him a soft kiss. One turned into two, two into long, sweeps of his tongue against mine. Finally, I pulled back and looked at him. "Do you want me to?"

"What do you think?" he said with a smug grin on his ridiculously handsome face.

I smiled, because I knew the answer to that.

CHAPTER TWENTY-TWO

GARRETT

The last ten hours of my life felt like they'd been ripped from some cliché book where the hero is shown a glimpse of the wonderful thing he's been missing, and once he realizes just how stupid he's been, he vows to change his life so that he never misses it again.

That was me. I was the hero.

Not only because I was pound-my-chest, sublimely relaxed in the middle of my bed with Rory curled into me, but because I felt vaguely heroic after the stamina I'd shown during those ten hours. Even laying perfectly still, so I could watch her sleep next to me, muscles in my abs and legs still held a slight burn from … umm, overexertion.

And she met me for every second of it. I'd learned firsthand just how sleekly strong she was somewhere around two a.m. when she rose up over me, looking every inch like a goddess, a celestial warrior with the tangled hair that fell around her shoulders like a golden curtain.

In the light of day, Rory was stunning. But in the dim light of my bedroom, unabashedly unclothed, she was otherworldly.

When she slept, curled on her side with her hands tucked into her chest, she looked like pure perfection.

You've met your match, a voice whispered in my head. It couldn't have been my subconscious, because I wasn't aware of making that decision. Of looking at her and feeling the smooth peace of choice. But even if I hadn't, the thought was there all the same, and it didn't scare me.

With a careful finger, I swept a smooth lock of hair off her cheekbone so I could see her face more clearly. The patrician slope of her nose and the perfect curve of her upper lip, the long sweep of her dark lashes against her flawless skin, they all called to me.

They had since the day I met her and lost my breath.

I'd muted it since then, in the days and weeks and months and years since she put me in my place, but it was always simmering under the surface. The ability to freely indulge it made me feel like a grade A creeper, watching her sleep for the last hour when I should have been doing the same, but I never questioned stopping.

I followed the curve of the back of her skull, down her toned back, counted the bumps of her spine as my finger brushed each one. When I hit the tiny dimples at the bend of her lower back, I grinned, tracing circles around them and watching her shift slightly in her deep sleep.

Rory pulled a slow breath through her nose, the deep inhale making her upper body expand underneath my fingers.

"Why am I not surprised to find you groping me in my sleep?" she said with a sleep-thick voice.

"Because I'm creepy."

She turned slightly, so my hand was forced to slip from her back to the arc of her waist. Then she smiled, and my heart hiccupped in my chest. One smile and the voice in my head started an endless chant that I was powerless to ignore.

My match.

My match.

My match.

I couldn't meet her eyes because I was terrified she'd see it there. Terrified that it wouldn't be reflected back at me. But what if it was? What if she'd felt the pure magic arcing between us all through the night?

So I looked. Her face still held that tiny smile, the minute lift of her lips that did strange things to me, like we shared a secret. We did, I guessed.

No one but us had been holed up in my room. No one had felt what we'd done to each other, how we'd touched each other with reverence and mind-numbing passion.

That was only ours. And she knew it, too. I saw it in her eyes.

"You're not creepy," she whispered, lifting her hand so she could drag her fingers along the stubble on my jaw. She ran them in the opposite direction, making them rasp against her fingertips like sandpaper. Goosebumps popped up on my arm and I struggled to not tackle the hell out of her right then and there.

"Nicest thing you've ever said to me, Anderson."

For a second, she narrowed her eyes. I held my breath, waiting for her to snap something back at me, but she started laughing instead.

"You know what's sad? You might be right."

"I'm always right."

"Humble too."

"It's one of my many good qualities," I said sagely, and was rewarded by her quick smile.

"This is how I envisioned you, if you were lying in bed with a woman. Telling her how amazing you are."

I wagged a finger at her, which she batted away. "So you thought about what I'd be like in bed. Naughty girl." To my surprise, Rory ducked her head like she was embarrassed. Instead of laughing or calling her out, I cupped her chin so she looked at me again. "Come on now, don't hide that pretty face from me."

We kissed, this time softer and sweeter than the night before. My hands slipped down her back with familiarity and when she dragged the edge of her thumbnail against the line of my jaw at the end of the kiss, I smiled against her mouth.

"Is it weird to you?" she asked, drawing back just far enough that her features weren't fuzzy from how close we were.

"Is what?" I dropped my eyes so I could feel the hard edge of her collarbone under the soft, golden skin of her chest.

"This. Us."

It probably would have surprised Rory if I told her that not one second of it felt anything other than perfect. That weird was not something that had crossed my mind since the moment she walked through the front door looking like she belonged in my home, even with her visible nerves.

Instead of saying all that, I kept it simple. Kept it honest. "No. Not weird."

If I was waiting for her to say that it wasn't for her either, I might have been disappointed in her lack of a response, but Rory usually held her cards pretty close to the chest.

And what a spectacular chest it was.

"Do you need help cleaning up in the kitchen before I leave?"

"Who said you're going anywhere?" I asked before pressing her back into the bed and peppering her face, neck and shoulder with kisses.

She laughed, a husky, breathless laugh that tightened every inch of skin on my body. "I said. Mia is visiting, so I can't ditch her all day."

"Okay, I'll allow this on one condition." That elicited a deep sigh from Rory, but she motioned for me to continue. "You go home and shower the smell of sex off of you and spend the day with your cousin."

Rory raised an eyebrow. "What kind of condition is that?"

Tapping the end of her nose with my finger, I smiled. "And then tonight, around seven, I'll pick you up and take you out to dinner. If you think Mia will be okay to fend for herself for a couple hours, that is."

"You're asking me out on a date?"

"Does that surprise you so much?"

Idly, her fingers traced the edge of my pecs as she peered into my face. "No. I guess it doesn't."

When a relieved breath pushed from my mouth, I realized just how much it meant to me that she answered that way. Of course, I knew that most people would have been surprised if they knew how traditional I was when it came to women. Being like this with Rory, when I hadn't even taken her out somewhere, wasn't how I operated.

She'd probably laugh if she knew that Michael the manwhore had tossed the condoms in my nightstand after he'd gotten to the house to screw with me.

Despite my age, and how my generation viewed sex as a casual transaction, I wasn't like that. I never had been. And it wasn't even that I judged people who did, everyone had to make their own choices about how they lived their life, but it never worked for me.

Seeing someone like I was seeing Rory right now was an intimacy that meant something to me. If you literally laid yourself bare in front of another person, to share whispers and passion and trust, you were making yourself vulnerable to them. Right now with her, I was more vulnerable than I'd been in years, because she had the power to reach through my chest and yank my heart out, if she wanted to.

"Good," I said, my voice sounding like my throat was coated in sandpaper.

She sat up and stretched her arms over her head with a groan, her hair a tangled mess down her back. "And you're taking me somewhere nice where you can't wear clothes with holes in them?"

I clucked my tongue. "Such a snob."

Very slowly, she turned her head to pin me with a narrow-eyed glare over her bare shoulder. "Excuse me?"

I sat up next to her and bumped her shoulder with mine, while the gray sheets from my bed pooled around our legs. "I'm not complaining. If you're picky, then it's a compliment to me."

She laughed. "I suppose it is."

"Want me to make you some breakfast before you go?"

Rory shook her head and stood from the bed, then propped her hands on her hips. "Where's my dress?"

I grinned. "Probably in the other bathroom still. Is it weird that I want to watch you strut naked through my house to go get it?"

She rolled her eyes but smiled. Then with her head held high, she waltzed right out of my bedroom. I fell back onto the bed with a tortured groan. It was quite possible that Aurora Anderson would completely decimate me. And if how I felt right then was any indication, I'd let her do it with a smile on my face.

CHAPTER TWENTY-THREE

AURORA

Mia was already on the couch, sitting cross-legged in the corner, when I came out of my bedroom with a towel wrapped around my hair. Her hair was parted neatly down the center and then wrapped in pigtails on either side of her grinning face.

"You look gooooood, cousin," she drawled as I sank into the off-white, velvet arm chair to the right of the couch. My cheeks were flaming, I could tell, but I smiled back at her.

"It doesn't look like your night was too rough either," I said, peering at the mark on her neck. She hummed into her coffee, giving a dramatic shiver that made me laugh. "Wow, that good, huh?"

"That good."

"Does that mean you'll be visiting me more now?"

Her eyes widened comically. "No! Lordy, no."

"So Michael didn't convert you to try a relationship?"

"Why?" she tossed back. "Did Garrett convert *you*?"

"Maybe he did," I answered honestly. She was surprised, I could tell. But she took another sip of her coffee and gave me a long look.

Pulling the towel off of my hair and starting to comb through the damp strands with my fingers, I gave her one right back. "What?"

"Just seems like a fast leap to make with the guy who you couldn't stand two months ago. And happens to be your boss."

"Inconvenient, right?"

Mia made a thoughtful face, but then shook her head slowly. "I don't think that's the right word."

I snorted. "How could it not be?"

"Well, what about it is inconvenient. I mean, really? You have a lot in common, Rory. He's smart and funny, not to mention in a great job, at a place that you happen to love. He's hot as hell, and looks at you with little flames shooting out of his eyeballs."

"And that's a good thing?" I asked, but still blushed at her assessment.

"If Garrett's eyes had the power to remove clothing, you would have been stark-ass naked the second you walked through that door. Boy is smitten." But she leaned forward and gave me a serious look. "But none of that matters if you're not feeling it too. Don't feel pressured to go with him tonight because you think it'll be awkward at work."

"No," I said quickly. "That's not it at all. Last night was because I wanted him. He brings out a side of me that I really like. And it's one that no one else has been able to tap into before." When I said 'tap', Mia made a thrusting movement with her pelvis, so I threw my towel at her. "Can you not act like a teenage boy, please?"

"So you like him."

I nodded. "I do."

"And you're willing to carve time in your life for a relationship with him? If that's what he wants to do," she added when she saw me hesitate.

"I am. Because, even though I've known him for so long, I don't know this Garrett. The one who was sexy and sweet and respectful, who turns me into this ... greedy, insatiable person that I've never been."

"Hell yeah he did." Mia nodded. "Greedy and insatiable are two of my favorite words. Especially when they're applied to you."

I couldn't help but laugh at that, because she was right. The closest that I'd come to either one of those things was insatiable. But only for work, which was definitely not Mia-approved. But proving myself in that arena was as important to me as when I'd walked out of my parents' house. And I'd done it.

Everything that I'd worked for since the day I turned eighteen was laid out right in front of me. Just because having a man at my side hadn't been in my original vision of what my life should be didn't mean that I couldn't adjust it now.

And the crazy thing was that Garrett made me want to adjust it. Nothing about it felt too sudden or ill-timed. Maybe Mia was right. Maybe inconvenient wasn't the right word to use at all, maybe he and I were coming together at just the exact right time.

If Rich hadn't died, I thought with a dull thud in my stomach, I never would have gone to his house the day before. Never would have kissed him in the dark room at the gym. Never would have felt the unbelievable high he'd brought me to, never heard him tell me I was perfect against the skin of my temple when I was trembling against his body.

Inexplicably, tears heated my eyes and I blinked rapidly to dispel them. If the mere thought, the hypothetical alternate reality, of not experiencing Garrett the way I had the night before brought tears to my eyes, then I knew it wasn't wrong to want to pursue it. It wasn't inconvenient at all.

"So," I said to Mia, "Are you going to help me pick out what to wear tonight?"

"Girl, we need to go buy something new for this date." She stood from the couch and held out a hand to pull me up. "Garrett won't know what hit him."

Mia was right. Unfortunately for me, I was the one who was going to have to walk in the high-waisted, sky blue, fitted mini skirt she forced on me, and try not to flash my goodies to everyone at the restaurant. I also had to do this while feeling more nervous than I could ever remember. More than the day I left my parents', more than the day I started my internship at CFS, and more than when I sat to hear Rich's will read out loud.

There was something that rolled over my skin, something slow and warm, when Garrett texted me that he was on his way in. I couldn't even call it simple nerves, because it was so much bigger than that. At thirty-three, nervous didn't cover it for a first date. It was the anticipation of something big. Something life-changing. Or at least, there was the possibility of one evening changing your life. For me, this was equivalent to stepping off the edge of a building with no notion of what was waiting for me at the bottom.

Garrett would either catch me with ease, or I'd end up broken on the hard, cold ground. A mental vision of my own limbs twitching against concrete settled my stomach a bit. So I stepped through my door instead of waiting for him.

Waiting was for chumps and wusses. I was neither.

But when I walked out of my building and caught Garrett's eyes, his jaw dropped, and the flurry of nerves swept back up with a single-minded vengeance.

The light silk tank that I'd decided to tuck into the skirt was covered in a subtle pattern of blues, greens, and golds. On my feet I wore four-inch nude wedges, bringing me only a couple inches shorter than Garrett.

Garrett shook his head and slowly scratched the side of his face. He'd shaved since that morning and I wanted very badly to know what it felt like against my hands.

"Rory," he said and then paused, laying a hand on his chest. "You've stopped my heart."

To break apart the swarm of bees in my stomach at his simple words, I lifted an eyebrow. "Did you practice that line on the way over?"

He grinned and offered his elbow to me, which I took gratefully. If there was the slightest chance that he was feeling the same breathless, stomach-tilting anticipation that I was, then maybe we could lean on each other through this.

We walked in companionable silence down one block from my condo to where he'd found a parking spot for his sleek black car. He opened the passenger door, but didn't let me in right away.

"I'd never try to prepare my reaction to seeing you. You steal my ability to speak far too easily, even when your intent is evisceration and not seduction."

"Such big words," I said with a sly smile. "And such sweet ones, as well. Who'd have thought it?"

Garrett leaned in, and I caught the potent smell of his soap and aftershave when he whispered in my ear. "Don't tell anyone."

Then he kissed my cheek and ushered me into the car. My heart was still thrumming when he took his seat and smiled over at me.

"Are you nervous?" I asked suddenly, needing to know that I wasn't alone in this body-locking free fall.

"It's a miracle I haven't puked yet," he said so earnestly that I burst out laughing. "You?"

I gave him a chagrined look before answering. "Mia made me take a shot before you picked me up because I was driving her insane."

Garrett hummed and leaned forward, laying a light kiss on my lips before slicking his tongue along my top lip. "Tequila?"

Stunned and beyond turned-on with that brief touch, I nodded. Garrett had put on dark jeans and a light blue oxford with the sleeves rolled up over his forearms, the ropes of muscles flexing underneath his skin when he steered the car down Grant Street.

"Where are we going?"

"The Ninth Door." He glanced over. "Have you been?"

I nodded with a relieved smile. "I love that place."

What I didn't need to tell him was that the few high, curved walls of the booths allowed me to eat my tapas without people giving me curious looks when I was by myself. Sometimes I brought a book and settled in for a couple hours with a glass of their sangria.

Garrett gave me an unsure look. "Do you want to go somewhere new? I'd hate to do something average. You'd never let me forget it."

"No, really, that sounds perfect. Tapas is good to share."

Even though there was a location closer to my condo, he drove us downtown instead to the one in LoDo, and I loved that. Like he wanted to extend our time together. The restaurant was busy, but Garrett leaned in to the hostess, who walked us straight through the dark, dimly lit restaurant to one of the booths that I favored. He waited for me to slide in first, and instead of staying on one side of the table so that I'd face him, I took a deep breath and stayed in the middle of the bench.

Garrett's face was angled away from me when he slid in, but his hand smoothed down my thigh as soon as he was next to me. The rough skin of his palm against the sensitive skin of my inner thigh made me close my eyes.

Finding this balance with him, outside of fighting in the office or finding purchase underneath the soft cotton of his bedsheets, might be more difficult than I imagined. Mainly because I had no clue what he was thinking as we sat underneath the wrought iron chandelier, plastered next to each other in the booth.

"I don't do casual," I found myself saying out loud as soon as the smiling waitress walked away with the drink order. "That's not me. I don't sleep around, so don't expect me to answer a late night text if that's all you're looking for."

"You think I'm gonna send you a booty call text?" He sounded so amused that I almost slapped him. But with us, that was as good as foreplay. And what with being in public and all, figured it probably wasn't a good idea. "Rory, I just ordered a fifty-dollar bottle of wine. This isn't casual for me either."

I lifted my chin, attempting cool when the relief almost pulled me under the table. "And what happens at the office?"

His arm snaked behind my back, anchoring me to him, as if I was pulling away. "Well, we do our jobs. Same as we did before."

"It's not that simple, and you know it."

"What worries you about it?" He didn't ask it in a sarcastic way, which was a relief.

I took a deep breath before I answered, and we both paused when the waitress brought the wine, filling both of our glasses with a few ounces to try. She left when we liked it, and I rolled the rich, dry liquid around my tongue while I gathered my thoughts.

"I've told you before how pivotal it was for me that your father respected me. That Cal did too. They were my superiors, yes, but they never treated me that way." I took a sip of wine, and he waited, somehow knowing I wasn't finished. "I need to know, that even though you'll see a far more casual side of me than anyone will at the office, that even though we're intimate, you'll respect me. Respect my position within the company. And I'll do the same with you. You may be Garrett who likes to feel me up in my sleep, but within those walls, you're the CEO. I need to know you'll still treat me as Rory the COO when we're there."

Garrett was searching my face while I spoke, soaking in everything I was saying. "I can respect your role, and you."

"Thank you." I smiled, tucking a piece of hair behind my ears. "Is that what you expected me to say?"

"No," he said on a laugh. "I figured you'd just ask for less yelling, a few less death threats."

"What's the fun in that?"

"Exactly. I'm not worried, Rory. I think we can figure it out. We're still *us* there, and outside of work, we can have something else. Something sexy," he leaned in and kissed my jaw, "something new," another kiss just to the right of my lips, "and something that I'm very much looking forward to exploring."

Yup. Okay, that sounded good. Check, check, check. One last flag crossed my heavy-lidded vision. "And no dating other people?"

Garrett pulled his head back. "Hell no. Pretty sure you're all I could handle anyway."

Some women might have been offended, but I felt the satisfied smile spread over my face as I leaned in to kiss him. "Good."

And it was.

The food and the wine was good. The conversation even better. He was funny and charming; he was interested in what I had to say; his hands on my skin was so much better than *good* that I almost mounted him in the booth.

"Last boyfriend," he asked around a mouthful of dátiles, licking a speck of drunken goat cheese off the edge of his lip and making my stomach curl deliciously. The question got lost when he popped the rest of the ham-wrapped date in his mouth and made this sexy as hell chewing motion that stretched his jaw muscle. My finger swept across it without me realizing that I'd intended to move at all. It felt so intimate, so natural for me to want to know what his skin felt like when he moved that way. "Rory?"

I blinked out of my lust-filled haze and caught his amused look when I dropped my hand. "Shut up."

"You want me *so* much, Anderson. It's almost embarrassing."

With a sniff and a steadying breath, I took a deep drink of my wine "Last boyfriend? That was the question?"

"Before you ogled me, yes."

Ignoring that, I lifted my eyebrows while I thought. "It's been a while," I hedged, not sure if I was ready to admit that it'd been years.

"Define a while."

"You tell me first."

He grinned. "I've never had a boyfriend."

"If you're going to joke, I won't answer."

"Woman, you make me work harder to get to know you than anything I've had to work for in my entire life."

With a laugh, I rolled my eyes. "Fine. But you can't make fun of me."

"I'd never," he said gravely.

"Three years," I answered on a rushed exhale and then looked away. "It's been three years since my last relationship."

To his credit, Garrett didn't have much of a visible reaction, just a simple lift of his eyebrows in response. "Why so long? Because I know it can't be because you didn't have anyone interested in you."

I blushed at that, snagging a patatas bravas from the long white plate in between us. When I was finished chewing, I glanced at him. "I did have men who were interested. In exactly what, I couldn't say, because it never got that far." I tilted my head, thinking through the past handful of years. "It was never worth my time, I guess. Everyone has a list of priorities; you know? That wasn't on mine."

"Simple as that, huh?" Oddly enough, Garrett didn't look like I needed to convince him.

"Simple as that." I pointed a finger at him. "Your turn."

"Not as long as you. But I've had to buy a couple new calendars since the last woman."

"Really?" I leaned back in surprise. "And here I was expecting you to say that it'd been such a *long* month with no one to laugh at your jokes or compliment how big your biceps are."

Garrett leaned in, staring at my mouth. "How big are they?"

I smiled and he brushed a kiss over my lips. When I went to deepen it, he pulled back with a smug grin on his chiseled face. "Big enough that you don't need me to tell you jack shit."

We both laughed. That was how good it felt to be with him like we were. It was easy, effortless. We ordered dessert and a carafe of sangria, in no hurry to leave. When the check came, Garrett slid his card to the waitress and then weaved his fingers through mine while we waited for her to bring it back. Nothing was said as he signed it, leaving her a generous tip. Or when he laid his hand on the small of back and we walked back to his car.

The drive home to my condo was charged, and my skin was fevered from the possessive way he held my thigh while he drove. So good. Everything about our night was so good.

But by the time he walked me to my door, I was ready for good to become mind-blowing. I dropped my purse onto the ground and gripped his shirt with both of my hands.

"Aggressive. I like it," Garrett whispered when I backed us up against my front door and proceeded to kiss the hell out of him.

His hands were good, one gripping the back of my neck and the other lifting my thigh so he could press against me. Very, very good. The kisses were hot and deep, his tongue tangling with mine in a way that I never, ever wanted him to stop. The pleasant haze of wine and food and Garrett made me giddy, so when I whispered against his earlobe that he should come in, I almost didn't register that he was lowering my leg off of him and pulling back.

"Not tonight." If he hadn't sounded so pained about it, I might have forced him. Grabbed him by the shirt and dragged him into my place anyway.

"Why not tonight?" I whispered against his mouth, tightening my grip on his shirt.

He groaned. "Because I don't usually do things backwards like this. I don't want you to think I don't respect you." Oh, well if he was going to go ahead and say the perfect thing. "If it helps, I'll be hating myself the entire drive home."

"It does help," I admitted, eyeing him up and down with regret. "But I really I wanted to wear that shirt in the morning."

He hissed, gripping my face and giving me a goodbye kiss that rocked a whimper out of me, so deep that it had me seeing stars behind my eyelids. "Evil, evil woman," he whispered against my smiling mouth. "I'll see you tomorrow at the office."

Ah yes. Tomorrow. At the office.

"Shit," I whispered and slumped against the door while I watched him walk away.

CHAPTER TWENTY-FOUR

GARRETT

When I saw Rory at work that next day, she gave me this secret little smile that launched a submarine through my heart. If I'd felt a massive crush on her when I met her, and wanted to cement her to me after our first kiss, then our night together followed by the most perfect first date I'd ever experienced in my *life* had shoved me off the first step of falling for her.

Yeah, that fall. The big one. The one that had always petrified me before. Now I couldn't figure out what was so scary about it.

That she had the power to rip my soul out via my heart? So what. Looking at her now, across the conference room table from me only ten days after that first date, I'd take that chance a million times to know what I did about Rory now.

I knew that she slept curled in a ball on her side, always in underwear and a tank top. I knew that she ate oatmeal for breakfast almost every single morning. I knew that she had to have seven pencils lined up by her computer at work and at home and she rarely ever watched TV unless it was the news. I knew that she gave the most incredible kisses, and hid the passionate side of herself so well at work that it almost freaked me out when she unleashed it later.

I knew that she was the kind of smart that was almost scary, observant and patient with our employees, and so beautiful that every single morning, it took me about thirty minutes to get used to being around her again. Thirty minutes before I could look at her in a way that people might not be able to see how wholly she was embedded under my skin.

Rory nodded at me across the table and I gave her as polite of a smile as I could manage. Oh yes, meeting. Work. Other people around us. "Right, so as long as everyone's comfortable with where we're at, then let's stick with the current investment model for that account. I don't think Max wants the flashy, big risk investments. Definitely think long-term, solid growth when it comes to his money."

"Thanks, everyone," Rory said while David and Bryce stood from their chairs and left the conference room. When the door shut behind Bryce, Rory leaned back in her chair and gave me a considering look.

"What?"

"Just trying to remember the guy who sat across my desk and said he was living a life that felt like he was in someone else's skin." The blue pen that she used in every single meeting that I'd been in with her spun in circles on the table in front of her, moved only by the tip of her slim finger. It was far, far easier to watch her make circles with a pen than think about the ramifications of what she was saying. Not once since the day my father died, had either of us brought up what my intentions were at the end of the twelve months. I wasn't even half done yet, but in the last month of showing up at the office every morning, I'd steadily begun to realize that I didn't hate the walls around me anymore. It had happened without a conscious choice from me.

"That feels like it was forever ago."

She hummed in agreement, staring at the pen against the high-shine of the lacquered table. "It kind of was. Do you feel like the same person?"

"No," I answered truthfully. "Do you?"

"I do, actually."

That didn't surprise me in the slightest. Of all the things I'd learned about Rory in the last handful of years, it was that she was more comfortable in her own skin than just about any person I'd met. She was unapologetic about her intelligence, and her motivation. I just wasn't sure whether that motivation was still aimed at the current job that I was holding. With a ticking clock hovering over the entire company, it was probably something I should have figured out by now. But if she said yes, then it was almost undeniable that it would shift the *us* part of Rory and Garrett into an uncomfortable spot.

"Do you have lunch plans?" I asked, chickening out from asking her.

From the way she narrowed her eyes thoughtfully, it was obvious that she knew I'd been thinking something else. But she didn't call me on it. Probably for the same reason that I didn't continue the conversation. Everything else was too good to risk upsetting it.

At least for now.

"I was going to eat at my desk." She shrugged one shoulder, pursing her lips at me. "Unless someone has a better offer for me."

I shifted in my seat, though there was no chance of me feeling comfortable with the visions of how sturdy my desk was running through my head. "Marjorie is off today."

"That so?" she asked with a coquettish tilt of her head.

"Mmmhmm."

"Well, I guess I could wander down in about," she flipped her wrist to look at her watch, "ten minutes?"

"Perfect." I stood from my chair and straightened the knot of the blue tie I was wearing. "And Rory?"

She lifted her head, the heat in her eyes almost knocking me back. "Yes?"

"Close the door to my office behind you when you come in."

"Does it lock?" she asked in between kisses. She'd barely cleared the door when I pressed her against the wall in my office.

"It's got to," I said, frantically fumbling with the doorknob and then crowing with victory when the latch turned. "I need to tell Marjorie to take days off more often."

Rory laughed while I pushed the hem of her skirt up with one hand. The other was anchored in her ponytail. I loved that she wore her hair like that every day. Mainly because I could use it to tilt her head in the perfect direction for whatever kind of kiss I wanted to give her.

Today's was the kind of kiss that was Rory's favorite. The full-bodied ones, where our hands and legs, tongues and teeth were all involved. The kind that made her whimper into my mouth when I wrapped her in my arms so tightly that she couldn't take a deep breath. She'd told me that just a few nights ago, and something about that made me feel like pounding my chest. I had the ability to limit her breathing capacity, to make the blood race so quickly in her veins that she needed to pull in more oxygen, but she couldn't do it. She was so firmly in my arms that she *couldn't.*

With frantic hands, Rory started unbuttoning my white dress shirt. "Why is it so hot when you run a meeting like that?"

I groaned when her fingers hit my skin. I wanted them there forever. Maybe I'd swap out her lotion for superglue so that the next time she touched me, she'd have to stay indefinitely.

It was either the creepiest idea I'd ever had, or flippin genius.

"Probably the same reason that it's so hot when you stand in the doorway of my office and ask if you can delegate monthly reports to someone else."

Rory broke away from my seeking mouth to bark out a laugh. "What?"

"I don't know what it is," I said fervently, using both hands to frame her face. "There's something on your face when you ask me a question that you expect me to say yes to. Like I don't have a choice, but you're still being polite about it. It makes me *crazy*."

She looked so delighted, so pleased by my strange answer that she smacked a kiss on my mouth. "I'll remember that for future use."

"Thank you for not wearing lipstick today," I said, nibbling along the edge of her lips, tracing the shape and committing it to memory.

Rory shoved at my chest, walking me backwards with a warrior's expression on her face. *Conquer me,* I wanted to roar, but I didn't. Maybe that wasn't manly enough for some men my age, but the thought of Rory devouring me whole, razing me to the point that I was barely standing sounded like the best possible outcome for me.

My calves hit one of the chairs that I used for more informal meetings, and I fell backwards into it with an oomph. Rory hiked up her skirt and wedged her knees in between my legs and the arms of the chair.

Her hands dug into my hair while she took my mouth, and my hands slid up her back into the ends of her hair, tangling the smooth strands between my fingers. Rory stopped to take a sip of the water that was sitting on the end table next to the chair. How she knew it was mine, I had no clue, but I didn't give a shit when she kissed me again and her tongue was cool and slick against my own.

The sound of voices outside my office made us both freeze, mouths panting against each other.

"I thought he was going to be in the office this afternoon," Marjorie's voice said, muffled through the thick door. Someone answered, but I didn't recognize their voice. The doorknob jiggled. "Huh. He never usually locks it during the day. Maybe he went out for lunch. Sorry about that."

My eyes pinched shut, and Rory laughed against the skin of my throat.

"That's it," I whispered. "She's fired. Early retirement for Marjorie."

Rory lifted her head and had such a sweet smile on her face that my heart fell down another step with a solid thud. Every single one of those that she gave me pushed me further and further down a path that I'd never be able to travel back up. If our date was the first step, her smiles were the second, then the perfectly sweet kiss that she dropped on the tip of my nose before wrapping her arms around my neck shoved me down steps three and four.

This could be my life, I thought. All of this.

Her and me, working together and playing together, making love and kissing in the morning before she dragged my ass out of bed to eat horrible oatmeal.

Whoever's skin I was living in now, I didn't want to leave it.

Ever.

But I had absolutely no clue whether Rory felt the same way.

"Hey," she said when Marjorie's voice receded and she'd moved to the chair across from me. Seriously, Marjorie was fiiiiiiired. Now Rory's skirt was smoothed down and she'd fixed her ponytail, everything set to rights after my hands did some serious damage. "I had an idea I wanted to run by you."

"Shoot."

"Well, obviously we haven't filled my former position yet, and there's hasn't been any extra strain on the rest of the department by spreading out my previous responsibilities between them. So we have this extra money in the budget from what we used to pay me." She took a deep breath, looking completely different from the woman who'd been rocking in my lap about three minutes earlier. "So we've always outsourced our marketing, right? And they do a good job, but I'd really like to have someone in-house, who's part of CFS and really understands our vision, who wants to be part of it with us."

I nodded. "Makes sense."

"I'd like to hire a full-time director of marketing instead of fill my old job. If we're still sticking with the five-year strategic plan that was put into place last year, then it'll help with the growth that we projected. I really think someone that's solely dedicated to CFS can help with that, because we set a pretty solid goal for the next five years as far as assets managed."

With no small amount of shame, I realized I didn't even remember specifics from the strategic plan. I'd had to sit in on the discussions, but thinking about CFS even a short five years in the future, had sounded awful to me. But the woman across from me had the thing memorized, apparently. And she hadn't been part of the meetings. It was the first time since my dad died that I felt a similar flash of embarrassment at how easily Rory made me feel like a lesser employee.

But that was my problem to deal with, my cross to bear. Everything she said made sense, so I smiled. "That's a great idea. Work with HR to write up a job description and post it. Start internally for a couple weeks, and if there are no takers, then go external."

"Thanks, Garrett," she said, sounding appreciative. "I'll let you know if you need to sit in on any interviews."

Knowing Marjorie was milling around, Rory smiled and stood, but paused before unlocking the door to give me a smile. I was still buttoning my shirt back up when she did. Mainly because, for some reason, it was too hard for me to watch her walk away and see how easily she'd slipped back into business Rory.

"I liked doing lunch in your office."

I smiled. "We didn't even eat."

She ducked her head, but I caught the grin anyway. "I know. But I liked it all the same."

Awesome, can we do it every day for the rest of our lives? I almost pleaded, but pressed the tip of my tongue against the back of my clenched teeth instead.

CHAPTER TWENTY-FIVE

AURORA

Blink and you'll miss it was an apt description for the two weeks of my life post-food fight in Garrett's kitchen. Time moved faster than it ever had for me before. My days at work were a happy, busy blur, my nights after work were even more so. Out of the last fourteen days, I'd spent every night but one with Garrett.

All but one night, wrapped around him in his bed or mine, soaking in the warmth of his smooth skin and solid muscles. It felt like a strange dream sequence if I thought about it too long or too hard. It was almost like my brain couldn't reconcile the life I was living. Neither could my heart. So when I sat down on my couch, alone for what seemed like the first time all week, thoughts and memories of Garrett seemed almost unreal.

My work week had only been forty-two hours, only half of my nights were spent in my own bed, there was a smile permanently fixed on my face, and I'd been touched more in the last month by his hands and his mouth, his teeth and his tongue than I could scarcely believe. And instead of feeling overwhelmed and over-stimulated, I was happy.

I wasn't in love with him yet, I had too many unanswered questions about our future to cut the last cord that held my heart back from Garrett. But the muscle behind my ribs that pumped the life force through my body was straining toward him with every single beat. Every *glug-glug, glug-glug* was pushing me faster and faster toward a place that was with Garrett. That wanted to be with Garrett.

Forever.

In truth, I wasn't sure how much longer I could fight it, unanswered questions or not. But nevertheless, when I was finally able to sit in silence, alone with only one light on in the kitchen, they were the things looping around my brain.

What happens at the end of twelve months?

He told me once he hated his job, what was the other thing he wanted?

If he leaves CFS, where does that leave us?

And biggest of all, the one I couldn't turn off when I looked at him, kissed him, slept with him, ate meals with him, *if I fall in love with him, what would I do if he wasn't in love with me?*

Of all the questions that I wanted answered, eventually, at least, that was the one that I had the least amount of control over. The first three could really be answered with a simple conversation, even though it hadn't been simple to bring it up with him.

That one conversation that neither of us had broached. Every once in a while, I caught a look in his eyes when we were in the same room at the office. Usually at times when we worked so well together that it knocked me back, I knew he was feeling it too. It wasn't even about power, or that his title was one notch higher than mine. That was the strangest part of all, I didn't begrudge him the added rung on the ladder. Because he respected me, respected my opinion, and not once in the months since he'd taken over had he overstepped his boundaries.

I pressed a hand on the skin above my heart and pushed down, feeling the same raw ache whenever I thought of him, thought of us together. Maybe I should have been terrified that I didn't want more space from him, that I didn't want a night of normalcy. The kind of night that I'd done a million times since leaving my parents' domain.

Making dinner for myself, enough to last two to three meals, pouring a glass or two of wine and either reading, or watching a documentary, going to the gym most of those nights, too.

With a soft laugh, I realized that neither Garrett or I had needed to go to the gym since we started dating. Gah. That word. It felt infantile to call it that considering we were both in our mid-thirties. But *lovers* sounded casual or like there was no intention behind it. Despite the fact that no one at work, including his mom or Anna, knew about our relationship, I could feel Garrett's intent every time he took me somewhere thoughtful, every time he brought me coffee in bed in the morning.

There was a design, a purpose, to everything we were doing together. Calling him my lover didn't cover it. So dating would have to do it. My boyfriend, Garrett, I would say, if I were to introduce him to someone. Mia already knew him, of course, and it's not like I'd ever have cause to bring him to meet the General or my mother.

That gave me pause, and in the space that I stepped back to think about whether that would ever happen, my cell phone rang from the end table next to the couch. My eyebrows almost hit my hairline, I lifted them so fast, because it was my mom's cell phone showing up on the display.

I cleared my throat, completely weirded out by the fact that she was calling. "Hello?"

"Aurora," she said in greeting. I was never Rory to her. Not to the General either.

"Hi, Mom." There was a long enough beat of silence where I wanted to say, *umm, you called me, remember?* "How are you?"

"Fine, fine. Still in Texas."

"That's good." Even though the General had retired in his early 50s, they liked the area around Laughlin AFB in Del Rio, and had lived there for the last decade. I'd never seen the house they lived in. Not once. "Probably pretty hot for you guys right now."

"Oh," her voice softened, just slightly. "A bit, a bit. And up by you?"

I closed my eyes at the awkwardness. We hadn't spoken in six months, and if I played along, we'd only ever talk about the weather. "Yeah, September is supposed to cool down. So I'm glad that's right around the corner. No snow up on the mountains right now, that's for sure."

"Are you still living in the same place?"

"I am." I looked around my space, wondered what they'd think about it. I'm sure the General would think my décor was too pretentious, far from the Spartan way we'd grown up. In fact, he'd choke if he knew how much money I had spent on most of the art covering my walls. He'd hate the contemporary feel to it, he'd hate the expensive materials of my furniture, the light fixtures that I'd picked out with wide drums in interesting fabrics. He'd hate the thick rugs in white and ivory that covered the dark hardwood floors of my condo. "I think you'd like it, Mom."

But she'd probably never see it.

"I'm sure I would."

Silence stretched between us again, and I blew out a slow breath through my nose, aiming my face up so that it might not be obvious to her. This was my mother. The woman who gave birth to me, who put Band-Aids on my scraped knees, who braided my hair for church on Sundays. And we'd exhausted our typical topics of conversation in about forty-seven seconds. Suddenly, that really pissed me off. It pissed me off that she didn't ask about work, or how I spent my time. If I was dating anyone. And just as suddenly, I wanted her to know it. I wanted the General to know it. There were these amazing things going on in my life, making me happier than I'd ever been. And it couldn't be placed on her to figure out what those things were.

Some of this was on me. I closed my eyes for a second, the truth of that ringing through me.

"I was promoted," I told her, choosing not to go into details about Rich, because Lord knows she wouldn't care. "I'm COO now, and," I took a deep breath in her silence, "I'm really good at my job. I love it."

"Congratulations, Aurora," she said quietly. "At the same company?"

"Yeah. Calder Financial Services. We're growing. It's a really exciting time to be working there, to see the changes we're making. And I know that you and Dad think it's a selfish, gluttonous industry to work in, but I am proud of what we do. We help people, Mom. We help them be smart with their money, to make sure it will be there for them when they retire or if something awful happens in their life." My words were rushing together and my heart was pounding in my chest, but I felt lighter. "I'm proud of myself. That's why I left, because I knew you'd never be proud of my ambitions, of the fact that I might want to live my life differently than yours. I knew you'd always try to make me into something I didn't want to be, even if I was miserable."

"I know why you left, Aurora," she said, still quietly, but with a slight edge. "And it's not that I'm not proud of what you've accomplished, I am." I let that settle in, let the shock of hearing her say she was proud of what I'd done. Not *we*, of course. She didn't say that *we* were proud. But it still smoothed some of the hackles that I always had up when I spoke to her. "But we don't fit in your life just as much you don't fit in ours. And it doesn't make sense to pretend that we do."

"I don't want you to pretend anything, Mom," I said after I finally found my voice somewhere down in my stomach. I tried to imagine having this conversation someday with a daughter of mine. Someone that I raised. And I couldn't. Couldn't imagine the separation that yawned between me and my parents if it were a child of mine. It made me wonder, not for the first time, what my mom's relationship was with *her* mother. "Have you had a happy life, Mom?"

In the silence that followed, I heard her take in a deep breath. I was nervous for her answer. It felt vital to me, in that little blip of time, that she give me an honest answer. I wasn't even sure how I'd know if she was being honest, given that I knew her so little. "People define happiness differently, Aurora. What makes me happy, what I find satisfactory will be quite different from what makes you happy."

"I'm not asking *what* makes you happy," I clarified. "I want to know if you've *been*, or are, happy."

"My life," she said slowly, and I knew I wouldn't like the answer, "has been perfectly fine."

"I can't imagine living that way." But that wasn't completely true either, because outside of my job, my life had been perfectly fine until I took a chance with Garrett. My time outside of the office was quiet and simple, but it wasn't bliss by any means. So I took a deep breath. "I'm in a relationship, too. His name is Garrett, and he's … he's a good man."

"He treats you well?"

I swallowed past a lump in my throat at her careful question. "He does."

"Well," she cleared her throat after a few seconds of silence. "Then I'm happy for you."

The confession portion of the evening was over and I heaved a sigh after we hung up and I thought about the way she described her life. Perfectly fine.

But I knew, so deep inside of my soul, that I'd never be satisfied with that type of life. Maybe even three months ago, I wouldn't have answered that way. Because I hadn't seen what was supposed to fill in the gaps of work, which could only provide so much to one person. But I'd seen it now. Maybe Garrett wasn't the person that I was supposed to be with for the rest of my life, but he was the person who'd opened my eyes.

I didn't want to have a life that was perfectly fine, constantly trying to prove my parents' wrong. I wanted to be happy. Not setting my phone down after my mom hung up with no promises of when we'd speak next, I pulled up Garrett's contact info and waited for him to pick up when the ringtone filled the speaker next to my ear.

"Hey, Blondie," he answered, his deep voice swept through me, wringing a relieved smile out of my face that felt like it'd been frozen in a frown since first seeing my mom's number on my phone. "Miss me already?"

"What are you up to?"

In the background, I could hear voices. "Guys came over to play some cards, maybe have a couple beers."

"Oh," I said, knowing I shouldn't have felt the dull thud of disappointment at his answer. "Well, have fun. Just thought I'd say hi."

"No way, you're coming over." I could hear the smile in his voice, and it warmed me in the places that always felt cold after an interaction with my mom.

"The guys won't mind?"

It was a token question. I was already off the couch and slipping on my sandals.

"Don't really care. It's my house, and I want your fine ass sitting on my lap while you help me run the table."

I heard groans and jeering in the background, and I laughed as I locked the door to my condo behind me. "Perfect."

"Drive safe. See you soon, Blondie."

CHAPTER TWENTY-SIX

GARRETT

"Ooooooh, your girlfriend is here," Michael said from the kitchen sink, where he was rinsing out his pint glass.

I flipped him off, but couldn't stop the satisfied smile from covering my face. Seeing Rory's name pop up on my cell was a surprise —a pleasant one, of course — but still a surprise. We'd spent so much time together in the last few weeks, days and nights blurring together in a fricken fantastic way. I'd figured she wanted some space, given how much of it she used to spend by herself.

The front door opened at the same time that she gave it a quiet knock and Michael walked over to pull it the rest of the way for her. She smiled at him, and it punched me in the damn gut.

Why was she so beautiful?

If I wasn't half in love with her, it probably would've pissed me off. But since I was the one making her see stars every night, there was no problem with it anymore.

She was still wearing the black shirt from earlier at the office, but she'd traded her red skirt for soft looking jeans and plain black sandals.

There was something about seeing her softened up after the hard work I knew she did every day. It felt intimate, this secret side of her that she showed to so few people.

"Hey," she said warmly, sliding a hand across my shoulders and leaning down to kiss me in greeting.

The guys whistled and yelled, someone drummed their hands on the table when I cupped the back of her neck to slip her some tongue. Her face was pink when she pulled back, which made me laugh.

"They're just jealous," I whispered in her ear while she sat sideways on my lap, my arms wrapping around her waist and resting easily on her thighs.

"Dylan has a girlfriend and Michael gets as much ass as Justin Bieber."

I leaned back. "How do *you* know how much ass Biebs gets?"

She lifted her eyebrows like it was obvious. "Just making an educated guess. I don't think they're jealous."

"Of course they are. Look at you."

Oh yeah, that gained me some points judging by the embarrassed smile and shake of her head. Her eyes though, they were sparkling at me. *Sparkling,* people.

"Thanks for letting me crash," she said to the guys after Michael sat down and looked at his cards.

"Of course," Dylan answered. "Kat normally comes, but she went out with some ladies from the clinic."

"Is Anna coming too?"

I flipped my eyes to Tristan, because now that Rory had pointed out the way he looked at my sister at the barbecue, I couldn't ignore her point. He stilled and cocked his head toward us, tucking a long piece of hair behind his ear, an uncharacteristically nervous gesture from a dude that was solid as a rock all the time.

"No," I answered, looking back at her with a smile. It was a smile that I was still getting used to unleashing on her. It was my *I know how much of a covers hog you are* smile. My *I know what kind of underwear you prefer* smile. My *I know you have a freckle on your left breast* smile.

And she loved it. So much that she gave me one right back. Her *I know how much you like to feel up my ass when you sleep* smile. Because I totally did. Any sane man with access to her *in*sane body every night would do the exact same thing. You could take that shit to the bank.

Cole cleared his throat and I glared at him over Rory's shoulder. "Patience is a virtue, Mallinson, and a virtue won't hurt you."

Rory shifted on my lap to be able to see Cole better. "Mallinson, that's your last name?"

He nodded. "Yeah. Why?"

"Just kind of a unique name. I mean, no offense or anything."

Thankfully Cole smiled. "It's fine. And you're right, it is. I don't think I've ever met someone saddled with this thing, besides my family."

"I have," Rory said, glancing at me. "One of my final three candidates for the director of marketing position. Her last name is Mallinson." Then she made a thoughtful noise in her throat. "Though I guess I've never technically met Julia. Only spoken to her on the ph— "

"What did you just say?" Cole interrupted her on a shocked whisper. Across the table, I met Dylan's eyes, then Michael's, then Tristan's. And if I had a mirror, I bet my face looked exactly like their shocked ones. Julia. Oh, holy shit. "Did you just say *Julia* Mallinson?"

Rory was understandably confused, because Cole was now staring at her like he had the gift of precognition. That whatever was about to come out of her mouth, he already knew the answer.

"I did," she said slowly. "I spoke to her on the phone a couple days ago."

"Where?" he yelled excitedly, leaning forward in his seat like he wasn't sure if he was going to stay in it or jump to his feet. "Do you know where she lives?"

"Did I do something wrong?" Rory asked under her breath, aiming it at me but keeping a careful eye on the unstable, tall man sitting next to her.

"No," I answered her and then lifted a hand to Cole. "Hey, man, chill out a bit. Rory has no clue who you're talking about."

"But you do," he accused me, then gave Rory an apologetic look. "Sorry, I know I sound insane right now. But Garret, come on, you're considering my *wife* for a job and didn't think it was important to tell me?"

"Your *wife*?" Rory asked.

"I had no idea, Cole," I said at the exact same time. "I have nothing to do with vetting the final candidates. If I step in, at any point, it'll be right at the end when it's down to two." I rubbed a hand on Rory's back, feeling the tension in every inch of her frame where she was still perched on my legs. "He's fine, don't worry. Just has mild emotional instability when it comes to her."

Cole laughed, his eyes looking a little manic. "You think? I haven't had a clue where she's been living for the last *six years*, and tonight I find out that she's trying to get a job thirty minutes away from me working for one of my best friends? Yeah, I feel a little unstable."

"But I didn't do anything wrong?" Rory asked again, relaxing slightly when I moved my hands underneath the thin material of her shirt so I could feel her skin.

"No," I said firmly.

"Wrong?" Cole asked, then smiled widely at her. "Rory, I think I might be in love with you."

"Hey," I barked in a warning tone. Then he stood, gripping Rory's shoulders and planting a smacking kiss on her lips. She let out a surprised squeak, wiping at her mouth and laughing when I shoved at Cole's hulking frame hard enough that he released her. "Hands *off*, dude."

"It's fine, Garrett," Rory said, standing off my lap. "I can defend myself from unwarranted physical attentions."

I knew that. I really did. But there was something bubbling under the surface of my skin, now that I felt a claim over her. I loved that Rory was the kind of woman who could eviscerate a man with one look, one sharply spoken line, but I wanted to be able to defend her too. Wanted to be able to stand in between her and whatever it was that was aimed at her.

"First," Rory started, squaring off with Cole even though he was a solid six inches taller than her. That didn't matter to my woman though, she tilted that stubborn-ass chin up like she was talking to a little kid. "I won't hire her simply because she has a history with you. If she's the best person for the job, then she'll get it."

Cole looked at me like, *can't you do anything*? I held up my hands and then jerked my chin at Rory. "But— "

"No buts," Rory said firmly. "That's not how I'll make hiring decisions, especially if I know she's got baggage with a personal connection for both me and Garrett. I won't hold that against her, I promise. But, if she's the best fit for the job and we make her an offer, I *will* fully disclose the relationship between you and Garrett. I absolutely *refuse* to blindside a new employee like that."

The ruthless, corporate Rory was so hot. So hot. I shifted in my seat, because it was a very inopportune time to feel that turned on by her.

Cole struggled for calm, I could see it. The other guys watched with quiet interest from the table, occasionally taking sips of their beers. Cards were tossed onto the table, because it was pretty clear that the game portion of the evening was over and we'd fully moved onto entertainment, featuring Cole Mallinson and his tortured soul.

"Second," she said, in a softer voice, "I think she said she was living in California, but moving back here because of some family stuff."

"Thank you." Cole smiled at Rory, then his shoulders slumped, seemingly unable to bear the weight of what he'd just learned. "Sorry, guys. I think I'm going to head home, I feel like I just got socked in the nuts."

"Want some company?" Tristan asked.

"Thanks for the offer though, but no thanks." He gave Rory a small smile. "Sorry for losing my mind. I swear I'm normally saner than this."

He said his goodbyes and when he closed my front door behind him, Michael made an explosion noise. "Well that was intense."

Tristan took a long sip of his beer. "Kinda feel bad for the guy, though."

Dylan nodded. "I do, for sure. It probably almost makes it worse now. When he didn't know where she was, what she was doing, he at least had a chance of moving on. Not now though."

"Sorry for bringing it up, guys," Rory said, still standing next to my chair.

Dylan waved her off. "Nothing to apologize for. He'll be fine. And it looks like you've got your head on straight, which is more than we can say for him sometimes."

"She won't make the wrong decision," I said firmly, grabbing her hand and intertwining our fingers together. Rory gave me a smile, and the flush in her cheeks from squaring off with Cole made heat climb up my neck. "Okay. You guys need to leave."

Michael groaned and Dylan rolled his eyes good-naturedly. Tristan just went about picking up his stuff. The legs of my chair made an indelicate scraping noise when I shoved back from the table. Rory grinned, standing between my legs when I spread my knees. I smoothed my hands up the sides of her thighs, cupping her backside while the guys filed out the door.

Right before the door clicked shut, Michael poked his head back in and made obscene kissing noises. Neither of us paid him a single bit of attention though.

"I didn't come here for this," Rory said as she straddled me, looping her arms around my neck.

"And it's not why I invited you." It was true. I held her eyes, so she could see it, judge it for herself. So she could see that this was so much more for me. I wanted Rory to feel so deeply that seeing her in her element was as sexy to me as any personal show she could give me. That those sides of her, the ones that most men might feel emasculated by, simply made me want to stand up and scream to the world that she was mine. On my lap, she made a tiny rocking motion that made me suck in a breath. "But … while you're here," I trailed off, moving my hands from her back to push her hair over her shoulders.

"While I'm here," she agreed.

Our mouths fit together in a slow, hot kiss. Her hands gripped the sides of my face, the sharp points of her nails scratching against my scalp when I sucked her tongue gently into my mouth. After bracing my hands under her bottom, I stood easily. Rory wrapped her legs around my waist while I walked us into my bedroom.

The light from the hallway poured into the open doorway and spilled across my bed. When I stopped at the foot of it, I kept Rory in my arms and kissed her chin, the edge of her jaw, along her top and bottom lip.

"You like it when I get bossy," she accused, unwrapping her legs one at a time until she was standing in front of me. Her hands smoothed up my chest and down my stomach, pushing my shirt up when they traveled north again. With one hand, I gripped the back of my shirt and yanked it off.

"That obvious?" I plucked at her shirt and she got the hint, using both hands to pull it over her head. Her simple black bra looked stark against her golden skin and I traced the edge of the cups with my fingertips.

"A little." She smirked as she shoved her jeans down her impossibly long legs. I did the same, holding her eyes while I kicked them off. Rory raised an eyebrow. Now what? I could read the challenge in her eyes so clearly, like she'd just lifted on her tiptoes and whispered it against my ear instead of moving one small facial muscle. I took my pointer finger and followed the line of her breastbone, so hard underneath the silk of her skin. Then I pushed.

She fell back, hair spread in a wave against the dark cover on my bed. When I covered her with my body, we rolled our hips against each other seamlessly. This was a dance we knew well now, but the breaths we traded between pressed-together lips felt deeper and harsher in the dimly lit room. Or maybe just mine were harsher because I felt like it was getting harder and harder to keep my feelings from spilling over.

Everything about her called to me. On a primal level that I'd never realized existed inside of me before I touched my lips to hers. There was something molecular under my skin and muscle and bone, something embedded in my blood that wanted her. Would always want her.

I knew that now. I'd always want her. I'd always need her. Need her pushing me, fighting me, laughing with me, supporting me, lighting the fire under me to make a choice and make the right one.

Instead of pulling back to follow the thoughts pulsing through my brain, I kissed her harder, anchoring our hands together above her head with one of mine.

A choice. Maybe it was as simple as that. Before, I hadn't made a choice about what I wanted. Where I was now— at CFS, with her— it was my choice. And the uncomfortable skin from months ago felt perfect. Like it had been custom made and measured just for me. All because I'd made the choice to do it and fit better just shifting one spot over, with Rory right by my side for all of it.

I tightened my grip on her hands and slanted my mouth over hers. Our tongues tangled, nothing sweet or practiced about it.

"Garrett," she moaned when I lined up and slid inside of her.

I couldn't speak though. If one single word left my lips, it would start an unending litany of how easily she'd toppled me. How deeply I'd fallen for her. All the things about her that were perfect to me.

Instead, my hands clutched at her skin harder, my lips kissed her more deeply, my body moved against hers, into hers, with less finesse and more pounding emotion.

And she did the same with me. Her clawing hands and gasped breaths against my shoulder, her arched back said things to me. Every movement was so full of meaning that we burst together at the exact same moment. One perfect, suspended moment where I flew with her.

When we settled around each, after catching our breath and the sweat started cooling on our bodies, I used one arm to tuck her into my body and knew without a single, lingering doubt that I'd never, ever get over Aurora Anderson.

CHAPTER TWENTY-SEVEN

AURORA

Usually Garrett woke before me, but not that morning. When I stretched my arms over my head and turned to bury my face into the pillow that smelled like him, I encountered warm skin and solid muscle.

In his sleep, one of his arms had flipped up over his head and was propped up on the massive headboard framing his bed. Garrett's face was turned toward me, his features smooth and peaceful, his breathing deep and even.

It was strange how well I knew his body now. The way his biceps curved out, held me with such ease. The way his chest expanded, the way the wide slabs of muscle over his heart and bones looked in the dark of his room. How his hands held more callouses then most men in white-collar jobs, the way they felt on my skin. The way his smile started in his eyes before it ever touched his lips.

I used the tip of my finger and felt the line that dissected his abs, just lightly enough that I could feel the heat of his skin, but not enough to wake him. He shifted at my touch, his breathing stuttering while he settled again, more onto his side than he was before. He'd faced me more fully and I smiled at how he calmed again when I ran my hand into his hair.

He was so affectionate, something that was completely foreign to me. Obviously my parents hadn't been the touchy feely type. And the fact that all my dating experiences were the equivalent of dipping my toe into the ocean, for as deep as they were, hadn't ever gotten me to this point.

The wake up together part, where it's easy and comfortable and felt normal. It wasn't normal in that I felt complacent, and I didn't think he did either, but there was an ease to it that I didn't feel unsure about how to conduct myself.

I felt Garrett's eyes on me while I traced my fingers over his trim waist, relishing the feel of his muscles when they jumped under my light touch. I was about to hit the V that disappeared into his boxers when he grabbed my wrist.

"Good morning," he said, and then nuzzled his face into my neck. "Exploring, were you?"

We kissed briefly and I smiled when he tried to deepen it.

"I never wake before you, thought I'd enjoy myself."

He nodded, glancing over me. The white sheets were tucked under my arms and covering my chest. "Can't say I've never done that before."

"Oh yeah? And what did you explore, creeper?" I smiled so he knew I was kidding.

Over the sheet, he laid his hand on my ribs, exactly where my tattoo was. "You woke up when I got to the good parts, but this spot held my interest for a while the other morning."

"It's not like you've never seen it before."

"I know," he agreed, sliding the sheet over so that he exposed the script, but keeping me covered everywhere else. "That shocked the hell out of me at the gym, that first night I saw you there. Aurora Anderson with a tattoo. I could barely believe it."

I felt a blush on face at the way he said my name. "What did you think when you knew it was me?"

"That God was punishing me by sending me to the same place you were at."

I burst out laughing at his honesty, not offended in the slightest considering how tense things were for us that week. "Well if it makes you feel better, I almost fell off the treadmill when I saw it was you next to me."

"That does, actually."

I shoved his shoulder and he snatched my hand to pull me in for a kiss, rolling me over him in the same motion. My hair fell around us while we traded soft, languid kisses. It insulated us from the light outside, kept the noises muffled and our scents so closely intertwined that I couldn't tell what was me and what was Garrett.

"Wait," he said, pulling back and cupping the side of my face. "Don't distract me with your lips, devil woman. I was holding a meaningful conversation with you."

"You kissed *me*," I pointed out with a raised eyebrow.

He waved that away. "Whatever. Don't twist this up so I forget what I was saying."

With a hum, I rolled onto my knees so I could straddle him. The sheet slid off of my body, and he gave me a narrowed-eyed glare. "Do you remember what you were saying, Garrett?"

He swallowed and pushed his hands up my thighs. "Yup. Every word."

"Yeah?" I lifted my hands to twist my hair over one shoulder. "What was it?"

"Your tattoo," he answered easily, rubbing at the words with his thumb when he bracketed my waist with one large hand. "When did you get it?"

"When I was eighteen. On my birthday, actually." He was holding my eyes while I spoke, his hands firm on my skin, but not moving.

"Why that?"

"We're really having this conversation right now?"

"Yes," he said resolutely. "I've spent eighteen nights in the same bed as you, know exactly what you taste like first thing in the morning and that you're weird and condition your hair before you shampoo it. I know that you, quite impossibly, never get sick of oatmeal. But I still haven't heard much about your life before I met you."

It never failed to snatch my breath when Garrett did things to truly surprise me. Maybe because every aspect of my life before him was so predictable, by my own choosing. That when he flashed me some part of his personality that was so much more thoughtful or sweet than I'd expected from him, it shook something loose in me. No wonder I felt so upside down in the last few weeks. It was because of him, shaking things loose every single minute that we spent together. I vaguely wondered what would happen if I split my skin open, if I'd look different on the inside.

"It was predictable," I said slowly, making sure he was serious about talking about it. With me naked and sitting on top of him. Apparently he was, because he smiled when I answered. Was this us now? Would this be a normal Saturday morning for me and Garrett? Whispered conversations while the sun was still rising, tangled together away from the constraints of the office. My heart sped up, and my tongue desperately wanted to steer the conversation away from the General, but I took a deep breath and kept talking. "My father is in the Air Force, which I already told you. We moved a lot, which became predictable in its own right. My parents were," I paused, searching for the right word while I felt him smooth an encouraging hand up and down my thigh, "imperturbable."

"Do I need to get up and go get my dictionary?"

I laughed under my breath, placing my hand on his and squeezing. "Nothing ever fazed them. Nothing. My dad could be gone for months at a time, and I never saw it bother my mom. I remember in high school thinking that the term 'stiff upper lip' was probably coined in the Anderson house. Even if they were upset with me, which didn't happen much when I was younger because I was too afraid to step out of line, they did it quietly. A look was all I needed from them to know I'd done something wrong."

"Would it work if I tried that?"

"No," I said with a smile. Garrett nudged me up so he could shift to a sitting position with his back up against the headboard. I went to sit next to him, but he repositioned me onto his lap again so we were facing each other. Absently, I smoothed my hands up his forearms, since he'd wrapped his arms loosely around my lower back. The soft, crinkly hairs on his skin tickled my palms, and the heat of him seeped into me while I thought of a simple way to explain my childhood. "On one hand, the reason I'm so independent is because of them, they taught me to work hard and respect my elders, to appreciate the people who sacrifice to ensure our way of life. I know, without a doubt, that I get my backbone from both of them, and it's served me well."

"I'd say so." He tilted his head to regard me. "They must be proud of how much you've achieved."

There was a slight pinching in my heart at the way he said it, like it was a given. "I left right after I turned eighteen. And I haven't seen them since. I talk to my mom a few times a year, but I haven't exchanged one word with my father since the day I left."

"What? Why not?"

"They didn't agree with the kind of life I wanted. They think what I do feeds into a society of greed. That all we do is make the rich richer. I'm not contributing." I made air quotes around the last word, giving Garrett a rueful smile.

"That's bullshit," he said vehemently, holding me tighter, like it would chase away the things that formed me. "You're so smart, Rory. So damn smart that it scares the hell out of me sometimes. You're driven, and passionate, and you're amazing with our clients. They trust you, and so does everyone who works with us. You've achieved so much for how young you are. Don't they care about any of that?"

An iron ball wedged into my throat, and I worked to swallow around it as he spoke so passionately. About me. My eyes pricked while I stared at him, but I didn't dare blink. Just in case this was a sleep-induced mirage. Just in case the man in front of me, filling up every affection-starved part of my heart, wasn't real, I didn't want to miss a second. I didn't want to risk not experiencing it, because I couldn't deny for a single other second that I was falling in love with Garrett Calder. I held my eyes open as long as I could, keeping him firmly centered in my vision until my eyes burned. So I blinked, holding my eyes closed for a long second before opening them. He was still there, and still waiting to hear about everything I'd rather not talk about. "I don't really know. I mean, I actually talked to my mom last night for the first time in months. When I told her about what I'm doing now, she made it seem like maybe they were proud of me. They just don't see that it's necessary to tell me that. Maybe because I've made it apparent that their opinion doesn't mean much in my life."

"Now there's some more bullshit."

"Why do you say that? I left. How much more obvious can I be?"

With a bent brow, Garrett thought about that. His hands on my back moved up and down, like he couldn't keep them still. "So you got that tattoo to prove that you didn't need them in order to succeed, right? A visible reminder, every single day."

"Right," I agreed, trying to figure out where he was going with it.

"Rory," he said gently, "I know better than anyone what it's like to feel like a disappointment to your parents. We can posture all we want, yell to the rooftops that their approval doesn't make a lick of difference in our lives. But it does. You putting these words on your body, even if they'll never see them, is a constant reminder that you'll do anything in your power to prove them wrong. If your parents showed up to the office on Monday and said, we're proud of you, Rory, you'd feel the weight of those eighteen years vanish. Don't tell me you wouldn't."

"You weren't a disappointment to your dad." It was cowardly, but I chose to focus on the first part of what he'd said instead of dissect the rest of it. He was right, of course. Their opinion mattered greatly, and that's why I left. Because I couldn't have stood to be face to face with it for the rest of my life.

He smiled, but it was sad. "Yeah, I was. Not serious enough for him, not driven enough for him, and I didn't love my job the way he wanted me to."

"But you're doing right by him now," I reminded him gently. I couldn't imagine what it must feel like for him, to not have been able to ever hear that from his dad. But no matter what Garrett thought, I believed that Rich had been proud of him, had loved him without reservation.

"I suppose."

"You are. You could've walked away from that money and done something." I brushed my fingers over the side of his face, felt the prick of his facial hair against my skin when I did. "You told me once you hated working there. But every day, you're working hard to make sure your dad's company, his legacy, is successful. That the people he employed are happy and productive. That's no small thing, and he'd be proud of you, Garrett."

Garrett leaned his face into my hand, closing his eyes at my touch. "Do you remember me telling you that I felt like I was living in someone else's skin?"

"I do. You freaked the hell out of me by being so unguarded with me. Thought maybe you'd been taken over by pod people."

He smiled, taking my hand and pressing it to his mouth. "I realized something yesterday. I think so much of that stemmed from me feeling like I didn't have a choice, you know?"

"What do you mean?"

He let out a long breath. "I never felt like I had a choice in what I did. It was only right before he died that I felt like I could admit to him how unhappy I was. But, the thing is that I didn't even have something else in my head. Four months ago, if you'd asked me what else I wanted to do, I wouldn't have had an answer. Isn't that stupid?"

"No," I answered honestly. "Not at all."

"But I made a choice to take over. I could've walked away, taken that very generous check and found something else, something that I might have loved. But choosing to stay at CFS, choosing to do a good job after this very hot blonde marched into my office and told me I was being selfish, I think it changed how I looked at things. Changed how I looked at CFS."

"So you don't feel like you're in someone else's skin anymore?"

"I don't." He shrugged. He had both of my hands in his, playing with the edges of my fingertips. "Maybe that sounds simple, but I just don't. I like where I am, in all parts of my life."

Simple didn't mean that it wasn't powerful, because when he said that and punctuated his sentence by pulling me in for a deep, meaningful kiss, I sighed from the overwhelming feeling of being content. My heart was content, and for the most part, my brain was too. But there was still a niggling question of *but what next*? What would happen when Garrett made his decision, and where would I be when all the cards finished falling to the floor? If we broke up, no matter whose decision it might be, what would happen at work every day with the two of us as the ones running the company?

He pulled back, breathing hard from the kiss, and gripped the sides of my face. The look in his eyes was fervent, almost in contradiction to the slow, smooth way we'd been moving together.

"Do you know how much of that is because of you?"

I shook my head as much as I could in his tight hold. My heart raced at his tone, which was rushed and intense. "How much?"

"All of it," he said quietly, tracing my features with his eyes.

"You don't mean that."

"I do." He kissed me again, just a simple press of his lips like he couldn't not kiss me. When he pulled back, he licked his lips and locked eyes with me again. "Without you, I would've given up by now. Nobody but you could've gotten through to me."

"Marjorie or your mom—" I started, but he pressed his thumb against my mouth.

"Nobody but you."

He dropped his thumb and I took in a shaky breath. "Why?"

Before he spoke, he smoothed the hair back from my forehead and then traced a line down my forehead, down the slope of my nose and over my lips, watching his finger the entire way. "Because I am falling in love you, Aurora. And I know that's probably crazy to say so soon, not knowing what will happen seven months from now, but that doesn't mean it's not true. You are the best part of every single day."

My entire body froze against him, his words making my brain go blank and my heart shudder through a thick beat. "Garrett," I said on an exhale. But something made me not go any further. He put himself on the line, bared himself to the firing squad with absolutely no clue how I felt. "How did I not see you coming?"

If he was disappointed by me not saying it back, he didn't show it, because his smile was wide and genuine. "I'm sneaky like that."

"Yes," I said with a smile, wrapping my arms around his neck and pressing us so close together that I could feel his heartbeat against my breasts. "Yes, you are."

He kissed me, showing me everything that he'd just said with every push of his tongue and reverent touch of his hands on my body. I so desperately wanted to be the kind of woman who could say it right back, not feel any fear about the future and whether his decisions could put our relationship on shaky ground. But I wasn't. The guilt of that made my kisses harder, my hands rougher, and after I pushed Garrett so that he was laying on his back again, we didn't leave the bed for a few more hours.

CHAPTER TWENTY-EIGHT

GARRETT

You know how there are some days that you wake up and just know it's going to be one giant shit-show? Yeah. That was what happened to me when my alarm didn't go off. The second my feet hit the floor of my room and I was running an hour later than I should have been, I just knew it was going to be a horrible day.

Rory and I had spent the last two nights apart, after her showing up at my house for guys' night. So waking up Monday morning in an empty bed that still smelled like her, knowing I'd have to be respectful and not maul her in public had set me on edge instantly.

Like letting the words pour out of me had altered my ability to keep my hands off of her. I wasn't disappointed that she hadn't said it back, because I'd expected that. She was so self-possessed, so capable of controlling herself that I figured it would take her longer than me to put words to her feelings. Especially knowing what I did now of her upbringing. It explained so much about her, her unwavering drive and work ethic, her skill at being level-headed (read detached) when necessary. The thought of Rory, so warm and passionate, not having parents who could see or celebrate all sides of her absolutely slayed me.

So when she'd said she needed to get caught up on other things on Sunday, I didn't really question her need for some breathing room. Except when I woke on Monday morning, I felt off. Of course, it could have partially been the lateness in starting the morning, but my entire drive to work built tension in my spine. Traffic was shit heading into downtown, an accident slowing my arrival even further so that by the time I blew into the conference room for the senior management meeting, I was more than twenty minutes late.

Rory gave me a raised eyebrow when I plowed through the room to take my seat, I knew she was mildly annoyed that I'd missed almost half of it. The meeting went quickly once I was ready to go and had made my apologies to the team, but the rest of the day continued that way.

Marjorie sprung two last-minute meetings onto my calendar, when I barely had to time to breathe as it was. When I called her on it after the first meeting reminder, she told me to suck it up until she retired and then she could hire an assistant that cared about me being able to take an hour for lunch.

An hour after that, my credit card company called to tell me that someone had used it to make purchases at an electronics store in Manhattan, so clearly not me. My headache was already building by that point, so when my sister strode into my office unannounced, I was well past annoyed.

"Busy?" she asked, helping herself to the chair across from me.

"Yes, I am." I worked, very, very hard to keep the edge from my voice since I hadn't seen her more than once in the weeks that I'd been dating Rory. "What's up?"

She must have picked up on it anyway, because she lifted her chin and gave me the stubborn look that I was so familiar with from our childhood. "Like why couldn't I use the phone?"

"You said it," I mumbled, taking a sip of water from the glass on my desk.

"So you've been sitting behind that desk for, what? Almost four months now?"

I rubbed at my temples. "Anna, I do not have time for this today."

Her dark eyes narrowed at the weary sound of my voice, but I didn't really give a shit. "I want to ask my big brother a couple questions before I make a massive, life-changing decision. Can you make time for that?"

Okay. That had my attention. I dropped my hands and gave her another look. Anna looked tired, with slight dark circles under her eyes. Her hair was in a sloppy ponytail, which was unlike her. "Yeah, I can make time for that."

"Thank you." She shifted in the chair, worrying her fingers in her lap. "So, four months, right?"

I lifted my eyebrows while I counted back. "Yeah, just about."

"Do you regret doing what Dad asked?"

"No," I said easily. It was quite possibly the easiest question she could have asked me on such a shitty day. "You thinking about doing the same thing?"

Her eyes closed for few moments and her skin seemed to lose color before my very eyes. "I don't know."

"Anna," I said, leaning forward to brace my arms on the desk in front of me. I didn't continue until she opened her eyes at me again. "Did he do something to you? Because the way my day has gone, I'd happily inflict bodily harm on him if need be."

Actually, the more I thought about it, the better it sounded. Yeah, beating the shit out of Anna's absentee husband might be the perfect thing for my day. But she gave me a shake of her head, deflating my bloody visions. Damn it.

"No, he hasn't. But it's getting harder and harder for me to remember why I'm digging in my heels so much about this." She let out a long breath and then laughed humorlessly. "I'm married to someone who doesn't even see me when I'm in the room. Sometimes I'll just sit and stare at him to see how long it takes him to realize it. Last week it took him an hour. An *hour*, Garrett. I wasn't talking, just sitting in the chair across from him and staring at him."

"Yup. I think he needs a visit from your big brother." Honestly, I think my vision was tinged in red after hearing her say that.

"No, he doesn't."

"If he's pulling shit like that?" I stood from behind my desk, blood pumping furiously through my veins at the thought of my sister feeling ignored in her own home. By her husband. "Yeah, he really does."

"Stop," she said firmly. "And sit your ass back down so I can talk to you."

It took me a solid minute to do as she said, but she held my eyes the entire time. When I took my seat, gave me a grateful smile. I rolled my eyes, because she wasn't a big brother, she had no idea. "So what does me working at CFS have to do with it?"

"How long did you feel manipulated? Because honestly, Gare, even though I've stayed, I still feel like someone else is pulling the strings. Like it doesn't matter if I stay or not, because how do I know I'm not doing it just to be stubborn?"

I rubbed at the back of my neck. "I think I was too busy moping at the beginning to feel manipulated for long. Dad went easy on me, I still got some money. He wasn't leaving me completely high and dry."

"Yeah," she drawled. "What the hell is up with that?"

"He *really* hated your husband."

Anna groaned, but then started laughing. "He really did." After a second, I saw her eyes shine. "I miss him, even though stuff like this really makes me wish I could slap him."

The dull thud of grief hit my stomach when I saw her wipe under her eyes. "I do too."

"I'll figure out what to do. Eventually. At least he didn't give me a time limit on mine." She sniffed and blinked at me when her tears were gone. "Do you know what you're going to do yet?"

"I've got months to figure that out," I said, feeling a little testier than I should.

"So you haven't thought about it once?"

"No," I lied. I'd thought about it. Just had no freaking idea what I should do. Because the truth was, I knew Aurora would do amazingly in my job. I also knew that I enjoyed it way more than I'd expected. And I also knew that the further he and I got, the longer we were together, it would make the work dynamic between us that much more important. Could we be together, long term, and still run the company together? It was a question that I'd just never be able to answer until we actually tried it. Our current situation still held a flavor of impermanence. At any given moment, it could sway in either direction.

"That's stupid."

"Says the woman staying with a jackass husband for no good reason."

"Hey," she snapped, standing from the chair and pinning me with a glare. "I came here to get your advice."

"Perfect." I held my arms open. "Don't stay. That's my advice."

For a second, I thought about asking her if she noticed how Tristan looked at her. Women usually sensed that stuff before men. But if she hadn't noticed, then it would complicate her situation even more if I brought it up. So I bit down on my tongue.

"Thanks a lot." She snatched up her purse and turned to leave.

"You're welcome," I called out as the door slammed behind her. I shoved a hand in my hair and took a few deep breaths, trying to remember what I'd been working on before she came in. While I was doing that, my cell phone vibrated on the desk next to a stack of reports.

"What?" I barked into the speaker.

"Did you hire Julia yet?" Cole barked right back at me.

Awesome. Just what I needed. "I don't know, Cole."

"Then ask."

"I think they're still doing preliminary interviews."

"I'm crawling out of my skin here, Garrett," he groaned.

"And that's not my problem." See, that right there was how not to go about speaking to your friend who was on the edge of an ex-wife-inspired meltdown.

"So you're one of those CEOs who has no say in anything?"

"Don't be a dick, Cole." But his words made me roll my neck back and forth on my shoulders. I should've just hung up, because it was not the day for me to be having that conversation. Every minute, from the very first that my eyes were open, was rife with irritation. "Of course, I'm not."

"Seems like it."

"You wanna poke the bear, then keep going."

"Just tell me where she's living. Or her contact info. It would have to be on her resume."

"So you can stalk her? No way." I blew out a breath when he cursed in my ear. "I don't know whether she's getting an offer or not."

"So *make* her get an offer. That *is* within your power."

"Of course it is," I ground out. "Seriously, we need to have this conversation some other time, because I'm not in the mood, Cole."

"No, it's fine, I've got it. Your girlfriend just won't hire her because I made a big deal out of it. But it's good to know who wears the pants between the two of you. I'm sure she'll make a great CEO once you're gone."

"Hey," I shouted into the phone. "I get it, you're pissed and taking it out on me, but *I'm* the boss. *I'm* the CEO, and yes, I have the power to make whatever the hell decision I want. Not Rory. And if I say Julia gets the job, then she'll get it. If I say no, because you're being a giant dick, then she won't."

If I hadn't been so pissed off, I would've heard my office door open.

Unfortunately for me, I didn't. Not until she was already standing there, glaring at me.

CHAPTER TWENTY-NINE

AURORA

I'd had one brief moment where I considered stepping back out of his doorway, pretend like I hadn't just heard him say what he did. But then I remembered that I wasn't a pansy-ass. So I propped one hand on my hip and stared him down, my heart thundering in my chest and my blood roaring in my ears.

"Cole," he said into the phone, holding my eyes with color high in his cheeks. "I need to go." There was talking on the other end of the phone, and I saw Garrett clench his jaw. "I heard you, and I'm hanging up now."

I took enough of a step so that I could quietly close the door behind me. The office was fully Garrett now, not a single thing remained from when it had been Rich's, except the massive wooden desk. It was imposing. A true CEO's desk. And the hard-eyed man sitting behind it, in his three-piece suit with a striking blue tie looked every inch of one too.

"Rory," he started, and the chagrined pinch of his mouth was the only reason I wasn't losing it on him. "It wasn't like it sounded."

"Really."

"Really." He held up a hand, pushing his chair back from the desk so he could stand up. I lifted my chin, shoring up any internal armor I had at my disposal, because if he touched me, it would be so much worse. Every word I heard him say felt like he'd tossed grenades at me, lobbing them easily at my naked skin. And they'd hit accurately, all in my stomach and heart. The only thing unscathed, not bleeding out onto the floor was my brain. Because all along, that's what had held me back. "I've had the shittiest day in months, and Cole just kept pushing."

I nodded, taking a step backward when he rounded his desk. If he touched me, I'd explode from the inside out. Not because it would make me cave. Because I'd kick his *ass*. If Garrett laid one hand on me in an effort to console, to smooth it over, I'd aim for his balls first. It was the only thought keeping me from feeling the stunning, cold punch of betrayal. He knew. He *knew* exactly how much I craved respect from the people I worked for. The fact that he was my boyfriend made it doubly important. "It's perfectly fine to have a shitty day, Garrett. We all have them." Then I swallowed, feeling my stomach tumble when I thought about the hard anger in the words I'd heard. "But it's *not* an excuse for what you just said."

"Let me explain." He must have seen my hesitation, seen the anger simmering in my eyes, because he held up two hands in concession. "Please."

"Go ahead."

"Will you sit?"

"No," I said firmly. "Please start explaining, because it sounded an awful lot like you just horribly disrespected me to one of your friends."

Garrett blinked, and I saw the first sign of panic in his eyes. "No, Rory, I *didn't*."

"Really? So I misheard you? I have the power to make whatever the hell decision I want. Not Rory. And if I say Julia gets the job, then she'll get it." As I said the words back to him, I felt the embarrassing crawl of tears up my throat. "Did I hear wrong, Garrett? And don't you *dare* lie to me."

"Rory," he begged, stepping toward me. "Please."

"Did I hear wrong? I am giving you the chance to tell me that I did. That you didn't actually say that to one of your friends."

He blew out a breath in one hard puff, and I knew. I'd known when I heard it. "No. You didn't hear wrong."

I rubbed a hand on my chest, pulling in air through my nose while I blinked through the awful flash of pain. "Wow, Garrett."

"Shit, Rory," he said, reaching for me. He stopped short when I glared at him. "I'm so sorry, I wasn't thinking about what I said, I swear."

"You made me sound inconsequential, Garrett. Insignificant." I shook my head, wanting so badly to be able to hold on to the white-hot anger from a few minutes ago. Because it was so, so much worse to feel the hurt. The sucking, draining feel of betrayal. His respect, his trust in my abilities, of any of my superiors was everything to me.

"I didn't mean to, though." He wanted to scoop me up, press himself against me so tightly so that I'd have no choice but to believe him, I could see it in his eyes, in the tight way he held himself in check.

"It doesn't matter if you didn't mean to. Don't you get that? Your intent doesn't *matter*, Garrett, because you still did it. If I hadn't heard you, then Cole still would have. He would have heard you say that you don't respect my position, respect *me*."

"Hang on a second," he argued, fire flashing in his dark eyes. "I respect you, Rory. I more than respect you. I had a terrible day, everything went wrong, and he just wouldn't stop pushing about Julia, taunting me about how it wasn't up to me."

"So then tell him to go screw himself and hang up!" I yelled. "I am not just some random employee who heard something she wasn't supposed to."

"I know that," he yelled right back, ripping his jacket off with rough movements and whipping it into one of the empty chairs. "Sue me, Rory, I had a bad day and I mouthed off to my *friend*. I'm not perfect."

"That's not what I'm asking for," I cried and he lifted his eyebrows in response.

"Really? Because not everyone is capable of complete emotional lockdown when they've had a shit day."

"Excuse me?" I whispered. "You're blaming *me* for this?"

"*Shit*. No!" He grabbed the back of his neck with both hands, like he needed to do something with them. "No, Rory, I'm not blaming you. I just … obviously I don't do well when everything's piled up on me like it was today. I'm sorry I don't react in the perfect way every single damn time."

"You don't *have* to, Garrett." I pointed a finger at him, hating how it shook when I did. "I am not asking for perfection, and you know it. But you told me you were falling in *love* with me less than forty-eight hours ago."

"I know that," he said, voice breaking on the last word. "Do you think I forgot?"

"I don't know," I answered honestly, my voice thick with unshed tears and my eyes hot. "I've never been in a relationship where that word was used before, Garrett. Not until you." He whispered my name, dropping his hands and hunching his shoulders in like I punched him. "So I may be new at this, but I *do* know you're not supposed to talk about the woman you're in love with like that. I don't care how bad of a day you had. And it makes we wonder how we can do this."

"Do what? No, Rory, come on, just hear me out." He walked up to me, cupping my face with shaking hands. For a moment, I let him. For a moment, the heat in his hands pushed through my cold skin, and it felt like he might warm me from the inside if I let him. So I stepped back and he shook his head. "I am so sorry."

"I believe you," I whispered. "I do."

"Why do I feel like that's not going to be enough right now?"

A tear hit my cheek and Garrett watched it, a look of such raw pain on his face that I almost wished I could have stopped it before it fell. But I couldn't. Just like he couldn't undo what he said.

"All weekend, I wondered how the rest of this year would play out," I said by way of explanation, because he was right. It wasn't. "If you decide to stay, and we don't work out, will I hate that you're in a position that you used to wish wasn't yours? Or if you go, will I feel like you're ripping my heart out when you walk away because I know what it's like to be here with you? And," I swallowed, holding his eyes, "what about something exactly like this? When we have a fight or if we break up, what happens with everything here? I couldn't figure it out in my head how we'd keep everything separate."

"God, Rory, stop, please. We have so much time until I need to make my decision."

"It's *not* that much time, Garrett. And I'm not the kind of person who can just go with flow, getting deeper and deeper with you when I don't know those things."

He wiped a hand over his mouth, looking completely exhausted when he spoke again. "So what now?"

My brain raced, and I pushed a hand on my stomach to try and settle whatever churning was going on in there. I'd never quit, that wasn't the way I was built. But I couldn't come back in the morning and pretend like none of the last twenty minutes had happened. "Well, I've got a lot of PTO stored up. I'm going to use some of it. I need … I just need some space."

He nodded. "Okay. How much time?"

"I've got about three months built up." His mouth opened when I said it and I held up a quick hand. "I'm not going to be gone that long. But, I think a couple weeks."

"And space will help you?"

I shrugged. "Maybe it sounds stupid to say yes. But all of this has been so fast, we've barely had a breath apart since that first night. And … and I think I need time to breathe."

"I hate this," he admitted, looking pale, like if I pushed him too hard, he'd fall right over.

"I do too." My voice hitched and I pressed a hand over my mouth. Garrett clenched his jaw and then went to reach for me again but I stepped back, begging him with my eyes, my raised hands. "Don't, Garrett. If you touch me, I'll cave. And I can't do that."

He was breathing hard, but he nodded. "Okay. I won't. I want to. Because I love you, Rory, I won't."

A sob threatened to push from my throat, but I trapped it by grinding my teeth together. I only loosened them when I could breathe again. "Thank you."

I turned and walked out before the tears broke, but I felt his eyes on me until the door clicked shut, and as I drove home in a daze, then crumpled into bed as the tears started, I wasn't entirely positive that I was doing the right thing.

CHAPTER THIRTY

AURORA

I'd made my way through every bingeable show on Netflix, worked out until my entire body screamed in protest, and slept more than I thought humanly possible. That was just in the first six days.

Day seven was when I started thinking that there was a reason I never used all my PTO. Because not working was boring as shit. Every single year that I'd been a full-time employee, I'd banked my paid time off, with the exception of a few days. And every year, on December 31st, everything that had been unused, and was eligible, rolled into the next year. Even after the thrilling seven days that I'd just used, I was the current owner of enough PTO that I could have sat on my couch for fifty-six more days.

But in the same token, I wasn't ready to go back. In hindsight, there was so much about what we'd done that confounded me. Starting with me dropping that damn towel in his bathroom. Evidently, Garrett Calder had sucked my mind out with his kisses. It was entirely unlike me to not demand some sort of definition of what we intended to be, to not clarify what might happen at work after the food-fight levity cleared from our brains.

Levity was an interesting concept, the more I thought about it. On day three, I'd looked it up, and the very first definition of the word actually made me lose my breath because of its accuracy.

Lightness of mind, character or behavior; lack of appropriate seriousness or earnestness.

Yes. Levity was exactly the precise word for how I'd behaved. How we'd behaved over the last couple months. Fighting with Garrett had been interesting, something unexpected and diverting that led into a passion that I hadn't known I possessed. The realization that he'd uncovered something inside of me, just by being himself, was sobering.

Naturally, that meant I had to start drinking.

So that's what started my Pinterest addiction, the decision to move on to alcohol if I intended to actually make it two weeks without work. Pinterest was not something that I really understood pre-Garrett. But post-Garrett, I totally got it. There were so many drink recipes, so many outfit ideas and DIY projects that I needed to attempt the second I purchased a circular saw. I pinned so many things in a twenty-four-hour time span that it was difficult to know where to start.

Oh yeah. Alcohol was where I needed to start. The first recipe that caught my eye was called a Cinnabon cocktail. Considering I hadn't indulged in anything starting with "cinn" in almost five years, I added that to the list on my grocery store app. About two hours later, I couldn't figure out why the recipe called for one-part Fireball to three parts cream soda. They must have meant a two-two ratio, because holy shit, I was the happiest I'd been in *days*.

Happy blurred into something blurry on my TV screen. I sat up too quickly, squinting at it.

"Holy shit," I gasped. "It's *The* mother-effing *Notebook*."

The beginning of it and everything. With a scowl on my face, I settled in, totally determined to laugh my ass off. I sent Mia a text and told her what I was watching. Me and my Cinnabon drink.

Ninety minutes and a painfully full bladder later, I was sobbing into a pillow.

So, it's not gonna be easy. It's gonna be really hard. We're gonna have to work at this every day, but I want to because I want you.

When tears pooled in my collarbone, I threw my soaked pillow at the TV mounted over my fireplace mantel, only to have it fall ineffectually onto the ground about two feet from the couch. "Oh, go *screw* yourself, Gosling."

The tears choked in my throat, imagining how easy it had been to fight with Garrett, kiss Garrett, let myself be me with Garrett. All of it had been easy. So easy that I'd ignored big things, big questions that needed to be answered. I'd ignored that nagging voice in my own head that normally would have been screaming at me that we had things to work out, roles that needed to be defined and conversations that we should have been having. Instead I'd morphed into one of those girls that bit her tongue when it begged to be let loose. Actually, I thought with a thud, that wasn't even true. I never even got to the point where I bit my tongue, because I too easily swept the thoughts away that made me question whether Garrett and I were a good idea. They'd only been brief wisps in my head that I'd effortlessly swatted away.

I sniffed, turning the TV off with a vicious punch of my finger onto the remote. The leggings that I'd thrown on that morning, or wait, maybe the day before, had two wet spots of whiskey on them. And nope, I totally didn't even give a shit.

This was vacation, bitches. And I was going to let loose.

My hands were remarkably steady as I glugged more Fireball into the lowball glass. I held it up to the light over my kitchen sink, trying to judge with squinted eyes whether I'd added the cream soda first.

With a shrug, I knocked it back and then coughed, my throat burning. "Nope, holy shit, nope there's no cream soda in that."

I stood by the sink, bracing my hands on the counter while I waited for the warm feeling to settle in my stomach. When it did, I shuffled back to the couch and sank into the corner. The screen of my phone kept blinking, but I chose not to look. The reason I chose not to look is because I knew it was probably Mia checking in to make sure I was a *Notebook* convert.

"Pffft," I blew air through my lips. "Keep dreamin', cuz," I said, even though she couldn't hear me. I shut my eyes and let my head flop back onto the couch, enjoying the way the room floated around my head. Or my head floated around the room.

Someone was playing drums. Or tap-dancing on my ceiling. It got louder and I curled my lip in the direction of the noise.

Bang bang bang bang. "Rory?" A woman's voice called out.

My eyes popped open. Maybe not tap-dancing since my name was now involved. I groaned, pushing myself up off the couch and then pausing when everything swam around me.

Bang bang bang bang bang.

"I'm coming, geez Louise," I mumbled, tripping on the corner of the rug under my dining table and taking a second to right myself. Squinting, I looked through the peephole. "Kat?"

The mop of blonde hair shifted. "Yeah, it's Kat. Can you let me in?"

My forehead rested on the cool, hard surface of my door and I stayed for a second, because it felt good on my hot skin. "Yeah. Hang on. I'm a little drunk."

She laughed, which made me smile. I don't think I'd smiled all day. When I swung the door open, gripping the side of it so I didn't go flying back on my ass, she was there with a grocery bag in her hands and a friendly smile on her face. "I come bearing gifts."

"Is it more alcohol?"

"No," she said decisively, shutting and locking the door behind her when I walked back over to the couch with a disappointed grunt. I watched her through the slits of both eyes while she lifted up the bottle of Fireball with wide eyes, then looked back over to me. "When did you open this bottle?"

"I dunno," I said around a yawn. "Like, two hours ago."

She whistled. "Explains a lot."

"How'd you know where I live?" Then I lifted my head and pinned her with a glare. "Did Garrett send you?"

I acted mad when I said it, but my heart did a slow tumble at the thought of him sending his friend to check up on me. Kat licked her lips while she pulled some things out of the brown paper grocery bag. "It was Mia, actually. She sent Michael a text to see if he could send me over here. She's the one who gave me your address."

"What a nosy bitch. Something wrong with the fact that I want to get drunk in the privacy of my own home?"

Kat laughed under her breath, coming over to join me on the couch. In her hands was a takeout container of Chinese. She smiled as I took it. "I think your cousin is worried, Rory. She said you hadn't answered a text in three hours."

"Well," I said, taking the fork from her hand and digging into the fragrant pad thai noodles from the place down the street from my condo, "you can report back that I'm alive."

Instead of answering, Kat watched me eat, then cast an interested look around the room. "Your place is beautiful. Exactly like I expected it to be."

"Mia says it's boring."

"It's classic," Kat argued, and I felt an unexpected flush of warmth at the fact that she liked my place. "You have impeccable taste, there's no doubt about that."

My chewing slowed down, and Kat handed me a bottle of water that I hadn't seen her carry over. "Are you sucking up to me so I'll talk to you about Garrett?"

She laughed and shook her head. "No. I think your sobriety is nonexistent enough that I wouldn't have to work very hard to get info out of you."

"You're so pretty," I blurted out. When I took a hurried sip of the water, she smiled at me. It was a kind smile, and I felt rotten about how I'd acted when I first met her. "I'm sorry I was a bitch the first day we met."

"It's okay. No apologies necessary."

"But they are. We'd just kissed for the first time the night before. And I … I don't know, just seeing that different side to Garrett made me feel weird. And even though I knew he was single, you showed up all cute and tiny and adorable with a crippled dog, for shit's sake." I gave her an earnest look and I could tell she was fighting not to laugh. "I'm sorry for saying your dog is crippled. That's probably not PC, huh?"

"Leonidas is a very forgiving creature."

"He's cute," I said glumly, and then stood up to go refill my glass with Fireball. Kat was right behind me, snatching the glass out of my hands.

"I'll make you one. I used to work at a bar." She uncapped the cream soda and poured a generous amount over the melted ice clinking around the bottom of the glass. "That's how I met Dylan."

When Kat poured a tiny splash of Fireball into the drink, I rolled my eyes, but still took it from her. "You guys look really good together."

"I know," she said on a happy sigh. "I mean, it's mainly him. He's so hot, isn't he?"

There was nothing artificial about her, and it was so refreshing. She wasn't asking to gauge whether she could trust me, or if I warranted her jealousy. Her only motivation was a deep-down appreciation of the man she loved.

"Yup," I agreed. "He really is."

We laughed at that. When she stopped, she asked if she could use a bathroom. I pointed out the door to her, and as soon as it clicked shut, I opened the Fireball and filled the rest of the glass.

When she came out, I was finishing an egg roll with a blissed out smile on my face. "Thanks for bringing me food. You didn't need to do that."

"Mia insisted when I called her. She loves you very much."

"She's been the only one my whole life," I found myself saying.

"That's not true anymore," Kat said gently. "I know someone who loves you very much."

I huffed out a dry laugh. "He can't be too happy with me right now."

"I think he's worried. And I think he misses you. He's been pretty mopey the last week."

My eyes fell shut and I rubbed at my chest. Even through the pleasant numbing haze of my drinks, there was such a deep ache in my heart when I thought about him being miserable. "Kat, he made me *so mad*." She laughed, but I lifted my eyebrows. "Like, if we'd been married and I was a little bit less sane, I would have gone Lorena Bobbitt on his ass."

That sobered her, but even though her smile dropped, her eyes still looked like they had laughter in them. "Well, then for both of your sakes, I'm glad that that didn't happen."

Whiskey swam in my head, making it harder to blink at a normal speed. I could hear the pounding of my heart in my ears, amplified so much that it was all over my body, thumping across my skin. "I think I drank too much."

"I think you might be right, Rory. How about you drink the rest of this water? Okay?"

With my eyes closed, I took it from her and downed the entire thing. "Thank you."

"Of course." She rubbed my shoulder. "Do you want to go get in bed? I can stay out here on the couch, make sure you're okay before I go home."

"Mmmmkay." With the assistance of Kat, I stood up and walked down the hallway to my bedroom. She kept the lights off, but helped me pull back the covers of my bed. It was so soft and so dark, so I pulled the blankets over myself and burrowed into my pillow. I peeled my eyes open, Kat's face bouncing in my vision. "Do you know what I keep thinking about before I go to bed every night?"

"What's that?" she asked softly and stroked the hair back from my forehead. It felt so maternal, so sweet, that my eyes burned.

"I love him too. And I didn't tell him."

Kat blinked rapidly. Maybe her eyes were burning too. "You can tell him soon."

"Do you think he knows?" I slurred, my words elongating as they came out of my mouth and I fell further and further into sleep.

"Go to sleep, Rory. I'll be right outside."

Visions of Garrett and cupcakes and kisses and treadmills and conference rooms swished through my head as I did exactly that.

CHAPTER THIRTY-ONE

GARRETT

Sleep.

Eat.

Remember to smile at people.

Shuffle papers and pretend to pay attention.

Watch clock on my office wall until I could go home and do it all again the next day.

Lay in bed, stare at the ceiling and think about Rory's smile, the way she kissed me when I made her laugh, the curve of her hip bones underneath the softest skin I'd ever felt. Do those things on repeat until my stomach threatens to revolt. Then think about her in my office. Think about her crying. Get up and take shots of whiskey and try to sleep.

Again and again. Over and over. For seven days, I followed my list religiously. Only, I didn't eat much, and I definitely didn't sleep well.

If this was love, if this was how it felt to walk around without your essential organs, without the ability to breathe properly, then I finally understood with perfectly clarity why I'd avoided it for so many years.

The only thing that changed on my list was late on day seven, when I started staring at my phone for hours at a time. I'd flip between Rory's Facebook, which gave me shit for clues, then move on to my camera roll to study the few candid shots that I had of the two of us. One in bed, smiling at the camera, one at the gym, her growling at me for snapping a picture of her, and one of us out to dinner. Dressed up and smiling at each other. Then I'd torture myself and pretend like I was going to call her. I'd press my thumb over her contact info, run through in my head what I'd say if she answered.

I miss you.

I'm an idiot.

I love you.

The thing I loved about work was having you there with me.

Also, I'm an idiot.

Don't ever leave me.

Days seven through ten were rough. Just so that I would have some sort of physical manifestation of what was happening in my heart, I stopped shaving. I looked like a horrible version of myself, which made sense, since that's what I'd turned into.

And as I laid in bed with day ten drawing to a close, I had an absent thought that maybe Rory had yanked my heart out when she left my office. I rubbed at the skin above my heart and wondered if I never saw her again, if I would ever stop feeling that way.

CHAPTER THIRTY-TWO

GARRETT

I showered on day eleven, tried my best to scrub away the sloth that had inhabited my body since day one. It should say something to me, I thought, that without Rory at work with me, I didn't hold the same love for it that I'd been feeling over the previous months.

Was it the fact that I'd made the choice to be there? Or was it her?

As I stared at my reflection in the mirror of my bathroom, trying valiantly not to remember how insanely beautiful Rory had looked when she'd walked in and dropped that towel the first night we were together. The first night I felt her skin and wanted to surgically attach my lips somewhere on her body.

I shook my head, tossing away that thought, because that cheapened it. Cheapened what I felt for her. It made it about the physical, when that was only one sliver of Rory, and one sliver of what she meant to me.

I loved her. And I didn't have a single clue how to balance giving her space and what I really wanted to do, which was pound at her door, not give up until she let me in.

But she'd asked for two weeks, at a minimum. So I hung my head in between my shoulders and let out a deep breath. Dylan had blackmailed me into coming over for a couple beers. And by blackmail, I meant that he told me Kat had seen Rory, but I wouldn't know how it went unless I showered, shaved and came over.

And since I was a sucker, willingly falling into the trap my friends had laid for me, I did just that. Even though they might have gone about it wrong by using Rory, I was glad the second I walked into Kat and Dylan's house. Leonidas ran crazy circles around my legs, his long, fluffy tail whacking into my knees while he did the high-pitched whine that meant he was excited.

"Hey, man," I said, leaning down to scratch underneath his jaw. "Miss me?"

"He cries about it every night," Kat told me with a wink. "And I'd know because someone has been letting him up into our bed at night."

Dylan held up his hands. "Can you say no to his eyes? Because I can't. He always comes to my side of the bed, so it's easy for you to act all tough."

"I'm glad you're here," Kat said, nudging my shoulder with hers.

"Under duress," I aimed at Dylan with a hard look. He simply grinned at me and wrapped an arm around Kat when she stepped next to him. "I'm here. Do I get the goods now?"

"Beer first," he said, handing me an already opened bottle of one of my favorites from a brewery out of Chicago. Almost impossible to find. "You doing alright?"

"Define alright."

Tristan and Michael walked in, tipping their chins at me in an eerily identical way.

"Hey, man," Michael called, clapping me on the shoulder as he passed. "Good thing Mia's got my number, huh? Rory probably would've woken up on the bathroom floor if it hadn't been for Kat."

"*What*?" I roared and Michael widened his eyes in surprise. Kat smacked a hand on the back of his head and Tristan just rolled his eyes. "She would have what? Is she okay?"

"She's fine," Kat assured me, still giving Michael the evil eye. "Mia was worried because Rory wasn't answering texts. She asked if I would go check on her."

"And…"

"And, she was just a little," Kat shifted uncomfortably, "drunk."

"But she was okay?"

When Kat nodded, I let out a relieved breath. "You expect me to still give her space after this? How am I supposed to not go talk to her?"

Dylan laid a hand on my back, his face stretched in a sympathetic smile. "I get it. You know I do. You didn't do anything wrong by giving her space, man. It's what she asked for."

"I know. But doing nothing feels insane, Dylan."

"You're not doing nothing," Kat said quickly. "You're respecting her wishes. And that's a good thing."

"But if she's so messed up over this that she was wasted? That's not Rory."

Michael went into the family room, staring at the TV like it held the solution to the world's problems. Kat's phone rang, and she went to grab it off the counter, leaving me with Dylan and Tristan.

"Cole not coming?" Tristan asked, not really looking at either of us. Dylan lifted an eyebrow at me like I'd know.

"He and I haven't really talked since the whole thing." I peeled the loose edge of the label on my bottle. "So if he knows I'm here, he probably won't. Not that I really want to see him yet either."

"That bad?" Dylan asked.

While I sucked in a breath through my nose, I nodded. "He was pretty out of line. I get it's his ex-wife, and we all know how he is about her, but he pushed too hard." Then I scoffed. "Or I caved too easily, as evidenced by the predicament I'm in."

"It's not about caving or pushing," Tristan said, leveling me with the full brunt of his intense stare. Maybe it was weird to think of another guy's eyes as intense, but Tristan fit the bill. Locking eyes with him made you feel like you'd just been sighted by a friggin bear or something. "You didn't *cave* to Cole, you made a mistake. Just like he made a mistake in how he treated you. The difference is that yours cost you— temporarily, at least— the woman you're in love with. You know Rory well enough to know that she responds to strength. To loyalty. You weren't being loyal either when you ran your mouth to Cole. You just have to show her that you're still both. Just don't push too fast when you decide it's time."

Dylan leaned forward. "Shouldn't I be giving him the deep, cryptic thoughts on how to be patient when your woman needs space? Or is this going to fall into the Tristan vault where we have no clue why you're so well-versed on giving relationship advice?"

While I took a sip of my beer, I watched Tristan again, and he shuttered his eyes before he looked at Dylan. "In the vault, I guess."

"You revel in this, don't you?" Dylan asked. "Keeping us all guessing."

Tristan's face broke into a wide smile, which was a rarity for him.

"Holy shit, you have all your teeth. I was starting to wonder," I mused.

Dylan laughed. "He's right, Garrett. Her wanting space isn't a bad thing for either of you. You guys dove in head first without talking through a lot of things you should be figuring out."

"It was so much easier to ignore them though," I said glumly. "And now I have no clue what she's thinking."

"Well," Dylan said slowly, "it doesn't matter right now. You know what you're thinking. She gave both of you an opportunity to really think about what you want moving forward. What the best possible outcome is. And once you decide what that is, with her and with work, you take whatever steps you need to make it happen."

"And if our outcomes are different?" I asked, not really wanting to contemplate the idea.

Dylan smiled at me, the kind of smile that reminded me that he'd had to go over his own hurdles before settling into his love story with Kat. "You won't know until you ask."

Kat called his name from the living area, and he nodded at me before making his way to her.

After a beat of silence, I gave Tristan a serious look. Relationship talk was already on the table, so I figured it was as good a time as any. Plus, it didn't seem like I'd be the center of conversation any more. "So Rory said something to me a while back that I couldn't quite believe at first, but the more I think about it, the more it makes sense."

Tristan took his time opening his beer, tossing the cap and taking a long pull from it before lifting his eyebrows at my comment. "What's that?"

"That you're in love with my sister."

I'd never seen a person go so still, so quickly. His beer froze in front of his mouth, his eyes locked onto me. Then he blinked and it was gone. He took another drink, watched me while he set it back down on the granite. "Your sister is a married woman."

"That she is." I nodded, tipped my beer at him. "Is that my answer?"

His jaw flexed, and he stared at the wall beyond my shoulder. "No."

I snorted. "You know I love you, man, but Anna has enough complications in her life right now. Last thing she needs is a broody ass like you, with hair better than most supermodels, muddying the waters."

"That your protective big brother routine?" he asked, eyes hard and unrelenting. But there was something under the surface, something brewing that told me he did not like my answer.

"No," I laughed. "Do something to hurt her and I'll let you see it. Deal?"

He was about to say something, I could tell. But after a moment's hesitation, he just took another drink and walked into the other room. No nod, no deep, meaningful sigh, nothing. Just a slight narrowing of his eyes that gave me jack shit to decipher, and he walked away.

For a moment, it was a welcome reprieve from the Rory carousel that I couldn't get off of. For the rest of the night, I talked and laughed with my friends and it felt nice. I didn't want to be destined for a life like that, now that I knew what I'd been missing before.

It wasn't about knowing that I'd never disappoint Rory, like I'd been afraid of disappointing people before. My father was just one in a long line, unfortunately. If she gave me another chance, I'd probably screw up, and so would she.

But somehow, I had to pull my head out of my ass long enough to figure out what exactly it was that I wanted. When we all said our goodbyes and left Kat and Dylan's, I took my time walking back to my house.

It was a cloudy night, so I couldn't see a single star. Just a blanket of dark gray clouds obscuring the black sky above me, and the occasional streetlamp giving me circles of orange light to carve a path for me on the sidewalk.

When I climbed up my front porch, I didn't go inside right away, instead taking a seat on the top step and leaning up against one of the pine beams that propped up the overhang. Oddly enough, as I sat in the dark, listening to the occasional sounds of traffic and the punctuation of voices, I wished I could talk to my dad.

I wished I could figure out if he knew how unhappy I was, and if that's why he put me in the position that he did. Or if he thought forcing my hand would clear up my dilemma in a way I'd never have expected.

And then, I'd want to ask him what he thought I should do. About Rory, about CFS. All of it. There'd been a solid string of days and weeks, even months, that I'd found my groove at work, and I'd been so sure that it was because I'd made the choice to be there. But if the worst-case scenario happened, and Rory decided she didn't want me *or* her job, then what?

There was no way I could say that I'd feel the same about my job without her there next to me. I didn't doubt we could work together, we'd already proved that. But instead of hiding behind the perfect, mind-numbing happiness of what I'd felt with her, I needed to figure out what the hell I wanted to do with my life, and where I saw her in it.

I knew where, of course. I wanted her with me. But what piece of the puzzle would she fit into, outside of my relationship with her? *If* she wanted me back, I thought with no small amount of pain in my chest.

With a sigh, I tilted my head back and stared into the solid gray mass looming over me. Of all nights, I wished that I was capable of seeing the blanket of stars in the sky. That I could have picked one and stared at it, maybe make a juvenile wish on it in the hopes that I'd wake up in the morning and have a clear direction.

"Dad," I said, feeling like a giant tool for that fact that it felt so natural to speak it out loud like I was. "I have no idea if you can hear me, or how all of this works." I laughed, scratching the side of my cheek. "If you can see what's going on from wherever you are, you've probably wanted to kick my ass many times in the last few months. For a multitude of things. Which wouldn't be a whole lot different than what you wanted to do when you were alive, I guess. But this is different. This is so much more important than any feelings of discontent that I had when you were around."

I curled my hands into fists and propped them on my knees, waiting for a car to drive past my house before I kept going.

"If I can't figure out what it is I want from my life, besides her, I guess, then what business do I have gambling with yours anymore? You built it. From the ground up, and not once did I feel the pride in it that I know you did every single day. Not until recently. Even when I liked what I was doing, it was like that part of me was snuffed out. But I don't know if it was because I refused to see it, just like you said."

As I said it, I knew it was true. Rory had been a very pleasant blindfold when it came to how I looked at my job, but it didn't mean that once I removed it, I wouldn't see the same picture in front of me.

I smiled up at the sky, feeling less like a tool and more like I was having a conversation that I should have had with him in the weeks leading up to his death. That I should have had the balls to do right from the beginning.

"I wish I'd had the chance to say goodbye to you, Dad. To thank you for pushing me so hard." I let out a rueful laugh. "Actually, you taught Rory quite well in that regard. I wish you could see how amazing she is for me." I blinked away the moisture building, swallowing past the emotion that crept up my throat. "I just need to figure out a way to make things right with her. I couldn't do that with you, and I'll never stop wishing that I'd been able to."

I dropped my head and closed my eyes, feeling a weight dissolve from my shoulders, from my gut, and from my heart. My dad would be proud of me for following my heart, no matter where that led me. Of course I knew that he'd have loved to see me happy at CFS for the rest of my life. But at the end of the day, it's what he'd done. He'd taken a risk and did what felt right for him. He'd have been proud of me for doing the same. And Rory. Oh Rory, that beautiful leggy blonde who would have my heart for the rest of my life, she'd see me on day fourteen, with some magical speech and perfectly laid out plan that I had three days to think of to win her back.

"No big deal, Garrett," I said under my breath. "Just your entire future happiness depends on it."

CHAPTER THIRTY-THREE

AURORA

Day Fourteen

My eyes were gritty and my back hurt by the time I got out of my car in front of my condo and yanked my carry-on suitcase out of the backseat, but I couldn't expect much more than that after a last-minute, thirty-six-hour trip to Del Rio, Texas to have lunch with my parents.

Yeah. I know.

So even though it wasn't bad, per se, it was still a little awkward, and I was a lot tired. So when I was digging through my purse to pull out my keys, I was less than prepared to see Garrett sitting with his back up against my front door, eyes closed like he was sleeping and a wilted bouquet of roses wrapped in green floral paper.

He looked … awful. Handsome, but completely exhausted. With a tiny smile on my face, I wheeled my suitcase to a stop and cleared my throat. Garrett jumped and blinked up at me.

"Rory."

"How long have you been sitting here?"

Now that he was looking up at me, I could see the dark circles underneath his dark eyes and the slightly manic look in them at seeing me. I knew the feeling, but I breathed through it, still not sure what he was doing at my place.

But my heart, oh my heart absolutely leapt at the idea that he waited for me with flowers. Something so simple, probably to most women. But to me, it wasn't. It was exactly what I needed to see after the last day and a half.

"Umm, four hours, I think."

I crossed my arms over my chest and narrowed my eyes, not ready for him to see how much I was vibrating inside at the simple pleasure of seeing him. "And this is your idea of giving me space?"

Garrett swallowed, and then clenched his jaw. As I watched, he seemed to make a decision. With careful movements, he stood, holding the flowers out to me. It looked like a dozen; red, orange and deep lavender. A few hours ago, I'm sure they were stunning, but now they were crumpled and tired-looking from a lack of water.

"These are for you," he said, holding my eyes until I carefully took them from him. "I'll take your suitcase for you."

I nodded, rifling through my keys until I found the one for the deadbolt. "You still didn't answer my question."

From behind me, he answered, the rumbling deepness of his voice at my ear popping goosebumps on my neck. "Well, I figured it'd be easier when we're inside, that way if you want to jump me, you can do it without people watching."

I bit down on the smile, refusing to be outwardly charmed by him. "Thoughtful of you."

"It's a burden, but I wear it well, I think."

My eyes closed as I walked into my condo, feeling a pang of melancholy when I realized that he sounded like the old Garrett. The pre-Rory Garrett. It wasn't melancholy because I didn't like that Garrett. It was because it had been so long since I'd heard that teasing, cocky tone of voice.

"Well," I said, turning to face him. "We're inside. What did you want to say to me?"

He lifted his chin at the roses still clutched in my hands. "You should put those in water. No point in giving up on them just yet."

His carefully chosen words echoed through my head while I turned to pull a vase from the cabinet over my fridge. Neither of us said anything while I unwrapped the Kelly green paper from around the thorny stems and placed them in the cold water. Garrett was staring at my suitcase when I turned back around, and he smiled when he realized I caught him doing it.

"My flight was delayed out of San Antonio. Otherwise you might not have had to wait as long."

"It's okay," he answered slowly. "I don't mind waiting."

"Uh-huh." I lifted an eyebrow. When I did that, the side of his mouth quirked in a smile so unrepentant, that a grin broke free before I could stop it. "Really, Garrett, why are you here right now?"

"Well, I've missed you." He rolled his shoulders, and I admired the way the thin material of his black long sleeve t-shirt stretched across his muscles. It was easier to focus on that than the intense, searching look in his eyes. "I knew it might be a bad idea to just show up. But then I thought," he shrugged, "what the hell? I love her. And it's worth the risk that she might kick my ass back to my car as soon as she sees me."

I had to swallow back the rush of *everything* that hit me when he said it. Garrett's words, ones that he'd clearly taken the time to choose before he said them, hit me in every vulnerable spot that I had left. In all the days that I'd been apart from him, letting my thoughts shift, come in and out of focus, I hadn't realized just how many parts of me were left without armor.

He found every single one in four sentences. My hands were shaking, and I turned to open the fridge. "I guess it's good for you that I'm too tired to kick anyone's ass tonight." I looked over my shoulder at him. "I'm pouring a glass of wine. Would you like one?"

"Ah, no, thank you." When I gave him a surprised look, he grinned.

"Want to keep a clear head for my pitch."

"Oh goody. Is there a PowerPoint?"

"So many things to figure out how to work. I gave up after the first slide where I listed all the reasons you should keep me around."

"Must have been a short slide."

"Ouch," he moaned, doubling over like I had socked him in the stomach. But he was smiling. I was too. When I sat in the corner of the couch, watching him over the rim of my wine glass, he sat on the cushion next to me. Not on the opposite end of the couch like I'd expected. Cheeky. Not like I could really be surprised. "Did you see your parents?"

I didn't even ask how he knew. I was almost positive that Mia was behind his new fountain of knowledge. "Hmm. Briefly. I didn't tell them I was coming until I landed in San Antonio."

"Ballsy."

"Cowardly," I confessed, thinking back on how I felt when I got off the plane, contemplated turning right back around and catching a return flight to Denver. "But it was … okay. We had lunch at their favorite Mexican restaurant. My father let me pay," I said on a shocked laugh. "They gave me a tour of their house, we had a glass of iced tea on their back patio and then I left."

"Why did you decide to go?"

While I thought about that, Garrett leaned forward and carefully wrapped his fingers around mine so he moved the wine glass toward his mouth. My heart thundered in my chest just from that innocent touch, from watching him touch his lips to the glass and take a mouthful while I still held the stem.

"It was time," I said after I'd steadied myself enough to speak without sounding completely breathless. "The last time I talked to my mom, I realized that it wasn't fair for me to begrudge them not visiting or reaching out to me if I wasn't willing to do the same. My mom was right, the last time we talked. I don't fit in their life, and they don't fit in mine. We'll never have the tight relationship that a daughter is supposed to have with her parents. And that's okay. I guess I just needed to … I don't know, see for myself as an adult. To hear them say they'd call more when I apologized for not doing the same. Look them in the eye and tell them that I'm happy."

"You were able to tell them that? That you're happy?" His voice sounded rough when he asked and I sighed at how that must have sounded.

"You know what I mean." I pinched the bridge of my nose at my snippy tone. "I'm sorry, Garrett. I didn't mean it like it sounded. I'm just so tired that my brain isn't even working right anymore. I didn't sleep well last night. I need the entire bottle of wine I just opened, a hot bath and about sixteen hours of sleep."

The irony was not lost on me that I was apologizing for saying something I didn't mean, the exact reason that I'd stormed out of his office, albeit on a much smaller scale. It turned my stomach. In a rush, Garrett stood off the couch and I cursed in my head for not immediately telling him what was on my mind. But he didn't walk toward the door to leave. Instead, he headed in the direction of my master bathroom.

"Where are you going?"

"Running you a bath," he called over his shoulder while I gaped at him in response.

Of course he was. With a sigh, my head fell backwards. I didn't even have it in me to argue with him. So a few minutes later when he said my name from the bathroom, I made my way back there without a second thought.

I pointed at him where he stood testing the water temperature that must have been underneath the massive foaming bubbles. "You're not staying in here while I do this."

"I'd never dare," he mock-gasped. Then he swept his arm to my bedroom. "But, I'm allowed to stay in there."

"Why?"

"Can I just stay and talk to you?" When I gave him a wary look, he held up three fingers. "Scout's honor, I won't peek."

"Yeah," I said quietly. "You can stay."

The fact was, I wanted him to. I wanted to hear his voice, to know he was nearby. While I stripped my clothes, Garrett positioned himself on the floor with his back against the wall that faced out into my bedroom. From where I sank into the perfectly hot water, I could see his feet and part of his jean-clad legs. When I was fully submerged, I let out a quiet sigh.

"Thank you for doing this," I told him.

There was a quiet thudding noise, like he was banging his head against the wall, which made me giggle. "Don't you dare make that sound, Anderson. I'm hanging by a thread as it is."

"Sorry."

"No you're not."

I grinned. "No, I'm not."

We fell into silence for a bit, and with each minute in the tub, I could feel the stress seep from my pores. I was almost asleep when he started talking. But he only let out one word before I interrupted him.

"Wait, Garrett."

"Okay," he said in a tight voice.

"Before you say anything, I want to apologize."

"For what?"

My fingers slipped through the water, pulling up a handful of bubbles while I let out a breath. "Just now, before you came to run me a bath, I snipped because I'm tired and wasn't even really thinking about how it sounded when I said the words. And I think … I think I get why it was so awful for you when you realized I overheard you."

"Rory," he groaned and I heard his head hitting again. "Please don't make excuses for me, I have every intention of apologizing."

"And I'll accept it gladly," I told him quietly. "But I let my insecurities keep a vice grip on my heart, I should have been able to see it from your perspective. And I didn't. So I'm sorry for that. I really needed you to hear that before you say what you were going to."

"Apology accepted," he said in a voice full of gritty emotion. "Can I say my spiel now? I practiced."

"Sure." I smiled, sinking deeper into the water.

"I'm so sorry, Rory. I wish I could even put into words how sorry I am that I said what I did to Cole. Seeing you look at me like you did," he paused, and the bridge of my nose tingled, "I've never felt that *awful* about myself. And I don't blame you for wanting space, I really don't. It was good for me too." More thudding on the wall, and even though I could have said something, I swished my hand through the water again and let him finish. "It forced me to think about what I want. What the best possible scenario is for me. For what I want out of life."

I sniffed while that settled in. He still hadn't said anything about us, and it was so hard for me not to jump out of the water and wrap myself around Garrett, but I gripped the sides of the tub so I wouldn't.

Then all of a sudden, he was in the bathroom.

"Hey," I said, feeling a flush cover my chest and neck, "you're supposed to be out there."

"There's enough bubbles in that tub to cover four of you. I can't see anything." He blew out a breath. "Unfortunately."

He crouched next to the bathtub, tangling his fingers with mine on the porcelain edge and pinned with me a look so intense that I squirmed in the water, conscious of every inch of my skin that he could see.

"There's only one that I want. Only one that matters."

"What?" I whispered and he stared at my mouth when I did.

"You and me," he said simply. "At the end of the day, it doesn't matter what job I'm in, or if you decide you want me to be your sugar daddy for the rest of our lives. If you want to have seven little Garretts and be my sugar momma so I can stay home and change their diapers, it doesn't matter. All I need is you and me. Everything else is just details."

"Garrett." I shook my head, overwhelmed with how right it sounded. Apart from seven kids. That sounded awful. "They're not just minor details though."

"I know. But the point is that we'll talk them out together. We didn't do that before."

"We didn't," I admitted. Just as I was about to open my mouth again, he pressed a gentle thumb to the center of my lips, stopping me.

"I meant it when I said it really doesn't matter what job I'm in, as long as I have you to come home to." He swallowed, searching my face while he traced the edge of my bottom lip. "But I'd really like to go to work with you every day, too."

"Really?" I whispered, feeling a cautious swell of hope. I hadn't even realized how much I wanted him to decide to stay until I heard him say the words.

"Really." His thumb pinched my chin and he lifted it so my face was turned completely toward him. "So, this is the part where you tell me whether you see it being you and me too." His face was serious, a vulnerability in his eyes that I'd never seen before. All I did was smile at him.

Garrett blinked when I did, then dove forward and kissed me, groaning when I gripped the sides of his face and pushed my tongue against his. In the next beat, he lunged up and jumped into the tub with me.

Fully clothed.

Water sloshed out onto the tile floor while he pulled me up onto his lap, wrapping his arms around my soap-slick body.

"You are crazy," I laughed into his mouth.

Garrett pulled back, bubbles clinging to his jaw. His smile was so big that it carved lines in his cheeks. "Damn right."

He kissed me again, with so much passion that his whole body shook from it. So did mine.

I broke away from his mouth, but he followed me, biting along my jaw and down my neck. "Wait, Garrett, stop."

"Why?" he whined, sliding his hands up and down my back. He didn't stop, so I grabbed his face with both hands, forcing him to look at me.

"Because I want to see your eyes when I tell you I love you too. I hated that I didn't tell you before. And this whole time we were apart, it weighed on me that you didn't know."

He blinked, searching my face. "Really?"

I nodded, smoothing my hands over the soaked fabric of his shirt that was clinging to the muscles of his shoulders. "Really. And I should have told you sooner. As soon as I felt it, I should have told you."

"Say it again," he urged, nipping at my lips.

"I love you."

Then he smiled. "Just don't forget who said it first."

EPILOGUE

GARRETT

Twelve months later

"Put it away, Rory."

"Just one more." Her thumbs flew over the screen of her phone, and her forehead furrowed like it always did when she was concentrating.

"Put it away, wife."

She stopped just long enough to give me a dry look. "I do have a name, *husband*."

I settled back into the lounge chair and sighed contentedly under the hot sun. "Aurora Anderson-Calder. Hottest hyphenation I've ever seen in my life." With the tip of my finger, I ran it up her tan, toned thigh. "Hottest wife I've ever seen, too. I think I'm going to make a spousal decree that you're only ever allowed to wear bikinis from now on."

She smiled, but I couldn't see her eyes behind her aviator sunglasses. "Might get awkward around the office."

I leaned over onto my elbow and slid my sunglasses down the

bridge of my nose. She was wearing an all-white bikini that showed all of her recently acquired tan from the first two days of our honeymoon.

We'd actually been married for a month— opting for a small, intimate ceremony with just our families, close friends, and a few coworkers— but in order for both of us to take the same week off, it took some finagling at the office to make it happen. It was worth it though, to have seven days of just me and her in a private beach cottage on Turtle Bay in Hawaii.

"The more I think about it," I said, leaning over her to kiss over the slope of her shoulder, "you shouldn't be wearing clothes at all."

Her skin was warm from the sun and tasted salty from our last dip into the ocean.

"It's good for you to have to work at something while we're here." Another click of her thumb, and she opened another email.

"Put it away, Rory."

"I'm almost done."

"I'll hide it from you if you don't put it *away*."

Her lips screwed up and I got the distinct impression that she was glaring at me behind the dark lenses. "Two minutes."

"One."

"Two."

"Okay," I sighed. "You asked for it."

"Asked for wha— "

I stood, snatching the phone from her hands and tossing it onto the chair I'd just vacated. When she reached for it, I slipped my arms underneath her knees and back, lifting her up while she squealed.

"Put me down." Her voice was breathless with laughter, so it made it easy to ignore her.

"Woman, I said no work this week. Do I need to fire you when we get back?"

She laughed, wrapping her arm around my shoulder while I walked across the sand toward the jewel-blue ocean. "Good luck with that. You couldn't function without me."

I waded in, shifting her in my arms so I could smack a kiss on her smiling lips. She tightened her grip on me and deepened it, slicking her tongue against mine and letting out a soft moan into my mouth.

Right before I tossed her into the water.

She came up sputtering and whipped her sunglasses off her face. "You're going to wish you didn't do that."

"Oh yeah?" I dunked myself under, slicking back my hair with both hands when I broke the surface. She was staring at my chest, at the tattoo of her name over my heart that I'd had done the day after our wedding. "What are you going to do about it?"

Her lips quirked in a smile that actually made me nervous. Especially when she held my eyes and started untying the white string that tied behind her back.

"Rory," I warned, walking toward her, only stopping when she held up a hand.

"You wanted me out of clothes, right?" She tossed the top at me and I caught it against my chest. Her head turned to look at me over her shoulder after she'd turned her back to me. "You got it. But now you're not allowed to touch."

I took off after her with a growl, and she laughed, diving into the shallow water and swimming away. I caught her ankle easily, yanking her toward me so I could wrap her in my arms. We pressed together in the warm water, kissing under the sun while the salt dried on our shoulders.

This little pocket of paradise should have made me dread the end of the week, but that was the thing about finding the perfect person for you.

I got to spend every day, living and working and loving with the most incredible woman I'd ever met. There wasn't a single day that I didn't look forward to. Because the best paradise I'd ever found was being with her.

The End

ACKNOWLEDGEMENTS

I'm going to try to keep these short and sweet.

My husband who let me sleep in *a lot* when writing this book made me see 1am more times than I can count. In no way do I take for granted the kind of support that he gives me.

My boys for taking naps for far longer in life than I expected, and knowing that momma needs to write when they do.

My mom, dad, sister and friends for being the best cheerleaders I could have asked for.

Najla Qamber Designs and Perrywinkle Photography for an amazing cover.

Jade Eby for pretty-ing up my pages.

Alexis Durbin, Ginelle Blanch, and Amanda Yeakel for proofreading.

My tribe of writers who keep me sane:

Whitney Barbetti for just … everything.

Katrina Kirkpatrick for letting me babble.

Brenda Rothert for knowing all the things.

Stephanie Reid who was allowed one reprieve as a beta for busyness but NEVER AGAIN.

Staci Hart for being my favorite verbal processor in da world.

Kandi Steiner for singlehandedly keeping me sane on Dylan's release day. I've never been more thankful to be stranded in the USA since it brought me you.

Jena Camp for making me laugh.

Zoe Lee, Amy Daws, Caitlin Terpstra and Christina Harris for beta reading and asking me tough questions.

My Savior. Nothing I have comes from anyone or anything but Him.

OTHER BOOKS BY KARLA SORENSEN

The Three Little Words Series

By Your Side
Light Me Up
Tell Them Lies

The Bachelors of the Ridge Series

Dylan

Garrett

Coming soon

Cole (book three in the Bachelors of the Ridge series) will release in the spring of 2017, followed by Michael in summer 2017and then Tristan in fall 2017.

For exclusive teasers, content and giveaways, join Karla's Facebook reader group,
The Sorensen Sorority
(https://www.facebook.com/groups/thesorensensorority)

ABOUT THE AUTHOR

Karla Sorensen has been an avid reader her entire life, preferring stories with a happily-ever-after over just about any other kind. And considering she has an entire line item in her budget for books, she realized it might just be cheaper to write her own stories. It doesn't take much to keep her happy…a book, a really big glass of wine, and at least thirty minutes of complete silence every day. She still keeps her toes in the world of health care marketing, where she made her living pre-babies. Now she stays home, writing and mommy-ing full time (this translates to almost every day being a 'pajama day' at the Sorensen household…don't judge). She lives in West Michigan with her husband and two exceptionally adorable sons.

Made in the USA
Las Vegas, NV
24 November 2022